"Okay, I'll consider relocating to the East Coast, but I think it's best if Kayla and I maintain our own residence. Kayla can visit back and forth between us, but I think it would be best for us to live under separate roofs."

Flex shook his head. *She just doesn't get it.* "No, Sweetness, you will live with me. We will live under the same roof, as a family."

Urgh! Sweetness! Why on earth is he picking this moment to call me Sweetness? Can't he just keep his attitude and keep calling me Deidre?

Deidre swallowed and inched away from him on the futon. The man was obviously a whole lot more dangerous than she'd originally thought, calling her Sweetness and whatnot. *What am I supposed to do with that? I have never had any defenses for his soul-filled chocolate-brown gaze combined with his seductive voice calling me Sweetness. Never.* Just the sound of his voice calling her by the loving nickname sent a soft, sweet sensation through her chest.

Indigo

An imprint of Genesis Press, Inc.
Publishing Company

Genesis Press, Inc.
P.O. Box 101
Columbus, MS 39703

Copyright © 2007 by Gwendolyn D. Pough

ISBN-13: 978-158571-206-9
ISBN-10: 1-58571-206-X
Manufactured in the United States of America

First Edition

Visit us at www.genesis-press.com
or call at 1-888-Indigo-1

SWEET SENSATION

GWYNETH BOLTON

Genesis Press, Inc.

DEDICATION

To my father
John Pough
August 17, 1946–May 4, 2003
I always loved you more than you knew. Rest in peace, Daddy. Writing this book made me grapple with how life would have been if you had gotten help. It has also provided closure for me in so many ways.

To all the b-girls, femcees, hip-hop feminists, hip-hop activists and hip-hop heads
Whoever said women didn't contribute anything of significance to hip-hop lied! This book is for all the women who love hip-hop and try to create spaces for women within the culture.

To my mother
Donna Pough
You mean the world to me. I thank God for giving me a mother as strong and as dedicated as you. You went through hell and back raising us by yourself. I love you.

ACKNOWLEDGMENTS

I thank God for granting me the talent and the will to write. Flex and Sweet Dee first came to me when I was in my MA program at Northeastern University. I was writing a creative writing thesis that was supposed to be a collection of short stories. One story about two teenagers who loved hip-hop refused to end, however. And that is how my thesis became the first hundred pages of a novel that I then called "Looking for the Spirit: A Hip-Hop Love Story." The novel has changed tremendously and most of the thesis has become their back-story. Still, I want to acknowledge my thesis advisors, Stuart Peterfreund and Joseph DeRoche. I also want to thank my good friend, LaTisha Fowlkes-Nwoye who read the thesis and fell in love with Flex and Sweet Dee way back then. I hope you still like them, girlfriend! Big thanks go out to my dynamic critique group, The Laptop Dancers. Suemarie, Jennifer, and Arlene, you ladies rock! Big shout outs and lots of love go out to my hubby, Cedric Bolton. I know you're getting sick of my deadlines. But I also know you support my dreams. I love you! I want to thank my mother, Donna Pough and my sisters, Jennifer Pough-Coleman, Cassandra Pough-Kitili, Michelle Pough, and Tashina Pough. And I also want to thank my aunts, Helen Hilliard, Deloris Reed, and Dianne Crawford. Much love and hugs go out to my in-laws, Ruby McCloud, Ervin McCloud, and Priscilla Bolton. Cheryl Johnson, we have a Muffin here. Let me know what you think of her. And finally, thanks to the Genesis Press family, especially my editor, Sidney Rickman.

PROLOGUE

"Superwoman"

That's right, I turn 'em out
You know my style
Rack 'em, stack 'em
Watch my money pile
Turn 'em out, that's the name of this tune
Chick so fly, make all the dudes swoon
Gear so fresh, all the girls throw shade
They mad and stuff 'cause they know I'm paid . . .

With the music blasting in her SUV, Deidre couldn't help singing along. She didn't usually ride down the street pumping her own music, but then every night wasn't like the night she'd just experienced. She'd had a chance to make things right and had blown it, big time. Listening to the remake of her past hit and singing along with it had an almost soothing effect.

Deidre "Sweet Dee" James had just gotten off of the plane from Miami where she'd performed for the first time in eleven years. The performance had gone well. After years away from hip-hop, it amazed her that she was still able to grab a microphone and rock a crowd with such ease. There were other parts of the evening that she could have done without, however, and they all had to do with running into her ex, Fredrick "Flex" Towns III.

Seeing him up-close and in the flesh again after all that time had shaken her more than she'd thought it would. Seeing him with a young hoochie mama bothered her more than she cared to admit. It had been all she could do to maintain her smile and cool demeanor with her insides churning and her heart pumping furiously.

He looked good. The years had certainly been kind to him. She told herself that she shouldn't get jealous of the fact that he had moved on. Things had ended for them a long time ago and she was the one who'd called it off. But telling herself and making her heart listen were two very different things. The fact was that Flex Towns would always touch the deepest part of her. Coming back into the limelight had been a mistake, a big mistake. The only thing she could do to salvage things was dive back into her reclusive life and hope that none of her students at the community college had seen her performing on the *Source Awards*.

She should have known better than to participate. Turning the volume down several notches when she pulled onto her street, she sighed. Back in Minneapolis where she belonged, she was going to put Flex Towns, Sweet Dee, and her past behind her, for good this time.

It's for the best. You can't change the past. Everything happens for a reason. You made your bed, now lie in it. The series of clichés ran through her mind, and not one of them made her feel any better.

She drove down the alley in back of her home, pushed the button for her detached garage, parked and got out. It was nice to be back to a life of relative obscurity.

Deidre opened the door to the cottage-style home she shared with her ten-year-old daughter. It wasn't elaborate, but it was home. The white stucco house with green shutters and trim had caught her eye five years ago when she got tired of renting and wanted a more secure home for her child. Although it was small with only two bedrooms, one and a half baths, dining room, living room, den, and eat-in kitchen, the hardwood floors and built-in bookshelves had stolen her heart. The older home made her feel cozy and safe and she needed to feel that.

"Mommy, I missed you so much." Her beautiful brown-skinned child with deep-chocolate eyes ran into her arms and gave her a giant hug. Kayla had on her pajamas and a night-scarf around her braided hair, but the vibrant smile and expectant glow in her eyes showed that she was nowhere near ready for sleep.

"Kayla, what are you still doing up?" Deidre hugged Kayla and tried to put a sternness that she didn't feel into her voice. Holding her child in her arms made it hard for her to feel anything but joy.

Seeing her made Deidre realize all the more why she was no longer involved with the life she'd left behind. Besides how dangerous the world of hip-hop had become, she would miss Kayla terribly if she had to go on the road all the time.

"Grandma said I could stay up and watch you perform with Lil' Niece and Sexy T on the *Source Awards*. Then she said I could wait up for you because I wanted to tell you how great you were. You looked so pretty, Mommy. I can't wait until I'm a big rap star like Lil' Niece!"

Deidre looked up and caught Lana James's eye. Since retiring from her job as a high school English teacher, Lana came from New Jersey to visit them more than she stayed home. The doting grandmother knew full well that Deidre didn't like Kayla listening to Lil' Niece and Sexy T.

Looking at Lana James was for Deidre almost like peering into a mirror and seeing how she might look in the future. She and the older woman shared the same golden-honey complexion, the same light brown eyes with flecks of gold that looked like tiger-eye stones, and the same sandy-brown hair with almost blonde highlights. Although Lana was a few inches shorter and a couple of sizes bigger than Deidre's size eight, the resemblance between mother and daughter was striking.

Deidre gave her mother an irritated stare. "Mom, it's so late. You know it's past her bedtime." *And you know she has no business watching a hip-hop awards show,* she added in her thoughts.

Deidre didn't even let her child listen to her own old rap recordings from the nineties. Kayla and her friend Lily thought they were going to be the first little girl rappers to make it big. As far as Deidre was concerned, her child would never be a rapper. If she did become one, it would be as an adult.

"The child wanted to see her mother perform, and I wanted to see my baby perform also. Besides, she doesn't have school tomorrow. You were great, by the way." Lana walked over and gave Deidre a hug.

SWEET SENSATION

"Thanks, Mom, but you know I don't want Kayla listening to some of that stuff. She shouldn't even be listening to 'Turn 'em Out.'" It was hard trying to raise a girl who clearly loved hip-hop culture and rap music as much as she had when she was growing up. Deidre had never thought she would turn into the moral police and criticize the culture and the music, but some of the things she heard on the radio made her cringe. She did her best to filter and control what Kayla was allowed to listen to.

Lana waved her arm dismissively and shrugged. "Please, she's going hear it with her friends or outside anyway. I say listen to it with her and then talk with her about it."

Deidre shook her head and thought, *This from the lady who wouldn't let me listen to Run DMC in the house. Good grief.* It never ceased to amaze her how laid back Lana had become now that Deidre was the one trying to raise a child. Then she smiled and patted her own daughter on the head.

She was more than happy to stick to her life as Deidre James, single mother and community college writing instructor and leave Sweet Dee behind. It really was for the best.

Deidre sighed. "Okay, young lady, you got a chance to stay up way past your bedtime, but now it's time for you to go to sleep. Go to your room and I'll be right there to tuck you in."

Kayla pouted and put on a pleading face. "Oh, but I wanted to stay up hear all about the famous people you saw tonight."

"I'll tell you later. Bed. Now."

"Oh, okay." Kayla gave her grandmother a hug and a kiss. "Thanks for letting me stay up, Grandmommy."

"You're welcome, sweetie pie, you're welcome. Thanks for keeping me company." Lana smiled and held Kayla extra tight.

Deidre shook her head as she placed her hand on her daughter's back and walked her to her bedroom.

Turning, Deidre found her mother staring at her. Although the expression on Lana's face said she wanted to talk, talking was the last thing Deidre wanted to do. She'd had her chance to talk with Flex and

4

had let it pass. Rehashing the night's events with Lana wouldn't change a thing.

Hoping that Lana would put off her inquisition until the morning, Deidre yawned and stretched. "It's late, Mom. Shouldn't you be hitting the sack also?"

"Well, I was just wondering if you saw Flex tonight. Did you get a chance to talk with him?" Lana James simply leaned against the wall.

I knew she wanted to talk about that. Maybe I should try getting a job as one of those telephone psychics, Deidre thought wryly. She'd really hoped that the woman would have the decency to wait until the morning to try to squeeze her for information.

"Oh, I saw Flex with one of his hoochies and I said hello and goodbye. That was the extent of anything I had to say to him." She feigned nonchalance, but inside she was feeling things that she couldn't name.

Really, she thought, *what was I going to say to the man? Hey, Flex, listen. You remember when we were in love all those years ago and I broke it off? Well there's something I've been meaning to tell you . . .*

Flex was not the same man she'd left all those years ago. In fact he hadn't been the same man since she'd left him. She'd lost track of all the beautiful models she'd seen him with in magazines and on television since he went from Flex the deejay for The Real Deal to Flex, super producer and record label owner. A man of money and power, his life held all the trappings that went along with it. Sure that he had long since removed her or anything she might have meant to him from his heart, Deidre turned to face her mother.

Lana's eyes held the unspoken questions that mother and daughter had argued over and disagreed about for a while and Deidre was in no mood to go there.

Deidre shrugged. "Mom, things are fine the way they are. I've left that life behind me. Attending that awards show tonight just let me know that I made the right decision leaving that madness."

"But—" The elder James woman was about to sing the same tune about Flex but Deidre didn't want to hear it.

"Trust me, Mom, everything is for the best." She'd told herself that so much that she almost believed it. The truth was, she didn't know. That was a part of the problem. She didn't know, and she didn't have the guts to find out for sure.

Lana shot Deidre an all-too-knowing look, the kind that made her feel as if she were fourteen again and had just been caught lying about cutting school to hang out at the mall.

"Is it really for the best, or are you making it easy for yourself?"

Leaning against the closet door, Deidre let out a sigh. "Ma, I don't want to talk about this now. Please, let's just agree to disagree and give it a rest."

"Deidre, every man is not like your father. Even he is not the same man he used to be. You can't keep running away because you're scared that you're going to end up like us—"

Lana's eyes took on a sad expression that pierced Deidre's heart. She had to stop the conversation before they ended up bringing out old skeletons that Deidre was determined should stay in the closet. She couldn't do it, not after just seeing Flex again. "Mom, I said I don't want to talk about this. Please, go to bed. I'm fine. Kayla's fine. She has us. We're all she needs. I'm going to bed."

Deidre peeped into her daughter's room. Kayla was fast asleep. It hadn't taken her long at all to drift off. Kayla was her heart and Deidre didn't want to lose her. It was too late to tell Flex—too late to start up that particular drama again. She had gotten herself out of that life and she just had to make sure that she stayed out. Things were going to be fine. She'd taken care of herself and her child for ten years and she would continue to do so.

CHAPTER 1

"Who Can I Run To?"

Two Years Later

Deidre rushed in the back door to her home, dropped her bag of groceries on the floor and rushed to the phone. She had no idea how long it had been ringing and she wanted to catch it before the answering machine picked up.

"Hello." She panted the word out and tried to catch her breath at the same time.

"Dee Dee, girl, you've got to see this. Turn your TV to Music Television. They're talking about you." It was her mom calling from New Jersey.

"What are they talking about me for?" She went into her den and turned the television to the Music Television channel. She sat on her kente cloth-covered futon and took off her shoes while she waited to see what her mom was talking about.

One of those 'whatever happened to them' shows was on, and Deidre sucked her teeth. The producers for that show had been after her for months to get her to do an interview, and she'd turned them down.

The beauty of being a female hip-hop artist in hiding was that, for the most part, no one came looking for you. Every once in a while there was a special on television about hip-hop, and it devoted five minutes or so to women. When they were persistent enough to find her in the Midwest, Deidre just declined. Ever since she'd done the *Source Awards*, she'd received all kinds of requests to talk about the status of women in hip-hop and she'd turned them all down.

The realization that she should have never performed had hit her quickly. So, she did the only thing she could do in the aftermath—pray that the interest in her would die down. Besides the fact that she found most of the 'whatever happened to them' shows corny, she knew that the Music Television special wouldn't help her maintain her low profile and had declined the interview. It looked as if they hadn't needed her cooperation to do a show.

They were giving her story based on old interviews, archived photos, music videos, and performance footage. They played up every bit of the drama and controversy in her life. They had a field day with the fact that she was a former debutante who graduated from a prestigious black women's college and she became a hot and steamy rapper down with a crew of gangsta rappers. They also played up her tumultuous relationship with former deejay and super producer Flex Towns. They had pictures of her coming out at the Links debutante ball in Teaneck, New Jersey, pictures of her pledge line for Zeta, and her graduation picture from Spelman. Clips from her videos were interspersed with old shots of her and Flex attending various parties and premiers while they were a couple. It was weird seeing herself made up as Sweet Dee with jeans, hooded sweatshirts, bandanas, and shades. At least she had clothes on, which was a lot more than she could say for contemporary women entertainers.

As the montage of clips and photographs ran, a voice-over asked the question, "How did a Black American princess go from debutante to hard-core gangster rapper?" They also spouted off a series of observations about how intriguing it was that most so-called gangsta rappers were actually middle-class black kids who had no idea of what life in the hood was like. None of that bothered Deidre. It was old news. The media had done a number on Sweet Dee years ago, when her second album dropped. Back then, the controversy surrounding her less-than-gangsta beginnings had actually made for huge record sales.

The program worked to sensationalize her life story to the tenth degree. However, the old footage and tabloid-style retelling of her life story was not the problem. The problem was the new footage they were showing.

The black Barbie-like host with bleached blonde hair spoke in a pseudo-reporter tone that came across as more gossipy than factual. "Ms. James declined our offer to interview her, but our people found her living as a little-known poet and instructor at a community college in Minneapolis with her daughter." They showed footage of her leaving Minneapolis Technical and Community College and getting in her SUV.

Deidre smarted. *Can they give out that kind of information on television?*

"While Sweet Dee, née Deidre James, last performed in public two years ago at the *Source Awards*, we were able to obtain footage of her going about her life as a former rap star. Here she is picking up her daughter from an after-school program. And we here at *Hey, What Ever Happened To . . . ?* find it really interesting that Sweet Dee's daughter looks a lot like super producer and record label owner Fredrick 'Flex' Towns."

Deidre's mouth fell open and her eyes sprang wide. The jerks even went so far as to take a recent school picture of Kayla and place it side by side with a picture of Flex when he was a boy. They had the same oval-shaped faces, the same dark chocolate eyes, the same button noses, the same serious expressions and half-smiles on similar lips. The resemblance was undeniable.

She gripped the arm of the futon with one hand and clutched the phone with the other. "Oh, my, God. They don't have the right! Who gave them the right?"

"Needless to say, we here at *Hey, What Ever Happened To . . . ?* now know why Sweet Dee, née Deidre James, has been hiding out all these years. We wonder if Flex Towns knows about his striking resemblance to Sweet Dee's love child?"

Shocked, Deidre turned off the television and leaned back into the futon. One hand still held the phone and the other covered her mouth.

"Oh, baby, what are you going to do? You have to tell Fredrick now. I just hope that you can tell him before he hears it from someone else. Or, God forbid, he sees it on this show." Lana James's voice broke through the fear-laden haze that had started to cover Deidre's mind.

Deidre stared blankly into space. She felt as if she had to be in some parallel universe, the Twilight Zone or something, because there was no way she could have seen what she thought she'd just seen. *Is it that easy to change the course of someone's life? It can't be, can it?*

Lana screamed through the phone, "Dee Dee, did you hear me? What are you going to do? Are you going to try to tell Flex before he hears it from someone else?"

Deidre blinked and then heaved a sigh. She was holding a phone, but she had no clue how to speak. Somehow she found her voice and managed to put together words. "Mom, I . . . well . . . I just think it might not be necessary. I mean, how many people watch this kind of thing? I know that Flex probably doesn't. He's way too busy to watch this kind of crap. Really Mom, all they did was show a picture of my child and imply that she could be Flex's. They don't have any DNA proof, and I will deny it until the grave. If Flex should happen to call or inquire, I'll just tell him it's not true. Yeah, I'll just deny it. Yeah, that could work." She was trying to convince herself more than she was trying to convince Lana.

The tsk and cluck that came across the phone lines spoke volumes; Lana wasn't buying it any more than she was.

Deidre sighed again.

Deidre could hear the *mmm, mmm, mmm*, even though Lana didn't say a word.

"Now you know I'm not one to try and tell you what to do or how to live your life."

When Deidre heard those words, she knew she was in for it then.

"But Dee Dee, I wouldn't be a mother if I didn't point out to you when you were making a grave mistake."

Deidre leaned her head back on the futon and vowed never to use the *I wouldn't be a mother if . . .* line on Kayla.

"You can be irritated and zone me out if you want to, but I am going to speak my mind. You need to also consider Kayla here. What are you going to tell her if one of her little friends sees the program and shares with her that she may be Flex Towns' daughter?"

Deidre opened her mouth and closed it. She didn't have a clue what she would tell Kayla. When Kayla was younger, Deidre had always been able to get around the daddy question with her child by being evasive and vague whenever questions came up. She'd known that the questions would get harder and harder to answer the older Kayla became, but she hadn't banked on that coming up so soon. She didn't know what she would say to the direct question, *Is rap super producer Flex Towns my father?*

Can I lie to my child? She knew as soon as she thought the words that she never could tell an outright lie to her daughter. The fact that she had hidden the truth all these years ate at her soul enough. She wished that she had had the courage to come clean two years ago when she saw Flex at the *Source Awards* or even twelve years ago when Kayla was born, but she hadn't, and now she had to pay the price.

"I'm not trying to be a pain, and I'm not trying to get in your business, Dee Dee, but I don't think you're thinking about all the implications of this. I have no doubt that someone is eventually going to tell Kayla about the show, or she may even see it for herself. I think you want to think really carefully about what you'll tell her about it."

Deidre shut her eyes tight and waited a moment before opening then. She was sure that when she opened them, her life would certainly be right side up again. *What kind of crazy alternative earth have I been transplanted to? This is not my life.*

"Do you really think I should tell Kayla who her father is?" Deidre mumbled the question.

"I think you should tell Kayla who her father is, and tell Flex he has a daughter."

She didn't need to see Lana James's face to see the I-told-you-so expression on it. It amazed her that such a non-verbal form of communication could somehow make it through the phone line.

"One thing at a time, Mom. If Flex doesn't know yet, he won't die if he has to wait a little while longer. I'm not ready for that conversation. I'm not even ready to talk to my child about this." *It's wrong, and believe me I know it, but one crisis at a time, please.*

Deidre heard a small gasp and she turned to see Kayla standing in the doorway of the den.

Kayla's jacket was open and her pigtails were sticking out every which way on her head. The girl looked as if she'd been running, and worse, the dried tears that streaked her face and the fresh tears running down it gave her a very distraught appearance. Her eyes were wide and accusing. The usually bright and bubbly mocha-complexioned young lady sported a sad expression that had even burnt out the light in her brown eyes.

"Mom, I'll call you back later." Deidre hung up the phone.

She looked in her child's eyes, saw the unspoken question there, and knew that her mother was right. It was way past time to come clean, at least with her daughter. She just hoped she would be able to face it, because there was nowhere to run this time.

CHAPTER 2

"Left Me Lonely"

Flex Towns sat in his office, reading over more paperwork than he cared to. The business side of owning his own record label interested him about as much as having to live in the public eye as a hot hip-hop producer. He was more interested in being in the studio, working with artists, and creating good music. Living his life as a superstar was just one of the annoyances he had to put up with to ensure that Flex Time Records stayed on top and he continued to be in control of the product that he put out. Control was a major issue for him. He'd given up control one time in the past, and he'd always regretted it. A life had been lost, and other lives irrevocably changed, before he could make things right. He vowed he would never make that mistake again.

The buzz from his secretary momentarily pulled him out of his paperwork-induced stupor.

"Yes, Marcia," he said.

"Sir, you have a call from an Alicia Taylor-Whitman. She says it's urgent. I told her you were busy, but she insisted that you would want to hear what she has to tell you."

Flex smiled. He hadn't heard from Alicia in quite some time. They touched base on and off. Since she'd married Darren Whitman they didn't see each other as much as they once did when she was his date of choice at various awards shows. When the excitement of having a different model on his arm every few months started to wear thin, he'd luckily met up with Alicia and found a friend as well as a beautiful date.

Alicia was a knockout. Her looks would put most models to shame, and she was also cool. In fact, she was so cool, and such a good friend, that he at one time had almost thought she might be able to replace his one true love. Things hadn't worked out that way, but he was happy that his friend had found happiness with the love of her life.

Flex wondered what could be so urgent. She probably wanted him to do a profile in her magazine. Ever since taking over as arts and entertainment editor of her family's magazine, *Black Life Today*, she had been after him to do a feature.

He had done a good job of putting it off because he didn't want the attention, but he knew it would only be a matter of time before she caught up with him and made him do it.

He put his papers aside and smiled. "I'll take the call, Marcia, thanks."

"You're welcome, Mr. Towns. I'll put her through." Flex pressed the speaker button on his phone. "So, what's up, Shorty? To what do I owe the pleasure?"

"Hey, Flex. I was wondering if you'd seen Music Television's *Hey, What Ever Happened To . . . ?* They had a special on the other day about women rappers, and they actually featured Sweet Dee."

Flex rubbed his tired eyes. He knew good and well Alicia had not called him in the middle of a workday to get on him again about his past relationship with Deidre "Sweet Dee" James.

"I know you aren't calling me to share that information. And I *know* that's not what you're calling urgent."

He could hear her suck her teeth over the phone and he imagined the eye roll that went along with it.

"No, that's not the reason I'm calling. Judging from your calm demeanor, however, and your smart-aleck attitude, I would say that the answer is no. You haven't seen the most recent episode of the show."

"No, I haven't. So what gives? What's so urgent?"

"Well, for starters, you have a child."

"What?"

"Sweet Dee had a baby, and you're the father."

"Umm, I hate to burst your bubble, seeing as how you've called thinking you have broken some huge news flash, but Dee and I do not have a child. We haven't been together in quite some time, not that it's any of your business. If we did share a child, I'm sure I would know about it." Flex shook his head and studied his fingernails as he spoke.

"Really, you're sure? That's your story and you're sticking to it? Because I saw the program, and they put a picture of that girl and a picture of you when you were a child side by side, and she could have been your sister. She looks just like you. I mean, she has a little of Sweet Dee in her too, but the rest is all you. Like my Nana used to say, she looks like you spit her out!"

Flex frowned. Alicia must be playing some sort of practical joke, because there was no way Deidre would have had his child and not told him. No matter how badly things had ended between them, she still wouldn't have kept something so important a secret from him. Back then, he'd trusted her like no one else, even trusted her more than he trusted his own father. Deidre would never have betrayed him like that, no matter how pissed off she was at him.

"Stop playing, Shorty. Is this a bad idea of a joke? Do you have some cameras placed in my office to get my response? I know, it's a part of one of those reality TV setups where they play tricks on celebrities or something. When is the little white boy going to come out and tell me I've been punked? Are you in one of the other offices making this call?" Flex looked around for the hidden cameras, all the while chuckling. He didn't like the idea of being the butt of some television prank, but at least he'd figured it out before they got him on tape tracking down Deidre's phone number and calling her up to make a fool of himself.

"I'm not joking. I saw it with my own eyes, and you need to have your people look into having Music Television send you a tape of the show."

He stopped chuckling and searching for the hidden camera. Something in Alicia's voice signaled that she was not joking and wasn't playing a prank.

"You've got to be kidding. I know you're kidding, right?"

She let out an exasperated sigh. "Why would I call you and make something like this up?"

"Oh, I don't know, you do have an off sense of humor, and you can be a little crazy at times." He ran his hand across his closely cropped head. In an effort to make a fresh start, he'd recently cut the locs he'd been growing.

"You know what? This is why I don't usually get involved with other people's business."

Torn between telling his magazine writer and very nosey friend that she made a living getting involved in others' business, and finding out once and for all if there was any truth to what she was telling him, he opted to find out the truth.

"Okay, okay, I'll have Marcia get in contact with Music Television and have them send me a copy of the program. If this is some kind of a joke, then you can forget about that feature story."

"Again I ask, why would I make something like this up? My goodness. Just handle your business and get back to me with an apology when you find out that I was right. Then we will really have something to feature."

"I'll check you later, Shorty. Peace." Flex hung up the phone and buzzed his secretary.

"Yes, Mr. Towns?" Marcia came walking into the office with her pen and pad in hand.

"Marcia, I need you to get in touch with Music Television and have them send over a tape of the latest *Hey, What Ever Happened to . . .?* The one that featured Sweet Dee."

"Yes, sir. I'll call over there right away."

"Have them rush it. Send one of our own messengers to pick it up if necessary. I want it in my hands now."

"Yes, sir." Marcia rushed out of the office.

Flex couldn't focus on anything else. Alicia had to be mistaken. Because if she wasn't . . . Even though things did not end well with him and Deidre, she would have told him if she was pregnant. She would have told him if she'd had their child. He just couldn't believe that she would keep something like that a secret.

He got up and paced the floor of his spacious office. He looked out the window to the busy street in midtown Manhattan. As he gazed at the standstill traffic, he allowed himself to think about what Alicia had said. The more he thought about it, the more he knew it had to be false.

Deidre was his first true love. His only real love, if he was honest about it. He met her during his senior year of high school after being kicked out of boarding schools, prep schools, and even one military school. His father, a prominent judge and a single father, had finally had enough with Flex and told him that Teaneck High School was his last shot. If he got kicked out of there, then he would be out of luck.

He was pretty much a loner that year until he met Deidre James, a kindred spirit who had transferred to Teaneck High from St. Mary's. She'd gotten caught smoking in the girls' room and cursed out the nun who initially was only going to suspend her for two days.

Deidre made going to school every day suddenly worthwhile and they both managed to graduate from the public high school without any more trouble. He even went to college because of her. By his junior year of college, The Real Deal had a record contract and by senior year Deidre had a contract of her own based on guest spots she did on their album. Even with the touring schedules, they both managed to graduate, he from Morehouse and she from Spelman. He knew he wouldn't have gotten his bachelor of arts degree without her. If anyone had asked him then, he would have told them that he and Deidre were going to be together forever.

His train of thought was interrupted when Marcia brought in the tape from Music Television. He popped it into the VCR for the widescreen entertainment center he kept in the office to screen new music videos for his artists. It was weird to see all the old footage and interviews with Deidre. He was a little disappointed that they didn't have any new footage. He'd seen her two years earlier and she still looked great. He'd wanted to talk to her then, to touch base, make some kind of connection. But she'd rushed off so quickly that he'd barely had a chance to say hello. He still wondered what would have happened if he had gotten her to talk to him for a little while.

His jaw dropped when he saw the picture of Deidre's daughter. *My daughter.* She was a beautiful young lady, and all he had to do was look at the picture to tell who she was. Her complexion, a perfect combination of Deidre's golden-honey and his dark chocolate, was a smooth brown with red undertones. The oval shape of her face held miniature versions of his eyes, nose and mouth. He ran his hand across his head and his eyes narrowed so much he could barely see out of them.

How could she do this to me? To my child? Deidre was the woman he'd once considered his best friend. Now it appeared that she actually was his worst enemy. He picked up the phone. First he had to find where Deidre James was hiding. Then he would confront her and find out the reason behind her deception.

CHAPTER 3

"Just the 2 of Us"

Deidre sat on the edge of her daughter's canopy bed trying to come up with the words to make her understand why she'd made the choices she did. She thought she had strong and valid reasons at the time for not telling Flex that he was going to be a father. Sitting with her upset and distraught child, though, she just couldn't find the words to express how she'd felt at that time, or even how she felt at the current moment. After trying to make her twelve-year-old understand, she slowly came to realize that maybe her reasons hadn't been that good after all. The sulking child continued to give her the silent treatment.

The shock of it all continued to astound Deidre. One minute she had been going about her nice, quiet life, and the next minute everything became chaos. She didn't think things could get much worse than her daughter not speaking to her, but she knew better than to tempt fate by sending that thought out into the universe.

Sitting in Kayla's bedroom and yet again trying to get the child to talk, Deidre played with the frilly yellow comforter. "Kayla, baby, I'm sorry you had to find out about your father the way you did. Please say something, baby."

Kayla still refused to talk to her.

Deidre sighed. *Maybe she just needs time to process what she saw.* She got up from the bed and started toward the door.

"Why didn't you tell me? Why did you let me think that I didn't have a father?" Kayla huffed out the words.

Deidre turned around to find her darling daughter glaring at her. "Baby, I'm sorry. Honestly, I took the coward's way out and just assumed that you were fine with things the way they were, just the two of us."

Kayla heaved a sob and hiccupped. "I stopped asking when I was a kid because I thought that he must have been a horrible man who left us before I was born. He doesn't even know about me, does he?"

Deidre fiddled her hands and sat back on the bed. "No. He doesn't know about you. Or, he didn't know about you. He could very well know now that Music Television has aired that show."

"Were you ever going to tell me? If the show had never come on, if I had never asked, would you have told me?"

Deidre took a deep breath. The lies were over. She had to come clean with her child. The truth, no matter how wrong and how bleak, had to be spoken. "No, baby. I probably wouldn't have told you if you hadn't seen the show, or if you hadn't asked about your father. I . . . I'm sorry, Kayla. I know it wasn't right, but it's complicated. At the time I really thought I was doing the right thing. Now, I don't know . . ."

Deidre sat there until Kayla dropped off to sleep. The unsettling silence gave her plenty of time to think about and enumerate all the ways she'd messed up. Being young, scared, and upset with your boyfriend didn't cut it twelve years later when you were a thirty-five-year-old woman. She only hoped that she could find it within her to do what she needed to do for her daughter.

Once her child was finally sleeping, she watched her for a while and then went to her own room. She sank down on her brass bed, picked up the phone on the nightstand and called her mother.

Luckily, her mother answered the phone and Deidre didn't have to talk to her father. She had dodged having to say more than two words to Dr. Howard James for years, and she wasn't in the mood to break her streak by having to face him that evening.

"I was waiting for you to call me back, baby. How is Kayla? Do you need me to come?" Lana's voice was a soothing balm.

"Mom, I just don't know what to do. She's so upset. She isn't talking. I never thought . . . Oh, Mom, I've really messed this up. What am I going to do?" The words rushed out of her mouth before she could think.

She felt a sense of hopelessness and failure. Her reasons for keeping her secret years ago now seemed silly when compared to her child's haunting look of betrayal. Deidre needed to feel that there was something she could do to right the wrong she'd done.

"Dee Dee, I really think that you should try and get in touch with Fredrick. It's time to come clean. Perhaps once Kayla has met her father the three of you can work this out together. She deserves to have her father in her life and he deserves to have his daughter. Maybe the television program was a good thing, the universe's way of righting a mistake." Lana's voice, which had soothed her only moments before, now had the opposite effect on her.

Of all the things Deidre expected her to say . . . of all the times she needed Lana to be on her side . . . She didn't understand why Lana was picking that moment to bring up Flex.

"Mom, I can't get in touch with Flex. I need you to tell me how I can reach Kayla, how I can work things out with Kayla. Flex is—"

"Fredrick is her father, and it's time to come clean. You need to be a woman, set an example for the child. If you don't do this correctly, then how can you expect Kayla to forgive you? You need to model forgiveness for her. Whatever Fredrick did to make you keep his child from him, you need to forgive it. You need to bring them together and hope that your actions will spark the forgiveness in them both." Lana's voice was still soft but it had picked up just a hint of a lecturing tone.

Deidre sat in silence, soaking in Lana's words and what they meant for the life she'd created for herself and Kayla.

From the moment she found out she was pregnant with Kayla, she'd known that she wanted her, that she would always do what was best for her. At the time she was maxed out with the music business and yearned for a life away from the spotlight. She loved Flex, but she knew that if she stayed with him, even if she never performed as a rapper again, he could never leave the business. He loved it.

Music was in his soul. From the time he was a high school and college deejay to the time The Real Deal recorded their first record, his love of making music was always present. She couldn't ask him to give up what he loved and she couldn't stay. Worrying about the violence that began to surround Body Bag Records, and seeing firsthand what fame was doing to Flex, was not the way Deidre wanted to spend her pregnancy. So she left.

From what she could see watching him and his various model and hoochie mama dates on television, she had made a good decision. No sooner had she left him, than he began to date an endless string of women. The media reporting on his numerous women increased even more when he became the head of his own label.

She couldn't have gone back after that. He probably wouldn't have wanted her back anyway.

If Lana was right, however, in her thinking that the only way to make things right with Kayla was to make things right with Flex, then she would have to try. She just wasn't ready to voice the decision yet.

"I don't know. I mean, Flex might not even see the show. He might never find out. Kayla knows now. I could always let her go to him once she's old enough to handle it. What if he rejects her?" Her silent fear came bubbling up. The main reason she'd kept her child a secret from Flex was that she knew her heart couldn't take it if he rejected their child.

"If Fredrick can look at that beautiful young lady and not want to be a part of her life, then she would be better off knowing that than building up some dream of a father for years, only to be rejected. It would be rough, but as her mother you would help her through it. As your mother, I would help you through it."

Deidre snuggled into her bed pillow, trying to pretend it was Lana's lap, and trying to feel a loving embrace wash over her again. Either she was tired or Lana was really making a lot of sense.

"Thanks, Mom. I'm going to check on Kayla before I go to sleep. I'll call you later to let you know how things go."

"Goodnight, baby. Remember, things will be fine. You'll make the best decision. I have faith in that."

Glad that one of them had faith, because she was running low on it, Deidre didn't have a clue how she was going to face the next day.

Instead of sleeping that night, she just kept thinking about her relationship with Flex and where they'd gone wrong. She couldn't help thinking about the way they'd met and how things used to be. She sighed and remembered what their lives had been like before she became a hot female rapper and he became the country's most sought after deejay and super producer. When they were teenagers and everything was new . . .

CHAPTER 4

"A Teenage Love"

Deidre looked at the words in her notebook and let out a sigh. She knew she wasn't finished writing the poem, but her mind wandered. She felt out of place in her parents' home. They seemed happy, but she still remembered the fights and lived in fear of them starting again and not being able to protect her mother.

No matter how much she wrote in the journal that her mother had recommended, she still couldn't find away to make peace with her feelings or with their move back into her father's house. Even though the fighting had stopped, she still didn't want to live with him. She liked it better and felt safer when she and her mother lived alone.

She couldn't wait to leave home and go to college. That was the only reason she stopped acting up in school. She needed to get into college so she could get away. She lived her life from day to day, just going through the motions. Then Fredrick "Flex" Towns III transferred to Teaneck High. Flex was a known rebel and the son of a prominent black lawyer. He enrolled in Teaneck High partway into his senior year in an effort to get at least a high school diploma.

She, like almost every other girl at Teaneck High, noticed Flex the first day he came to school. She noticed him, but figured she was nowhere near cool enough to catch his attention. Deidre had always straddled the fence between hard worker and slacker, rule follower and rule breaker, geek and cool. In spite of being able to fit in with any crowd, Deidre spent most of her time alone.

She always used her lunch hour to write in the journal that Lana had given her so that she could express her feelings about the two of them moving back in with her father, Dr. James. As an English teacher at an inner-city high school, Lana James had always encouraged Deidre to write down her thoughts. Deidre usually jotted down her random thoughts, and some poetry, in the journal. She had another notebook that she wrote rhymes and raps in, but she usually left that one at home, hidden under her mattress. She didn't tell anyone that she wrote raps, mostly because even though her friends listened to rap music, they probably wouldn't understand her wanting to rap.

She was completing a poem when she heard someone behind her say, "That's a nice little rhyme you got there. You got any longer ones?"

She turned around to see Flex looking over her shoulder. He was over six feet tall, bony as a skeleton, and walked around with a permanent frown.

"Excuse me," she said, not sure whether to be angry for the intrusion or happy that Flex was paying her some attention. If he thought the stupid poem was good, she wondered what he would say if she showed him her notebook where she kept her *real* rhymes.

"I said you got nice rhymes. You know, like lyrics. You know what I mean by rhymes?" Flex asked, as he took a seat beside her.

Of course, I know what rhymes are, she thought, but she couldn't find the words to answer him, couldn't believe he was actually talking to her.

She noticed that he was wearing his usual attire—jeans hanging off his behind so that his boxer shorts showed and a hooded sweatshirt that covered his rarely combed head of hair.

"Do I know what you mean by rhyme?" She repeated the question, a little nervous that Flex was sitting so close to her.

"You know, rhyme, rap, emcee," he said. He started staring at her as if she was from another planet.

Can I tell him about the notebook? No, then he'll probably ask me to rap or something, and what if I can't remember my rhymes? I've never really rapped in front of another person before.

"Oh, rap. No, I don't rap," she lied. "I listen to rap music and stuff." She started to close her binder. She was going to get up and walk away. Flex wouldn't be interested in a girl like her.

"Yo, wait a minute. My name is Flex. I mean, you know, that's what they call me, because I'm a deejay and I'm so flexible on the wheels of steel. I'd like to look at your stuff, you know. I mean, if it's not a problem. I like that rhyme you wrote. Can I have your phone number? 'Cause I figure we can get together, you know, and talk." He sounded as unsure as she felt.

She scribbled her phone number on a piece of notebook paper, ripped it out, and placed it in his hand. *What does it matter, he probably won't call,* she thought. She shyly glanced at him and rushed off before he could change his mind.

She spent the entire Christmas break waiting for Flex to call. She wrote more rap songs and practiced them in the mirror. She paid more attention to the rappers in the videos and on the radio. The more she listened, the more she realized that she was just as good, if not better. She even liked the way her voice sounded when she said her rhymes. She was more than ready when Flex finally called her.

"Hello. May I speak to Deidre?" he asked in a hesitant voice.

She immediately recognized his voice. It was so deep and so smooth. "This is Deidre."

"Hi, Deidre. This is Flex."

"Hi, Flex. What's up?" she asked in a shaky and very nervous voice.

"Nothing much. I was wondering if you wanted to take a ride with me over to P-Town. I deejay over there, and we have practice today." He sounded hesitant.

"Where's P-Town?" As soon as she asked the question, she wished that she could take it back.

"Oh, boy. You don't know where P-Town is?" he asked in a voice that sounded half-shocked and half-amazed.

"I've never heard of P-Town."

"You never heard of Paterson?" His voice had a hint of I-don't-believe-you-in it.

"Oh. Paterson. Yeah, I heard of Paterson. That's like, like an inner city, right?" Deidre almost said ghetto, but she thought inner city was a more appropriate term.

"Oh, boy. Look, maybe this was a bad idea. I'll get with you later."

"No. No. I want to go to Paterson. I mean, I've never really been there. I mean, I think I rode through there once on the way to Willowbrook Mall, when Route 80 was under repair. But I'd like to go." She uttered the words so quickly she could barely understand her own voice. She didn't want Flex to hang up and not call again.

"Well, all right. What's your address?"

"Oh, I live on Argonne Court."

"What's the house number?"

"Oh, it's 450 Argonne Court. It's a big white and black house," she said, wondering if she was giving Flex her address in vain.

"All right, I know where that is. I should be there in about fifteen minutes," Flex mumbled.

"Fifteen minutes? Oh . . . okay. See you then."

"Yeah, see ya." Flex hung up.

Deidre picked up one of the rap songs she had been memorizing. Reading the rap one more time before placing it back on her nightstand, she looked in the mirror and decided that the outfit she had on needed a little changing. She took off the white cashmere sweater and put on a black, hooded sweatshirt. Deciding to keep on her tight blue jeans, she took her long hair out of the ponytail holder, quickly brushed it back and put on a black baseball cap. After taking one last look at herself in the mirror, she sat on her bed and put on the brand new black sneakers she'd had to beg Lana to buy. She had just finished tying her laces when the doorbell rang. She grabbed her jacket and ran downstairs. Luckily, her parents were out, so she quickly left them a note telling them that she was going out with friends from school.

She didn't even bother to ask who was at the door because she wanted it to be Flex so badly. She flung the door open and couldn't hide the big grin that came to her face when she saw him standing there.

Flex smiled back at her. "So, you ready to take a walk on the fly side, Teaneck girl?"

"I guess so," she said, letting the door slam behind her.

They got into Flex's brand new black car and drove off. They sped down Route 4 through Bergen, Paramus, and Fairlawn, blasting loud rap music. She wondered if the police would stop them. A part of her wanted to get stopped.

Flex wasn't saying anything. He just bobbed his head to the music and drove.

She had never heard the songs before, so she assumed that Flex's group had recorded them. She began to wonder if he remembered that she was in the car. Just as she was about to open her mouth to speak, he took the tape out. She felt a hollow echo in her ear with the sudden silence.

"So, how did you like the tape?" he asked in an excited voice.

"Oh, it was good!" she tried to sound extra excited, not wanting to say anything that would make him regret that he'd decided to hang out with her.

"Good?" His voice had the same puzzled and hesitant sound it had earlier on the phone.

"Well, I mean, it was fresh, dope. You know what I mean. What group is that? They're fly. Word!" she said quickly, trying to dress up her original lack of coolness.

"Oh, that's me and my crew, The Real Deal Niggas. That's part of our demo. We just need a few more cuts and we can start shopping it around."

"The Real Deal Niggers?" Shocked, she couldn't believe that they were calling themselves by that derogatory term.

"Yeah. That's dope, ain't it?"

"*Niggers*?" She felt her facade of coolness slipping away. Yes, she listened to rap music as much as the next person, and she knew that those kinds of words got used often. Naming a group that, however, seemed outrageous.

"Nah, niggas. Girl, you really ain't up on much, are you?" His voice went from excited back to puzzled and hesitant. "You know, I usually don't deal with Teaneck girls. They're too prissy, goody-goody, and just plain stuck-up most of the time. They spend every minute they can at the mall. I don't know. I was watching you for a while. I watched the way you used to sit in the cafeteria and write in that notebook. I never saw you hanging around those other dizzy girls. You seemed deeper than them. Then I sneaked a peek at those rhymes and saw that you have some lyrical skills. So I thought I'd try to talk to you to see where your head was."

Offended, her eyes narrowed in on him. "You talk about Teaneck as if you aren't from Teaneck!"

"Don't you know, it ain't where you're from, it's where you're at? It's where you're at mentally, girl. If you're down with those snotty suburbanites, then you're down with them. I'm not. I can go to P-Town and get much respect. They all know deejay Flex." He patted his chest in a self-important manner.

"That's all fine and well, but I don't know why you all have to call yourselves niggers," she mumbled, fiddling her fingers.

"It's not *niggers*. It's *niggas*. We taking that shit and defining it for ourselves."

"You're defining yourselves as niggers?" she asked sarcastically.

"No, N-I-G-G-A-S, New Improved Gangsters Going After Society," Flex stated in a voice that suggested finality.

"Going after society?"

"You damn right! The Real Deal Niggas, and we mean business." His voice was filled with excitement.

"Whatever," she said in a sarcastic voice.

"Yo. Like I said, I thought you were down. I mean, I can take you back to Teaneck and hang out at the mall with your friends," he said in an equally sarcastic voice.

"Look, why don't we just change the subject? Tell me more about your group." She realized that she was blowing her chances at impressing Flex. He was the total opposite of any guy she had ever dated. He was so different from her father, or any boy that he would approve of, that it made her want to hang out with him all the more.

"I don't have to. You can meet them for yourself. We're here," Flex said as he steered the car into the parking lot of the Christopher Columbus projects.

It amazed Deidre how quickly they had arrived. Paterson and Teaneck seemed to be worlds apart, but it had taken less than 20 minutes to drive from one place to the other. That was North Jersey for you; a city block could separate one town from another, the suburbs from the inner city.

She looked at the twelve big brick buildings and gulped. The buildings were lined up one behind the other in rows of six. Deidre counted fifteen stories on one side and at least twenty-five on the other side. She and Flex were parked in the parking lot of the smaller buildings.

"Why are these smaller than those over there?" she asked, pointing to the larger buildings.

"'Cause these are the projects, the Christopher Columbus projects better known as CCP. Those other buildings are called the towers," Flex explained as he turned off the engine and took the key out of the ignition.

"Oh," she said, looking at all the people standing around. She had never seen that many black folks in one spot before, not even at church. It wasn't like it was warm outside. She wondered what it would be like in the summer.

"Aren't you scared to leave your car parked here?"

Flex let out a sigh, and she knew that she had asked the wrong question.

"No, I'm not scared to leave my car here! Because the people who matter down here know it's my car. Look, girl, I think I better try and school you before you go in there and say something to offend somebody. First of all, have you ever heard of gangs?" Flex turned around and faced Deidre.

"Yeah. I mean, they kill people, right?" She knew that she was saying all the wrong things and losing all her cool points, but she couldn't seem to stop herself.

"Oh, brother. No, they don't just go around killing people. Please, don't go in there and let that fall out of your mouth." He threw his hands up.

"Why?" she asked.

"Because you might offend somebody." He let out another exasperated sigh.

"Are gang members going to be there?" Her eyes grew large, and her mouth fell open.

Flex threw up his hands and shook his head. "Deidre, the whole group belongs to a gang called the Spades."

"You too?" she asked. Half of her wanted him to say no, and the other half wanted him to say yes.

"No, not really. That's not the point. The point is, I don't want you to go in there and embarrass me," he stated firmly.

"What do you mean?"

"I mean, don't go in there acting like no dizzy Teaneck girl. Try to be up on things." He ran his hand through his uncombed hair and hissed.

She sucked her teeth. "Oh, well, I'll try not to embarrass you!" she snapped.

"I'm serious. I worked really hard to build up my rep here," Flex snapped back.

"Okay, God!"

Flex started to say something else but inhaled his breath deeply instead. He was silent for at least a minute before he spoke again.

"Okay. We practice in the rec center in the basement of building six. Just follow me, and *don't* embarrass me." He got out of the car.

She got out and followed him. She found it hard to keep up with him because she was too busy looking around. Since she wasn't watching her step, Deidre almost tripped on a badly cracked sidewalk.

She followed Flex into building six, and was immediately hit by a strong scent of urine. Frowning so hard her nose turned up, she tried to hold her breath as they walked down the stairs. When they walked through the heavy metal doors of the recreation center, she was expecting more than a couple of pool tables and a broken down pinball machine.

They walked through the large, almost empty room and went through yet another large metal door into a room basically the same as the other. It had cement floors and walls. There were a few gray folding chairs, a table, deejay equipment, and two large speakers. The group was already in there waiting for Flex. She noticed that there were four guys and a girl. One guy was tall and fat. One was short, skinny, and had a straying eye. Another one could best be described as tall, dark, and handsome. One word described the overly muscled one, dangerous. Deidre found herself more than a little frightened of him.

The petite and pretty girl appeared to be bored and sat off in a corner doing her nails. She had big bright eyes and sported one of those asymmetrical haircuts that everyone had, and Lana wouldn't let Deidre get. She seemed to be around the same age as Deidre. So, Deidre figured, if that girl could hang out with those guys and not be scared, then she could also.

"'Bout time you got here! Who's the trick?" the tall, fat one said as he propped his feet on the metal chair in front of the one he was sitting on.

"Word. That's why he's always late. Messing around with those tricks." The skinny one got up from his chair and walked over to the fat one.

"Better not let Sharon catch you. You know that chick is crazy. Who's the trick?" the handsome one asked as he leaned against the wall and looked Deidre up and down.

The dangerous one barely glanced at her and simply glanced at his very expensive-looking watch, as if passing along some silent message.

The girl glanced up for a moment and gave Deidre the once-over. Deidre wondered if the girl was crazy Sharon. When the girl smiled at Deidre before turning her attention back to her fingernails, Deidre breathed a sigh of relief.

But the girl's smile did nothing to ease Deidre's discomfort about the guys and their comments, however. Her first instinct was to curse them out and tell them that she wasn't a trick. Her mouth opened but no words came out.

"Yo, y'all chill out. This is Deidre. She's the girl from Teaneck I was telling y'all about. Deidre this is the group. That's Teddy B.K.A. Ted-Ski." Flex pointed to the tall fat one. "That's Louie B.K.A. Loose-Eye."

Flex pointed to the skinny one with the straying eye. "That's the god Divine." Flex pointed at the good-looking one. "That's Stacks. He's not in the group. But he believes in us and has invested a lot into our demo." Flex pointed at the mean and dangerous looking one. "And the girl over there painting her nails is my cousin, Sasha. She's not in the group either, but we let her hang around *sometimes*."

Sasha glanced up again and crossed her eyes at Flex before smiling at Deidre. "Don't mind them, girl. They're all bark and no bite. And they don't *let* me hang out anywhere. I hang out when and wherever I please." She stuck out her tongue at Flex.

"Oh, the Teaneck girl. The one that you said could rhyme." Divine ran his hand across his chin and let his eyes roam Deidre's body.

She noticed that while Divine spoke to Flex, he continued to stare at her. She glanced uncomfortably at Flex and saw that he was watching Divine.

"Yeah," Flex said.

"That trick don't look like she can flow," Teddy snapped. He just glared at Deidre.

Deidre's mouth was still wide open, and she still couldn't say a word. The only thing she could do was look at the people talking. She could not respond.

Louie slapped hands with Teddy. "She sure don't look like she can flow, too pretty and prissy-looking to rhyme."

"She can, man. Don't sleep on her. She's got crazy lyrical skills," Flex said, his eyes still on Divine.

"Man, get that trick-ass trick the hell out of here. Bad enough we in here practicing on New Year's Eve. I ain't got no time for this stuff. I could be somewhere getting blunted." Teddy jumped up out of his chair, and it folded with his sudden movement.

"I'm telling y'all she can rhyme," Flex said.

Deidre snapped out of her shocked daze. "Who are you calling a trick?" Her eyes went from wide to piercing, aimed at Teddy.

"Oh, snap! It's on!" Louie started jumping around and slapped hands with Teddy.

"Yo, y'all chill," Flex pleaded. "Deidre, chill. They don't mean any harm."

"They don't mean any harm! Forget that! I am not going to just stand here and let them disrespect me." Her eyes shot piercing looks at each of the four guys before landing on Flex.

"Deidre, just chill, all right?" Flex said.

"Hell no!" Not thinking about the words she said, they just left her mouth in a flood.

"Look, little Teaneck girl, we really don't mean no disrespect. We just got a lot of work to do. It's New Year's Eve, and we really don't want to be here. We have to finish our demo. If you ain't gonna do nothing but sit your pretty behind in here and distract us, then you gots to go." Divine was still leaning against the wall and staring at her when he spoke.

Deidre wanted to tell them that they didn't appear to be distracted by the other pretty girl in the room, but she didn't want to alienate her only female ally.

"Yo, I told y'all, the girl's got skills. I wouldn't bring her here if she didn't," Flex said. He dug his hands further in his pockets.

"Why don't y'all just let her rap then? Are you scared she might blow y'all away?" Sasha winked at Deidre.

"Fine, if she got skills, then put the trick on the mike," Teddy said, pointing to the equipment.

"Yeah. Put the trick on the mike," Louie agreed.

"Man. . . ." Flex started.

"Nah, man. Put her on the mike. If she can't flow, then she gotta go," Divine said. He had a strange smile on his face.

Flex turned to her. "Do you want to get on the mike?"

Heated, she felt an enormous surge of energy run through her. "Hell, yeah!"

"Aw, shoot! Somebody get the pooper scooper 'cause the trick is popping shit!" Louie started jumping around again.

"Well, go on with yourself," Teddy snapped.

"Get 'em, girl! Show them what a female can do. I tried to school them, but they act like they can't hear you if you ain't rhyming. Take them out, girlfriend!" Sasha stood up and walked over, blowing her nails dry between words.

Flex and Deidre took off their jackets. They all walked to the back of the room where the turntables and speakers were.

Flex went behind the table and started looking through a crate of records.

"What kind of beat do you want?" Flex looked up from the crate at Deidre.

"Whatever," she snapped.

"Aw snap," Louie said, laughing.

Divine and Teddy were standing by each other with their arms folded across their chests. Stacks just stood against the wall watching her with minimal interest. Sasha stood by Stacks.

Flex handed Deidre a microphone. "Look, Deidre, you don't have to rap if you don't want to. I can take you home."

"I want to!" She snatched the microphone.

"Aw snap," Louie repeated.

"Well, cut the bull and let the trick rap. I ain't got all day. Start flowing, trick!" Teddy snapped, as he turned up his nose.

"Yeah, put on the beat. We ain't got all day," Divine agreed.

She glared at them. She had never felt so much anger in her life, so much that she couldn't remember one line from the raps she had written. She started to change her mind, but when she took the microphone, it felt so right.

Flex put a record on each turntable, the headphones on his head, and the music started. He was cutting and scratching without even looking at the records. His eyes remained on her. She had no idea that he was such a good deejay.

Deidre felt a current run through her body. She recognized the beat right away. It was an old school slow one, "Heartbeat." Flex kept bringing it back to the same six chords, over and over, doo, doo, da, da, da, da. Her shoulders rocked back and forth and then he scratched and brought in the boom, boom, boom, boom of the heartbeat and flipped it back to the six chords. Not able to remember any of her rhymes, she had to free-style. She opened her mouth and words flowed out.

You so-called niggas done messed up now
Let a chick grab the mike and show you how
It's done and that's a fact
'Cause my skills are unsurpassed
You thought a prissy chick from Teaneck
Couldn't spank that ass
Too bad punks, you underestimated this
You messed up and messed with the wrong chick
It's time to school you
And I'm holding no prisoners
Screw you, you, you, you and yeah, you too, nigga
The Real Deal?
I think you're real ill
And I don't mean dope, fresh, fly or chill
I mean wack
You need help?
I'll define that
It's what you get with wannabe gangstas that can't rap
So, all y'all punks can just
Kiss what I twist
I'm Sweet Dee, niggas
Not your average trick!

"Woo-wee, go on, girl! Nice pick this time, cuz. I like her much better than that ole stupid Sharon." Sasha rushed up and gave Deidre a hug.

"Aw shit. You heard that shit?" Louie ran over to the others. "Yo, she dissed us."

Stacks finally spoke, and when he did the sound of his voice sent a deadly chill down her spine but she maintained her cool facade. "Yo, the trick can stay. Shit. Y'all niggas hurry up and get that demo done. Time is my money, and I don't let nobody mess with my money. Come on, Sasha, let's let these chumps practice."

Deidre watched as Sasha left with Stacks, and she wondered for a moment why Flex would let his cousin hang out with such an obviously dangerous guy. Then she figured Stacks must not be as dangerous as he looked; otherwise, Flex wouldn't let his cousin hang out with him.

Divine followed Teddy over to the table and picked up a microphone. "Let's practice. Yo, Sweet Dee, you wanna flow on our demo?"

"Yeah, whatever." Her voice sounded nonchalant, but her heart was racing. She knew that she was probably smiling from ear to ear. She couldn't help it. Her smiled widened even more when she looked at Flex and he winked at her.

The guys had a hard time prying her off the microphone. She remembered the rhymes she had written and they liked them, but they wanted her to flow hard like she did in her battle rap. They told her that her grimy style was fly.

Even though she was uncomfortable using the word nigga, and more than a little unsure how she felt about the word trick, especially in reference to herself, there was something about being in that basement with all those guys and having their approval that was very intoxicating. She made a conscious decision from that moment on to ignore her discomfort in exchange for their nods of approval, pats on the back, and sometimes pats on the backside when they thought Flex wasn't looking.

Deidre felt at home when she was on the microphone, as she had never felt before. For a while she even felt at home with her new crew, The Real Deal. It would be years before the warm fuzziness of belonging would die off, before she would tire of *bitch* and *ho* being substitutes for *woman*. Before she grew tired of being the only female in a crew of guys that only seemed to respect her when she was doing exactly what they wanted and representing them in the way they wanted her to. She knew it wouldn't, and couldn't, last forever, especially once she finished her bachelor of arts degree and The Real Deal got their recording contract and she got her own contract.

CHAPTER 5

"Dear Mama"

Kayla rubbed her eyes and sat up in bed. The last thing she wanted to do was go to school. She wondered how many of the kids, besides her best friend Lily, had seen the special or heard about it.

She'd always wondered who her father was. She'd stopped asking her mother about him, because she figured her mother would've told her if she thought she should know him. Kayla took the fact that Deidre never mentioned her father to mean that he didn't want her, that he had left them because he didn't want to be a dad.

She'd always thought that having Deidre was enough. Now she wasn't so sure, and she didn't like the feeling. She loved her mother more than anything and thought she was the coolest mom ever. Finding out that she had kept such a secret for so long made her seem a little less cool. Kayla just wanted to go back to the days when, at least in her eyes, her mother could do no wrong.

She walked over to her closet, pulled down an outfit and put it on the chair for her mother's inspection. They had a nice system in place where Kayla was able to pick out her own clothes to wear to school, but her mother got to look over the outfit and make any changes she thought suitable.

Each morning while Kayla took her shower and brushed her teeth, her mother would come into her room and look over whatever Kayla had put out. Most of the time she didn't make any changes, except to add some thermals or extra layers for the Minnesota winters. Every once in a while she would object to an outfit being too grown-up, or match the colors better. Today would be no different, no matter how Kayla felt about it.

Kayla sighed and walked out of her room to the bathroom. When she was done with her shower she returned to find her mother sitting on her bed.

Deidre smiled at her but Kayla couldn't smile back. *Why did she have to lie?*

Kayla walked past her and began to get dressed, not saying a word.

"Kayla, baby, we're going to have to talk about this. I need to know what you are feeling so that we can get past this."

Deidre sounded upset and Kayla didn't like to make her upset, but she felt so confused.

"Why do you need to know how I'm feeling now? You didn't care what I was feeling before." The words rushed out of Kayla's mouth, and it was only after she'd voiced what she was thinking that she realized that she was being a little too smart-mouthed and could find herself in big trouble.

Kayla looked at Deidre and noticed that she looked just as upset as Kayla herself felt. She didn't like seeing Deidre upset, and didn't like feeling that she was somehow the cause.

Kayla finished putting on her clothes, waiting for her mother to tell her that she needed to watch her mouth, that she was not too old to be punished. Deidre just sat on the bed, however, and said nothing.

The quiet was getting to Kayla and once she laced up her tennis shoes she sat down next to Deidre on the bed.

Deidre placed her hand on Kayla's leg and cleared her throat. She rubbed Kayla's leg as she spoke.

"I know that I made a mistake, Kayla. I thought about it all last night. If I had it to do over again, I would probably make a different decision. I don't know. This has all happened so suddenly. I want you to know that I love you. I'm going to try and make this right."

Kayla took a deep breath. "Are you going to tell him?"

Deidre was silent for a moment. She moved her hand from Kayla's leg and started to wring her hands together. "Do you want me to tell him?"

Kayla thought about it for a moment. Did she want Deidre to tell Flex Towns about her? She had a father. If he didn't already know, it was on television. What if he didn't want a child, or a daughter, or her for a daughter?

"I don't know, Mom. I mean, I always used to wonder about who my dad was. I guess I've always wanted a dad. I've also liked it being just the two of us and having Grandma when she visits. Having Flex Towns for a dad could be cool." She stopped and thought for a moment. "I mean, he's famous and maybe he could give me a record deal on his label—you know like Lil' Pablo's dad Super C." Kayla could feel herself getting excited and almost forgetting all her other fears.

"Now hold on, little lady. Just because your father owns his own record label does *not* mean that you're going to be a rapper. You know how I feel about that. When you become an adult you can do whatever you want. Until then, you're going to go to school and get good grades, and then go to college and get even better grades." Deidre's stern voice accompanied with a pointed look erased most of Kayla's excitement.

Leave it to Mommy to burst the happy bubble, Kayla thought.

"But, Mom, I have skills. You won't even listen to me." Kayla didn't know why she continued to try to convince Deidre that she could really rap. They'd had this conversation many times before, and it always ended up the same. Deidre really wasn't listening to her at all. Maybe Flex Towns would be different.

"That's not the point. The point is, I don't want you to think meeting your father is going to jumpstart some dream you have for a rap career."

"I was just thinking that if my father heard me rap and liked it, he could produce an album for me, and I'd finally be able to blow those little boy rappers out of the water."

"Is that the only reason you want to meet your dad?" Deidre looked worried and a little stern, never a good combination.

Kayla tilted her head as she thought about the question. "No, I just want to meet him. But I'm scared. What if he doesn't like me? Or what if he doesn't want to be my dad?"

"I don't think that he's going to deny you, Kayla. I really think that he won't be able to help loving you. You're a wonderful kid." Deidre hugged her and then planted kisses on her forehead.

Lately, Kayla pulled away whenever Deidre got all mushy. *It was so-oo un-cool.* This time she decided to hug Deidre back. "You're not so bad, as far as moms go."

"So, are we okay? Are we going to be all right?" Deidre found herself holding her breath as she waited for Kayla to answer her. She knew that it would serve her right if Kayla held on to her anger a little bit longer. She'd really messed up this one, and she dreaded having to face Flex.

If she had to in order to salvage things between herself and her child, she would. She would do just about anything to make things right between them, even face someone she now was willing to admit she'd wronged.

Kayla's face took on the serious expression that always reminded Deidre of Flex. It amazed her that their child had so many of his little facial quirks, and that sometimes, especially when quiet and contemplative, Kayla looked so much like Flex.

"Yeah, Mom, we're fine. When are we going to go to New York?"

Stunned, Deidre paused for a moment. She'd thought she would have a little more time before she had to face Flex. Then she figured the sooner she got it over with, the better.

"We can head out this weekend, if you'd like."

"That's so far away."

"It's only two days away, Kayla. Besides, you wouldn't want to miss school, would you?"

"Wanna bet? The kids are probably going to tease me about this nonstop."

Deidre sighed. This was going to be hard for Kayla. There was nothing she could do now to make up for it. "I'm sorry, sweetie, but you still have to go to school."

"I don't want to go. I just know that they are going to come up all kinds of jokes."

"Well, you're a pretty smart kid—funny and quick on your feet. I'm sure you'll give them a run for their money. Think of it as a free-style battle. I know you can come up with some witty one-liners. You can practice those skills you keep telling me you have." Deidre couldn't help running her hand across her child's cheek as she spoke. Sometimes she just had to touch Kayla to make sure she was real and that she was hers. She loved her daughter.

When Kayla didn't brush off Deidre's hand, as she did more and more now that she was in her preteen years, Deidre smiled.

"Hey, yeah, good idea, Mom! I can come up with snaps for whoever wants some. Thanks." Kayla actually appeared to be happy and content for the first time since coming home distraught.

Deidre didn't know how she felt about encouraging her daughter to use rap, the one thing she was trying to discourage, as a means of shielding herself from cruel kids. As a former rapper known for being good at free-styling, she knew it was a powerful weapon. It wouldn't hurt Kayla to become adept at thinking fast on her feet and if it worked for school, she was more than happy to have come up with the suggestion. As long as the kid wasn't running off to become the next American idol, or rap superstar, it was probably okay.

Deidre looked down at her watch. There was no way Kayla was going to be able to walk to school and make it on time. She was going to have to drive her.

"Look at the time, Pumpkin. I'll have to drive you to school this morning."

Kayla made a point of looking at the raggedy sweatpants, t-shirt, and dusty house slippers Deidre wore around the house.

Deidre rolled her eyes. "I'll be in the car. Don't worry, none of your friends will see what I'm wearing. Goodness gracious, you would think the kid would just be happy to be getting a ride to school."

"I am, but I have enough things for the kids at school to tease me about. I don't need them teasing me about my mom's raggedy ponytail, busted sweat pants, and t-shirt. And why do you still wear those slippers? They are *so-oo* cruddy."

"I'll have you know this is my lounge wear, darling daughter. All the real divas are wearing this ensemble this season." She stood and did a half spin as she modeled her attire.

"Yeah, well, put on a jacket, please. Stay in the car." Kayla rolled her eyes dramatically and followed it with a smile.

Deciding to let the sly eye-roll slide since the kid was acting like herself again, she breathed a sigh of relief. As they walked out of the bedroom hand in hand, Deidre marveled at her twelve-year-old's reaction to her clothing. She would have thought that she had a few more years before Kayla started being embarrassed by her. She wondered what it would be like once Kayla became a teenager, or once Kayla was introduced to the suave and ultra rich world of Flex Towns, super producer. Panic filled her at the thought of what could happen once Kayla and Flex met.

Taking several deep, calming breaths, Deidre bit her lip and threw on a light spring jacket over the ensemble that Kayla wanted so desperately to hide. She supposed the t-shirt and sweats had seen better days, but they were comfortable, much like the life she'd had just a few days ago.

CHAPTER 6

"Always on Time"

Once she dropped Kayla off, she stopped at the independently owned coffee shop to grab a cup of fresh brewed coffee and a chocolate croissant to have for breakfast instead of the wheat grain and skim milk waiting for her at home. It was May, and while she had a stack of final papers to grade, the semester was over and she didn't have to make the trek to campus to teach her classes. For the first time in years she was not teaching a summer class, and once school was out for Kayla, she planned on making the most of the summer with her child. That included lots of trips to Camp Snoopy in the Mall of America, if her budding preteen hadn't outgrown it already. She supposed that she was going to have to factor in Flex somewhere in the equation. What if he wanted to spend the summer with Kayla? *Perish the thought!* She shuddered. He didn't seem like the parental type anyway, at least not the Flex she saw on television and read about in the gossip rags.

She ran a few errands while she was out in an attempt to delay the work that waited for her at home. She loved being able to work at home in her sweats and even though she didn't relish the stack of papers waiting for her, she knew that once she got settled at her "desk," à la the kitchen table, she would be all set. Being done for the summer so that she could get a jumpstart on her next poetry chapbook was a big motivating factor.

Deidre James, poet and teacher, was a far cry from Sweet Dee, the bold and sometimes vulgar female rap artist, and she liked it that way. Her life was quiet. No one got shot after a poetry reading. For the most part, the media wasn't trying to find out the latest dish on an up-and-coming poet.

Thinking of her simple life made the fact that in two days she was going to have to fly to New York and face Flex all the more stressful. *Maybe he'll be out of town. Maybe he'll be on tour or something like that.* She smiled at her wistful thoughts.

Deidre drove up the back alley, hit the garage door opener, and sailed into her small one-car garage. As she walked into the back door of her home, she could hear someone ringing the front doorbell. She wondered if it was the FedEx man. He always came when she wasn't home. She always filled out the back of the 'delivery attempted' card telling them to just leave future deliveries, but he never did. So, she ended up having to drive to the distribution center to pick up the package.

Determined to catch him this time, she ran to the front of the house, almost skidding across the polished hardwood floors. *Maybe Kayla is right. Maybe it is time for some new slippers. These have no traction whatsoever.*

Deidre banished the thought from her head. There was nothing wrong with her slippers. They had lasted her a good five years, and she believed they would last her another five.

She snatched open the door to see Flex Towns turning to walk away.

When the door opened, he turned back around and looked her dead in the eyes. Her mouth fell open and goose bumps suddenly traveled up and down her arms. Handsome was too mild a term to describe the man standing at her front door. He was tall, and had filled out with muscles in all the right places. The last time she'd seen him he'd had a headful of small locs. He now sported a close-cropped haircut. His dark chocolate complexion was still smooth and flawless. *Yikes. Not good.*

"Fredrick." Even though he would always be Flex to her, she called him Fredrick. At one time she did it because everyone else called him Flex and she wanted to be different. Later in their relationship, when she told herself she could care less about standing apart from all the groupies and hoochie mamas circulating in Flex's world and hanging around The Real Deal, she called him Fredrick simply because it got on his nerves.

"Deidre." His face was stoic. The stern stare made his always quiet demeanor scarier.

She realized that she was standing there with her mouth gaping, eyes wide, and the door open. She let out a hiss of air and tried to fight the dread knotting up in her belly. Flex had obviously seen the television special. There was no reason to try to lie. She was caught.

She opened the door a little wider and motioned for him to come inside. "Please come in."

Flex motioned for his bodyguards to stay outside and he followed her inside.

She surveyed the number of men traveling with Flex. *Why would he need that many bodyguards? Must be pretty dangerous being a record producer in hip-hop these days,* she thought wryly.

With her stomach churning and an uncomfortable heat traversing her body, she took what she hoped was a calming breath. It was no time for a panic attack. The little chat with Flex was going to be hard and she was in no way prepared. She led him into the living room and they each took a seat, she on the loveseat and he on the sofa right across from her.

Glad that the living room was the room least used in her home, and therefore always clean and tidy, she let her eyes roam every inch of the tiny space just to be able to look somewhere besides into Flex's accusing eyes. Taking in the cream sofa and loveseat, the Varnette P. Honeywood framed print *African Women* that hung over her fireplace, and the huge mud-cloth inspired rug that filled a large portion of the hardwood floor, she glanced occasionally at Flex to gauge his mood.

They said nothing to each other for what felt like hours but couldn't have been that long. She noticed that he seemed to be thinking as carefully about the words he was going to say as she was. Even though he was silent, his eyes roamed her body and seemed to penetrate her soul.

Deidre couldn't take it any more. "So, I take it you saw the television special."

His narrow-eyed gaze unshakable, he simply stared at her. Then she noticed one eyebrow slightly lift.

"Yes, I saw it. We need to have a serious talk, Deidre."

Deidre shivered. Flex had called her by her first name. *Not good.* He hardly ever called her that. Back in the day he only called her Sweetness or Dee, rarely Deidre. She could tell he was upset.

The average person would never be able to tell how upset he was. He appeared to be calm, cool, and collected. Ignorance would be welcomed at that moment since she truly regretted the fact that she knew him so well that she could read his every emotion. She wondered when, if ever, that kind of connection left a person.

She gave him a quick once-over. He looked good—damn good. The years had certainly been kind to him. He'd put on a few pounds, but it was all muscle. He'd come a long way from the tall lanky kid she'd met in high school. His close-cropped haircut and clean-shaven face showcased him as perfectly groomed. There was something else she noticed about him that made him even more appealing. He still exuded the same bad-boy confidence that had attracted her to him in the first place, but it was more subtle, making him all the more striking.

He looked every bit the high-powered businessman he'd become. His attire was dressy casual and clearly expensive. She was hard-pressed to find any semblance of the skinny, scraggly, roughneck kid. Noticing how dapper he looked made Deidre remember her own clothing. The last thing she wanted was to have her ex see her looking like this.

"So, to what do I owe this unannounced visit?" She tried to sound professional and strong, but she felt scared and on edge.

The glance that Flex gave her when the words came out of her mouth did not help her feel any better either.

Okay, so I know why you're here. That doesn't explain why you just popped up unannounced. We call first in polite society.

"Okay, maybe that came out wrong. I . . . well . . . I was going to fly to New York this weekend to talk to you . . . umm . . . about all of this . . . you know." Stammering, she crossed and uncrossed her arms as she spoke.

His expression didn't change a bit. He still stared at her as if he didn't believe a word she said.

She guessed that she couldn't blame him for doubting her. If she could have figured out a way not to tell him that he had a child, she would have done so. She knew she was wrong, but knowing you are wrong and being able to face it were two different things.

He sat back on the cream sofa, his eyes on her the whole time. She wished that he would say something, not just look at her as if she'd stolen something. *I guess technically I did steal someone from him, but I didn't think I had a choice.*

She sighed. "Say something. I've had it with the silent treatment for today." Dealing with Kayla in her silent mode had been nerve-wracking, to say the least. She couldn't take it from Flex as well.

His eyebrow lifted slightly, but he remained silent.

Going for broke, Deidre let out the breath she realized she'd been holding. "You know, things were really messed up between us at the end. Between the arguments and you spending so much time with Stacks and pushing me away . . . There was no way I wanted to raise a child in that kind of environment. I did what I thought was best at the time. Maybe it wasn't the best solution—"

"That's putting it mildly, don't you think? No matter how much you think things deteriorated between us at the end, I was always faithful to you—to us. I loved you, in spite of your lack of trust. I would never have kept our child from you. The fact that you kept my daughter from me for twelve years was more than just a poor solution. It's jacked up!"

Okay, I probably deserve that. He can get that off his chest. Maybe I should have just let him continue to sulk and steam. He always was a man of few words but once you got him upset about something and talking, oh brother.

She figured that it was her turn to be silent—to let Flex get things off his chest.

She never was any good at keeping her mouth shut, however. "I don't think it will do us any good to rehash old arguments about whether or not you were faithful. I'm just trying to get you to see what my state of mind was at the time so that you could maybe see that my decision—"

"I don't care what your state of mind was at the time. There is no excuse, no reason in the world that is going to justify what you have done to me—to my child. You took it upon yourself to decide whether I got to be a father, whether my child had a father. What gave you the right?" He leaned forward and pointed his finger as he spoke.

She swallowed and took a deep breath. "Were you ready to be a father then? We were what twenty-two years old? Your career with The Real Deal was taking you all over the world. Sasha had been murdered. Not to mention all the stuff that went down with Stacks. Everything was just too wild and too violent around you at that time. I didn't want my child around that. I *still* don't want my child around that."

He shook his head and laughed, only it didn't sound like a happy laugh. "You're really good at changing the focus, but not this time. What I need to know is why. After all we meant—all I thought we meant to one another—how could you do this to me? You betrayed me. You betrayed us. For what? Because you thought I was sleeping around? Because you didn't think I would choose you and our child over my career? What?"

Her breath caught in her throat. Hearing Flex voice his anger, his questions about her actions and the reasons behind them, made her go still. The last question especially felt like a razor scraping across her bones; it cut that close to her core, to inner feelings she hadn't even admitted to herself.

"Me wanting you to choose between us and hip-hop had nothing to do with my reasons for not telling you. That had nothing to do with it at all. I told you I thought I was making the right decision at the time. I now realize that it might not have been."

He let out that hollow laugh again. "Oh, and what made you realize that? Getting caught?"

She didn't know what she could do to make Flex understand. Getting tired of trying, she simply bit her lower lip and fiddled her hands. He had hit more than a few nerves and she felt wide open, emotionally raw.

CHAPTER 7

"Ex-Factor"

Flex had come to Deidre's house full of anger, and quickly became irritated by how fast it dissipated and was replaced by other stirrings. The simple truth was that these days he was more inclined to let most things slide as long as they didn't impact his business, his image, or the people he cared for. The fact that Deidre and his long-lost daughter now represented vulnerable people that others could hurt to get to him was not lost on him.

It was also hard to hold on to his anger with her looking so sexy in those old raggedy sweatpants and t-shirt, even harder once he realized that he still cared about her more that he was willing, or ready, to admit.

She'd filled out in all the right places. It was easy to see the imprint of her shapely behind in those sweats. While the t-shirt was a little loose, he could tell that her breasts were still perfect for his hands. Her slender arms were crossed on her knee. At thirty-five she was even more beautiful than she was years ago, even with her long light-brown hair pulled back in a ponytail. Her light brown eyes were flecked with gold and showcased all of her emotions; they were still capable of drawing him out of himself and into her. She represented beauty in a real and down-to-earth way that he realized he'd missed terribly.

Deidre was right. Things had gotten pretty intense between them in the end. Things in his life and career had been even crazier. He had spent a lot of time with Stanley "Stacks" Carter, his former 'friend'/record label owner/manager when his cousin Sasha was shot and killed. He'd wanted to find a way to prove that Stanley knew more about what happened to Sasha than he let on. The only thing he'd managed to do was gather evidence of Stacks violating parole and push

Deidre away. At the time he'd told himself that he was keeping her out of danger.

Feeling unable to protect the people he loved, he'd struggled all the more to keep Deidre safe. The stress of it all had been overwhelming, and it didn't help that Deidre did not take well to being put off and turned away. She'd pushed back, and wouldn't listen when all he was trying to do was keep her away from potentially dangerous situations. One night, things blew up and got so out of control that he scared her. It scared him so much that he immediately got counseling.

The thing was, he thought once things were handled with Stacks and he got the help he needed he would eventually get his woman back. That had never happened, and now they were sitting across from one another and Flex was trying like hell to remember that he had just cause to be pissed off at her.

"So, I'm hoping that we can deal with this in an amicable manner. I mean . . . I know that I should have told you about Kayla. But . . . well . . . I hope that eventually you will be able to at least understand my reasons . . ."

Rambling. She always rambled when she knew she was caught out there and dead wrong. *Understand her reasons? I will never understand her reasons. I might find it in myself to forgive her one day, but I will never understand.*

Flex let his eyes take in all of Deidre. She was still a dime piece. That was for certain. Even with her hair held back and wearing those slippers that could only be described as pink and dirty, she looked gorgeous.

Her pretty little face and please-understand-why-I-did-what-I-did demeanor were not going to make him forget why he was there. She'd had twelve years with their child, and he wanted his time with Kayla as well. It was only fair. He also needed to be able to protect them both, with Stacks getting out of jail any day now.

"I want my daughter, Deidre."

"You—you what? What do you mean, you want your daughter?"

"I mean what I said. I want a chance to be a father to my daughter."

She started fiddling with her hands in her lap. "But . . . well . . . of course. I think that's a good idea. We can make some sort of arrangement. I'm sure that she could visit you in New York. You know, on holidays, perhaps, or a week or two in the summer. It would be great for the two of you to get to know each other. I wouldn't want to stand in the way of that."

He gritted his teeth just thinking about her deception. She really was a piece of work, very diplomatic now that she'd been caught.

"I don't want to be a part-time dad to her. I want to be a full-time part of her life. I want her to live with me."

Deidre's jaw dropped and she sat straight up in her chair. By her facial expressions he could see his words rolling over in her head. Her lips twisted in so many different directions, she looked as if she were practicing a lip-sync routine. Only there was no sound. Unless of course you counted the hissing and sucking of teeth that sounded as if she were battling in a beat-box competition. Her eyes went from bulging in shock to narrowing in anger within seconds. It really was quite a sight to behold.

He folded his arms across his chest and waited for her one-woman facial expression routine to end.

"So, are you saying that you want to fight me for custody of my child?" Her back went ramrod straight and she peered at him through slanted eyes.

"Our child."

"You only just found out about her a minute ago and now you want to be a full-time daddy? What's that all about? You haven't even had any DNA testing done. She might not even be your child, for all you know. Most men would want some kind of proof. I have raised that girl all by myself, all her life. I'm all she knows—"

"Whose fault is that? You took it upon yourself to make decisions for us, for our child, without even considering how I might feel. You cut me out of my daughter's life. I am not willing to miss out on one minute more. I don't need any tests, Deidre. Unlike you, I trust the relationship we had. I can tell that she's mine." Flex leaned back in the sofa and studied her carefully. If looks could kill, he'd already be cremated and his ashes spread in the Atlantic. If he could get her to see reason, then he'd be able to insure the safety of both Deidre and their daughter.

He leaned forward again and placed his hands on his knees. "Unlike you, Deidre, I am not going to selfishly horde our child and keep her away from you. My mother died in childbirth and I never even knew her. I would never keep a child away from her mother. In fact, I'm a firm believer that, whenever possible, a child should have both parents at home."

She let out a sarcastic laugh. "Oh, now you're the poster child for family values."

He chuckled; even he could appreciate the irony. "Maybe not the poster child, but I certainly have some thoughts about how I want *my* child to be raised."

"News flash, Fredrick, I don't need your input. I've been doing just fine by myself." She shot daggers at him with her eyes.

"Things are about to change, because you and Kayla are no longer alone. I fully intend to be a full-time presence, a full-time dad."

"So what exactly are you saying? You want some sort of joint custody arrangement where she spends half the year with you and half the year with me?" She folded her arms across her chest.

"No, that's not what I'm saying at all."

"So you're going to sue me for full custody? I don't believe this!" Her eyes narrowed and her voice went up into a near screech.

"No, I don't want to take our daughter away from her mother."

"So, what are you saying?"

It's the best way and the only way to make sure that she and our daughter are protected, he told himself as he prepared to put all his cards on the table. "I'm saying that I want you to marry me, and I want us to give Kayla the two-parent home she should have had from the get-go."

Deidre found herself gripping the pillows of the loveseat. She couldn't believe what had just come out of Flex's mouth. *He must be out of his ever-loving mind. Marry him!* She jumped up, walked the few steps that it took to get from the loveseat to the sofa, and stood right in front of him.

"Have you lost your mind? We haven't been together in over a decade and you're talking about marriage? Why on earth would I marry you?"

"I can think of several reasons. The first and most important reason being you really want what's best for our child, and you realize the error of your ways, realize that you were wrong to keep us apart all those years. The second reason is you don't want to drag her through a big, ugly, public custody battle. Because I promise you, Deidre, there are really only a few ways this can play out right now.

"Either you marry me and move to the East Coast with our child, or you gracefully agree to grant me full custody with visitation for yourself. The other scenarios all end up with me keeping you in court for as long as it takes for me to get my child. While I know my dad worked out wonderful contract deals for you back in the day, your royalty checks don't pay enough to cover what it would cost you to go up against me." He studied his nails briefly before concluding. "I don't think your little community college instructor's salary or the money you make from your little poetry books will cover it, either. So let's just do this the easy way."

Stunned, she hadn't thought things could get worse. She should have known better. *Things can always get worse!* If Flex thought she was going to marry him, then he had another thought coming. She was not going to do it. She couldn't do it. How could he even ask her to? Marrying for the sake of a child never worked out. Her parents were a classic example of that, and she would *not* end up like them. He couldn't make her do that.

Surely he can be reasoned with. "I know you're upset. Okay, I admit you have good reason to be upset. You're right. What I did was wrong. It was jacked up, totally jacked up. Okay, I can own that. I *do* own it. But surely you see that the two of us getting married out of some anti-quated idea of what kind of family a kid needs is just wrong."

"I don't think it's wrong at all. I think that it's right. Growing up with just my dad was rough. He was always busy with work and his community obligations. I want my child to have two parents. I want her to live under the same roof as me." Flex crossed his arms across his chest. The firm tilt of his head that always struck her as a little *too* cocky was a sure sign to Deidre that he had made up his mind and he thought his idea was best and beyond reproach.

"Her life is here, her friends, her school." She threw up her arms instead of using them to pull him off the sofa and shake him as she wanted to.

"I'm not saying that it won't take a minute to adjust. I am saying that I want us to take that step." The matter-of-fact tone let her know that reasoning with him was going to be almost impossible.

"You know, you talk about a two-parent home like that is always the best thing. I grew up in a two-parent home and it was not all it was cracked up to be. In fact, it was hell. I don't want that for Kayla." She shuddered and blinked back the memories of hiding in the closet while her respectable doctor father beat her mother.

"She won't have that."

Flex more than anyone knew how her home life had been. For a while she'd thought he was the savior who was going to take her away from it all.

His gaze softened for a moment, then just as quickly went back to the firm my-way-or-the-highway stare. "We can be mature adults and put our own issues aside for our child's sake."

Barely able to stop herself from stamping her feet, she stood straight with her arms close at her side. "Well, I don't call this being mature. I call this being crazy. We don't have to get married just because we share a child. Word to the wise, it's a little too late for the shotgun."

"Look, I meant what I said. I want my child. So, if that means I have to take you too, then that's just the way it will have to be." He shrugged nonchalantly.

"Oh, how romantic. This is just the kind of proposal every girl dreams of. Not!" She walked away from him. Feeling as if her entire world was caving in and she was powerless to stop it infuriated her.

SWEET SENSATION

She knew that Flex was right about one thing. Fighting him for custody wouldn't be a piece of cake. Besides the fact that his father was one of the most prominent judges on the East Coast and had the contacts to prove it, Flex could afford to pay for the help that his father's colleagues would no doubt offer for free. She was not going to let those details, or the sexy man sitting in front of her, bully her into some sham of a marriage, however. *No way.*

She narrowed her eyes and let out a long, pronounced hiss. "I. Will. Not. Marry. You. Fredrick."

"He wants to marry you? Cool!" A twelve-year-old voice from the entryway made Deidre's heart skip a beat.

How long have I spent arguing with Flex? Kayla is out of school already? She spun around and looked at the wall clock before turning her gaze on her eavesdropping child. Three-forty. The girl was actually thirty minutes late. *I told her about coming straight home from school.* She made a note to herself to find out what had kept her daughter from coming home promptly this time.

Smiling wider than Deidre had seen her smile in days, Kayla's face looked the picture of happiness. Did Kayla want them to get married? Deidre let the possibility roll around in her head for a moment, and then quickly pushed it away. It didn't matter what her daughter wanted. It didn't matter what her daughter's father wanted. It mattered what was best. Clearly, she was the only one out of the trio who knew what that was. "No, Kayla—"

"Would you like for us to get married, sweetheart? Would you like to live with both of your parents?" Flex smoothly cut her off. He didn't even wait for her to at least introduce him to Kayla.

Deidre blew out a sharp breath from between twisted lips. She turned her gaze back to her child, because if she looked at Flex she was going to explode. She didn't want to do that in front of Kayla.

She didn't think it was possible, but Kayla's face lit up even more at Flex's question. "I think that would be *super cool.*"

Deidre relaxed her lips and released her scowl. *This is ridiculous,* she thought to herself. *I shouldn't let the two of them sway me. They don't know what's best.*

56

"Baby, I don't think—"

"Yes, Deidre, don't think. Your thinking has gotten us in the predicament we're in now. I think its time to move past that and do what's right, and I think that my daughter feels the same way that I do." Flex got up from the chair and walked over to Kayla. He held out his hand. "Hello, Kayla, my name is Flex Towns, and I'm your father. I want to start being a father to you, if that's all right with you. I know this is sudden. Hopefully we can spend time getting to know each other, and we can build on our relationship from there."

Kayla placed her hand in Flex's and Deidre watched, stunned.

"Hello, Fle—uh . . . Mr. Towns. I would like for us to get to know each other too. I think it would be nice if you married my mom. I always wanted a dad."

She always wanted a dad? Deidre sunk down on the sofa that Flex had vacated and placed her hands over her eyes.

CHAPTER 8

"Daddy's Little Girl"

Kayla smiled as she let go of Flex's hand. *My father. Dad. Daddy. Pops. I wonder if he'll let me call him Dad?*

She'd had a feeling when she came home and saw the huge SUV limo outside of their home. She'd hoped against hope that Flex Towns was inside, but never would she have dreamed that he was inside asking Deidre to get married. *He wants me and he wants my mom! Things couldn't be any better.*

"Thanks, Kayla, and you can call me Flex until you feel comfortable calling me Dad. I know this is as much a shock for you as it is for me. I'm really glad that I found out about you." He gently touched her cheek, and she felt all warm and mushy inside.

He wants me to call him Dad! She felt her lips spread into a wide grin; then she turned to Deidre.

Deidre didn't appear too excited. In fact, she didn't seem happy at all. She just looked weird—kind of sad, and almost scared.

"So, how about I take you two ladies out to dinner tonight and we can spend some time getting to know one another?" He smiled at Kayla, but she saw him throw a cautious glance at Deidre.

"Oh sure, I can see it now. We'll be eating and getting bum-rushed by your fans in between bites. Or we'll have to eat surrounded by your security team. We live simple lives. I don't want to raise a child around all that constant surveillance." Deidre huffed and fixed her eyes on Flex.

Kayla laughed, because she knew she would be in serious trouble for giving off as much attitude as Deidre was.

"It's okay, Mom. It should be fun. We could go to that small place on Lyndale you love that serves the Puerto Rican food you say reminds you of the East Coast. They're pretty small, and if we get a table in the back corner we won't have to worry about people crowding us." She knew she was gushing, but she couldn't help herself. She hoped happiness was contagious and some would rub off on Deidre.

Deidre sighed. Kayla almost felt bad because it seemed she was taking Flex's side against Deidre. She really wanted to get to know Flex better, and wanted Flex and Deidre to be together. Seeing them together and hearing Flex say he wanted to marry Deidre and have them be a family had sparked something in Kayla that she hadn't known was there. She wanted a father. She wanted *her* father.

She had a feeling that if she could get Deidre to spend more time with Flex, she would see that it would be a good idea for them to be a family and come around. So, she guessed that even if she was taking Flex's side, she wasn't *really* against Deidre. She just wanted Deidre to be happy, and hoped that Flex could make that happen.

"Come on, Deidre, it'll be fun. We can go out, have a nice meal, talk. I really would like to spend more time with you and Kayla."

Deidre's frown lightened just a little when Flex spoke that time. "How about we have dinner together here? I'll cook. You can come back in a few hours and we can have a nice relaxing dinner and conversation here."

"We will have to be out in public eventually, but if you want to stay in, we'll stay in. How about I send my guys over to that restaurant to pick up some takeout? That way you won't have to stress over cooking. If it's okay with you and Kayla, I'd like to stay and get to know her better until the food arrives." He smiled at Kayla when he spoke.

"That would be great. I'd love that." So excited that she could barely contain her composure, Kayla's words come out in a jumbled rush.

"Fine, if that's what you both want then I guess I don't really have a say." Deidre lacked any enthusiasm.

"You have a say. You can say no. I really hope you don't, because I would like to spend some more time getting to know this beautiful young lady." Flex gazed at Kayla as if she were the most precious girl in the world.

Kayla smiled. Before only Deidre and Lana had looked at her like that, sometimes her grandfather. But she didn't see him a lot. Having her father look at her like that was awesome.

Kayla gave Deidre a pleading look.

Deidre's shoulders slumped and she sighed. "Fine, Fredrick. Kayla knows the dishes that we usually order, and there should be a menu for the restaurant in the kitchen cabinet. I'm going to take a little nap so you two can spend some time getting to know one another."

Deidre left them standing there and went back to her bedroom.

Kayla sighed. It wasn't a good start. *How are they going to get together if she won't spend time with him?*

"So, should we go look over these menus so that we can order the food? I'm getting kind of hungry," Flex said.

She turned away from watching Deidre leave and returned Flex's smile. "Sure."

Flex couldn't believe he was sitting across from his daughter at the kitchen table. She was beautiful. He would have never thought that a child who looked so much like him could be so pretty, but she was. She had his features, but they were softened, and her beautiful brown-cinnamon skin tone was a blend of his and Deidre's coloring. She wore her thick hair in a ponytail with a curled bang in the front, and her smile could brighten any room.

He couldn't stop looking at her in wonder. The thought that he and Deidre had made her blew his mind. She was so smart. It was hard to believe that she was really only twelve years old.

He had a feeling that she was going to be crucial to his winning Deidre over. That was the ultimate goal. It was the only way to ensure that both Kayla and Deidre were safe. He had to get Deidre and Kayla close to him where he could protect them. He couldn't let anything happen to them now that he had found them.

"So, tell me about yourself, Kayla. What do you like to do? What are some of your favorite things? I want to know everything."

"Really?" She seemed hesitant.

"Of course. Do you like school? Are you a good student? Do you play a sport?" He pinched her nose playfully. "Who's your favorite music producer? You know, the crucial stuff."

Kayla laughed and, for a moment, something about the way her face lit up and the expression in her eyes made him think immediately of Deidre.

"Well, I like school a lot. I get really good grades and I'm pretty good at volleyball. I played on a team for girls under fourteen last summer. My favorite producers are . . ." She looked at him and smiled mischievously. "Let me see . . . that would probably be a tie between Diddy and Kanye. I can't forget Missy and Timberland. I *really lo-ve* Missy but then I also like—"

"Okay, okay, you're killing me." He clutched his heart as if in pain, then smiled. "Seriously, you seem to know a little something about music. Do you listen to a lot of hip-hop music? How do you know so much?"

"That's because I'm going to be the next little kid rapper, and I'm going to blow all those little boys out of the water."

Flex sat back in his chair. He hadn't expected his twelve-year-old daughter to rattle off the names of producers the way she did. Hearing that she wanted to be a rapper put it in perspective. Most kids with dreams like that knew all the players and already had a wish list of people they wanted to work with and get beats and tracks from.

She wanted to be a rapper. He wondered how Deidre felt about that. "Really, a rapper, huh? What makes you want to be a rapper?"

She shrugged. "I don't know. I guess it started out because Mom used to be one, and even though she doesn't rap anymore, sometimes when she does a poetry reading people will say that her work has a hip-hop feel to it. She doesn't let me listen to a lot of rap."

"So how do you know so much about the music?" Flex had a feeling he wasn't going to like the answer to that question.

She studied him carefully before answering. It was clear that she was trying to gauge whether or not she could trust him. She must have figured she could.

"Sometimes, when I'm with my friend Lily, we'll listen to rap music that her older brother, Patrick, has. He wants to be a producer. So he has a lot of music and he spends all his money on the newest and hottest stuff. We sneak and listen to it and watch the video channels after school when we're done with our homework. That's how I saw the Music Channel special on Mom and found out you were my dad." She looked him in the eye then. "Are you really okay with being my dad? You're not upset that I'm a girl, or that I'm not—"

Flex cut her off because he didn't want her to have any doubts. "Baby, I am overjoyed that you are my daughter and beyond happy to be your dad. From the moment I saw your picture on the screen I have been overcome with feelings of happiness. I feel like the luckiest man in the world to have such a beautiful and smart daughter."

"I'm not that pretty."

"Oh yes, you are. You are pretty and so precious, never doubt that I want you in my life. Now that I know about you, I'm not going to stop until we're together as a family."

"Is that why you want to marry Mom?"

"Partly." He wasn't about to get into an in-depth conversation with the daughter he'd just met about his mixed-up feelings for her mother, especially when he really hadn't sorted out what he was feeling anyway.

The doorbell rang, and Flex realized that his men had probably arrived with the food. Before either he or Kayla could make it to the door, Deidre was leading Rick in with a big bag of something that smelled heavenly. The sharp pungent spices of the Puerto Rican food seeped through the bags and right up his nostrils.

While still a little perturbed that Deidre wouldn't even consider going out to a restaurant with him, Flex somewhat understood her reasons.

During the last year of their relationship, when The Real Deal had reached a popularity that they had only dreamed of, things started to become strained between him and Deidre. She had her own success, and he'd thought they would be able to weather things until they calmed down a little.

He'd underestimated her tolerance, and then things got extra crazy with Stacks and the label. Before he knew it, he had lost the love of his life and had no way to get her back.

Looking at her now in the kitchen unpacking the food from the plastic bags and setting out the paper plates and plastic forks, he felt a surge travel from his gut to his dome. She hadn't changed her clothes. She was still wearing her sweats and her long brownish gold hair that was in a neat ponytail earlier was now almost sticking out all over the place. *That's my Sweetness, always keeping it real.*

Flex had to suppress a smile. Out of all the models and very beautiful women he'd dated after he and Deidre broke up, none of them could hold a candle to her at that moment. He was still pissed off about her keeping their child from him. He knew that they would have a long way to go before they could come to terms with, and properly deal with, their past. But, watching her at that moment, he knew without a doubt that he was going to dedicate himself to working things out with Deidre. They both owed it to Kayla, and each other, to try.

Taking a deep breath as the weight of what he had to accomplish in wooing Deidre overcame him, he let his gaze wander. It wouldn't do good to have her notice him staring at her, so he looked around the kitchen instead. It was a warm and cozy room painted a bright golden yellow. The appliances were all white and had a1950s retro style. The floor was checkered yellow and white linoleum. The dinette set was also retro style.

He cleared his throat. "So, did you have a nice rest?"

"Yes, it was fine." She barely glanced at him but he could tell by her defensive posture that she was very aware of him.

"We got all your favorites, Mom. The *arroz con pollo,* fried *plantinos,* and mashed *plantinos.*" Kayla smiled as she spoke and he could tell that she was a happy child.

"Great, I guess we should all just dig in." Deidre turned and smiled a little too brightly at Kayla.

Flex studied Deidre's face and saw that the last thing she wanted to do was enjoy dinner with him. *Well, too bad.*

CHAPTER 9

"Keep Your Head Up"

Deidre couldn't believe she was actually sitting through dinner with her ex and her child, like one of those family sitcoms they rerun on late night television or something. If it weren't happening in her out-of-control life, it would be funny.

All sunshine and smiles, Flex and Kayla were carrying on like the perfect father and daughter. Doting on Kayla already, Flex hung on her every word. The way Kayla had latched on to Flex so quickly made Deidre nervous. The daughter she had spent twelve years raising didn't even seem to be aware that she was in the room. Deidre finally understood what Lana had meant when she said motherhood was a thankless job.

"Mom! Can we, Mom, can we?" When Kayla finally paid some attention to her, Deidre was so lost in her own thoughts she had no idea where the conversation had headed.

She looked up from her still full plate when she heard her daughter's insistent plea. "Can we what?"

"Can we go and spend the weekend with Da-Flex?" Kayla grinned from ear to ear.

Deidre couldn't believe that Kayla had almost called Flex Dad. Things were moving way faster than she could ever have imagined, and she felt the overwhelming need to put the brakes on. "This weekend probably won't be good. You know I have to complete my final grades for the semester, and you're still in school. Maybe we can take a weekend to visit him this summer."

Kayla's face turned serious and contemplative and, at that moment, she looked just like Flex. "But we were going to go to New York this weekend anyway to tell him about me, face to face. You said it this morning, remember Mom?"

Traitorous child. "Well, he's here now, and he knows about you already. So we don't have to go and tell him."

Deidre almost felt bad when she saw the confused look come across her daughter's face, until she caught a glimpse of Flex giving her the evil eye. *Serves him right, coming in here making plans for people like he's running things!*

"If you were making plans to come and see me anyway, then I don't see why you can't come. If you're worried about the time it will take to make the arrangements, don't. My staff can handle that."

My staff can handle that. She couldn't help mimicking him in her head. "I can make travel arrangements for me and my child. That's not the point."

"What is the point?" He folded his arms across his chest and zeroed in on her with his eyes.

"The point is we need to talk and clear things up before you come in here making life-altering decisions about me and my child."

He tilted his head, and that expression that he and Kayla seemed to share crossed his face. "You mean the way you did about *us* and *our* child?"

Counting to ten in her head, she told herself that she was not going to scream in the middle of dinner in front of her child. She gave Flex a pointed look and took a deep breath.

"Can we please talk about this at another time?"

"Fine." He uncrossed his arms.

"Fine." She couldn't help herself. She wanted the last word.

Kayla gave her an uneasy look, and Deidre automatically regretted her desire for the last word.

Glancing back and forth from Deidre to Flex, Kayla stood. "Umm. Okay. So, how about I go do my homework so that the two of you can talk?"

"That's a great idea. I'll come and help you with it once your father *leaves.*" Deidre put extra emphasis on 'leaves', and regretted it as soon as she said it.

Both she and Flex watched their daughter exit the room and then turned their gazes on each other. She couldn't help thinking about how much it felt like a standoff. She didn't want it to be like that, but things were moving along way faster than she wanted them to.

"She's a great kid."

"Thanks."

"So, about this weekend."

"Yes, well, it's not like I'm trying to be difficult—"

"Really?" He smirked, a sexy smirk, but also a cocky, arrogant smirk.

Taking a deep, calming breath, she thought about her words carefully. She knew that she was wrong, and she knew that she should be bending over backwards to make things right. However, knowing it and doing it were two very different things.

"Really, I just need to take this a little slow. I mean, this is my life we are talking about. A few days ago I was living a relatively calm life, a life away from all the craziness, and all of a sudden, I have you telling me that I either have to marry you or lose my child and that I have to move to New York. Forgive me if I want to put the brakes on until we have a sane solution to our situation."

His appearance softened for a moment, and she almost thought she'd be able to talk some sense into him. Then he shook his head as if deliberately trying to change his mind or shake away his feelings.

"I want to be clear because I am only going to say this once. You and Kayla will be moving in with me. It's the only way I can be sure that you are both safe. Now, I'm trying to make an honest woman out of you and not have you shacking up. But hey, if you wanna be a twenty-first century woman and live in sin, that's up to you. Make no mistake, though, you and Kayla are moving in with me."

"You see, that's what I mean. You can't just dictate that kind of thing to me. I am my own woman. I make my own decisions. I like my life here in Minneapolis. I don't *need* protection *here*." She bit the words out with all the fury she felt.

"That was before the whole world found out that you're the mother of my child. I can't leave Kayla open for someone to hurt. This isn't up for discussion."

"That's the other thing, your lifestyle is too dangerous. I think that Kayla is safer not being around you." She hissed the words out even though she didn't really feel that way. She wanted Kayla and Flex to be able to get to know one another; she just didn't like the whirlwind of change that was storming through her life.

"Okay, you have two choices then. You can either marry me and move your behind to New York, or we can put everything in front of a judge and let him or her sort it out. The courts may agree with you. Or they might be open for persuasion on my behalf. Do you really want to take that chance?" He appeared so nonchalant that she wanted to scream.

"Threats, *Fredrick*? Come on, can't we just handle this like adults?"

"No, apparently we can't. We're at a standstill, *Deidre*, and I know I'm not budging."

"Marriage?" She couldn't keep her incredulous tone from surfacing. *The man is truly unbelievable.*

"Hey, you can move in with or without the ring and commitment. Just let the record show that I tried to do the right thing." He shrugged.

"The right thing would be to let Kayla and me continue our lives here and set up some reasonable visitation rights."

"No." Flex folded his arms across his chest.

She felt her eyes growing wider by the minute. "No?"

"No." He tilted his head in a definitive manner.

She sucked her teeth and then started, "Fred—"

"No." His eyes narrowed and his voice was final.

"Okay, let's try and compromise. How about I . . . Okay, we can come to your place this weekend. I'll just bring my students' papers with me and I can work on them while you and Kayla get to know one another better."

"That's a start. We can talk about when you guys are going to officially relocate this weekend. I'm getting tired of rehashing this."

The nerve of him! "You're tired of rehashing this? We haven't even really discussed it because you won't budge. These things take time. You can't just waltz into someone's home and expect her to change her life because you say so. I don't think you fully appreciate how unreasonable you're being."

"I do realize that it's going to take time for us to get used to it. I have thought about this, and the more I think about it, the more I know it's the right thing to do." He seemed so certain.

If she weren't so sure it would never work and not so dead set against it, she reasoned that he would be able to make a believer out of her. But she was not going to allow that to happen. "The more I think about it, the more I know it won't work."

"All the more reason for you to give yourself a chance to get used to the inevitable. We can discuss it this weekend when you and Kayla come to visit me."

"Fine," she snapped.

"Fine." A sly grin spread across his face and he looked like the cat that ate the proverbial canary.

The expression made her feel like a little bird staring into the eyes of a jungle cat—*a feisty* little bird. "I don't want to hold you up. I'm assuming you'll be heading back to New York."

"No, I'll be staying in town until Friday. We can all fly back together in my jet."

"I hope you don't think you're staying here. I mean—"

"Don't worry, I won't be imposing. I have a suite downtown at the Marriot. I plan to check out some of the local talent tonight and tomorrow night. You never know, the next Midwest wonder could be sitting here in Minneapolis waiting to be discovered. Would you care to join me?"

"No, thanks. My clubbing days are over. You know, being a *parent* and all." She added extra emphasis because she figured he needed to know that being a parent was a lifestyle change if there ever was one. All his talk about becoming a full-time dad needed some grounding in reality, and she was going to be sure to provide it.

His shook his head and then he chuckled softly. It was as if he was not going to let her get to him no matter how much she tried. "The job requires that I do a certain amount of clubbing still."

"Hmmm, well, all the more reason for us to think before we make any rash decisions. We are clearly moving in two very different worlds." *Reality check!*

He glanced at her, smiled and then shrugged. "You forget. I saw you at the *Source Awards*. You are just as capable of moving between the two worlds as I am. I think that our child, our situation, will require just that from both of us."

Reality bites. Leave it to him to bring my actions into this. "Oh yeah? We'll discuss it this weekend. Can I see you out?"

Flex laughed. "Yes, Deidre. I can see that I've overstayed my welcome."

She knew she was being rude, but she made no attempt to feign that she wasn't really extremely happy that he was finally leaving. She wanted him and his overwhelming presence gone so that she could think. From the moment he walked in the door, she'd felt as if she could barely keep her head above water. The fact that he was being more demanding and unyielding than she had ever known him to be was making her feel as if she were drowning while she was desperately trying to remain afloat.

"I'll see you out," was all she could manage to offer, that and a weak smile.

CHAPTER 10

"I'll Do For You"

When Flex got into his limousine after leaving Deidre's home, he immediately began planning. Deidre wasn't going to make it easy. That much was clear. But he was determined to see that she and Kayla were sufficiently protected. He tried to push aside the feelings that seeing her again had rekindled while he figured out a way to get her to do the right thing.

With Stacks being released from jail, protection was crucial. Although he and Deidre had discussed the issue of protection, it was clear she would use it as a reason against her and Kayla moving in with him. She wouldn't *exactly* agree to him making sure that they were protected. Based on their brief conversation, he knew she'd be angry if she found out. It would just add more fuel to her arguments against marrying him and moving back to the East Coast.

He turned to two of his best men. They knew the value of discretion, and he trusted them with his life. "Rick and Frank, I'm going to need you guys to hang out in Minneapolis for a while. I want someone watching out for Deidre and Kayla at all times." He sighed. "As long as they remain in Minneapolis, *you* guys are in Minneapolis."

He didn't like the covert nature of things. It would be much simpler if Deidre and Kayla could meet Rick and Frank and know that the men were there to protect them. He just didn't think Deidre would go for it.

"Remember to keep a low profile. They can't know that you're following them. If they make you, then you're not doing your job. The only time, and I mean the *only* time that you are to blow your cover, is if there is an immediate threat and you have to save them. If they're not being kidnapped, or if no one is holding a gun to their head, then you just keep it on the low."

"So we are basically shadowing them, no contact." Rick leaned forward and nodded as he bridged his hands in his lap. He spoke with a hint of a Jamaican accent.

Flex had trusted him for eight years.

Flex thought for a moment, and then nodded his head in the affirmative. "No contact whatsoever. If Deidre finds out, she'll have a fit, and that's drama I don't need right now."

"Got it. Any word on Stacks?" Frank asked. He had been around since the early days when Flex started Flex Time Records. Flex trusted the man more than anyone else on his staff, with the exception of Divine. When it came to having a guy around a woman he cared for, he probably trusted Frank more than he did Divine. Frank was an Italian-American whose taste in women was very different from Flex's, while Divine and Flex usually went for the same types.

"Not yet. He's due to be released any day now. I don't think he'll come at me right out of jail. Knowing him, he'll try to get his money right first. He has no idea how hard that's going to be." Flex had put several roadblocks in the works to put Stacks out of commission once and for all. Stacks wouldn't be able to connect with any of his old contacts, and he'd find it very hard to make new ones.

He might never be able to prove that Stacks killed Sasha, but he knew in his heart that Stacks was involved. For that he would pay. Flex just wished that he had known about Deidre and Kayla before he put his plans for Stacks' destruction in the works.

"Once he realizes that his money will never be the way it was before he got sent upstate, he'll be ready to strike out at someone. By then, Deidre and Kayla should be with me, and I'll make sure that he can't touch them." Flex hoped that everything went as planned. There was no room for mistakes.

"So are we still going to be assigned to them once they move in with you?" Frank asked.

"Yes. Your only job is to make sure that they're safe and to make sure that they don't know that you're there."

"That should be pretty simple." Rick leaned back in the seat, appearing a little too lax for Flex's taste.

Flex narrowed his eyes on Rick. "Yeah, simple, but you better not mess up. *Nothing* can happen to them."

"Got it." Rick sat up straight.

"Good." Flex then picked up his cell phone and made a phone call that he should have made hours ago.

"What's up?" Divine's voice boomed over loud music in the background.

Flex figured the man was out in the city clubs and on the prowl. "It's me. What's the word?"

"He's getting out tomorrow and Teddy's picking him up." The music slowly faded away in the background, and Flex figured Divine was moving to a quieter, more secure spot to talk from.

Flex loosened his shirt collar a little and leaned back in his seat. "You sure we can trust Teddy?"

"Trust me when I say he hates Stacks more than all of us put together." Divine chuckled a little.

Flex sighed. When Teddy didn't leave Body Bag with the rest of them, Flex figured he was loyal to Stacks and therefore cut him off. Even though he now knew differently, he still felt uneasy about trusting someone who had spent that much time with Stacks.

The irony of it didn't escape him, as he figured Deidre must have had the same feeling about him when he spent so much time with Stacks trying to bring him down after Sasha was killed.

At the time Deidre had taken to pleading with him not to spend so much time with Stacks. She'd even voiced what everyone else had been thinking, that Stacks had had something to do with Sasha's death. When her pleading didn't work, she'd started coming around when he was with Stacks and showing up at clubs when they were out. Flex couldn't allow that to happen, so he'd had to stop her. Stopping her had made her leave him.

"I wish he didn't have to link himself to that scumbag." Flex ran his hand across his head.

"Yeah, but it works for us. He'll be able to tell us whatever Stacks is planning. Plus, he's on the inside at Body Bag. We need a man on the inside. I trust Teddy with my life." The certainty in Divine's voice did nothing to sway Flex.

Flex wasn't ready to cosign on that statement, or Divine's faith in Teddy. Still wary about Teddy, he just hoped the man would hold up his end of the bargain and keep them posted on what was happening at Body Bag and what Stacks was up to.

When it came to his life and the lives of the people that mattered to him, Flex trusted only himself and a few others. That was why he had to get Deidre and Kayla under his protection as soon as possible.

"I hope he's trustworthy. We can't sleep on Stacks. We have to be on point and on guard. What happened to Sasha *cannot* happen to anyone else." Flex rested his eyes and massaged his left temple.

Divine sighed. "I'm with you, man. I'm with you. So, did you see Dee today?"

"Yeah, man."

"How is she?" Divine asked.

His sudden perkiness wasn't lost on Flex. Flex wasn't worried about it, however, because he knew that Divine had tried to make his move on Deidre the first night he met her and she'd shot him down. The memory of Divine's shocked face when she did so still cheered Flex up on bad days.

"The same. She's not going to make this easy. Right now she's not trying to hear anything about moving to the East Coast, let alone getting married and doing the right thing."

"Did she at least apologize? I mean, dang, that's some foul stuff to pull. She could have told you. It wasn't like you wouldn't have stood by her."

After going through the motions with Deidre, the last thing Flex wanted to do was to rehash things with Divine. "I know. I'm sure she thinks she had her reasons."

"You're taking it well. When you left here, you were pretty heated. I guess seeing Dee again calmed you down, huh?" The teasing quality of Divine's tone was not cute.

"Man, shut up."

"Yeah, I know. But don't forget that I know how the two of you were together. I couldn't even holla at Shorty because she was all about you." Divine laughed. "You wouldn't even get any groupie love on the road because you were all about her. Those kinds of feelings just don't disappear."

"Those feelings are dead, man. This is all about doing the right thing for my daughter." Flex replied even as something inside told him that it was about way more than that.

"So how is she? Is she a cool kid?"

A smile came across his face as he thought about the beautiful and bright young lady that he'd met for the first time that afternoon. "Yeah, man. She's wonderful. I still can't believe it, but it's true. Deidre and I have a child."

"I hope everything works out, and you and Deidre are able to recapture that love."

Flex could tell that Divine was sincere even without seeing his friend's face.

"This is not about love, Divine. It's about doing what's right. Deidre is just going to have to do the right thing for once." The music started to get louder over the line again. *Divine must be heading back into the club.*

"Yeah, player, tell yourself what you need to hear."

"Man, shut up. Just make sure we're cool with Teddy and I'll get with you later. I'm going to spend a little more time here in Minneapolis and work on Deidre a little bit more."

Divine chuckled. "All right, man. Peace."

Flex hung up the cell phone and sat up in his seat. He was in a much better position to protect the ones he cared for now. He just hoped that Deidre cooperated and let him do that.

CHAPTER 11

"Destroy and Rebuild"

As Stanley "Stacks" Carter waited outside of the maximum-security prison for his ride, he let his mind wander. Teddy was late. If he could have, he wouldn't have even dealt with the fat boy.

Teddy was the only one who had come to see him while he was locked up. All the rest of his so-called friends had disappeared. Teddy had at least stayed loyal to Body Bag Records and kept money in his commissary account. None of the others had.

Teddy's solo album had flopped big time. No one wanted to see or hear the fat boy from The Real Deal. The other punks in that group had jumped ship with that sucker deejay, Flex. For all the loyalty they showed, one would never have known that Stacks was the one who fronted them the cash for the demo. Stacks had put his money behind a label and put them down. They wouldn't have had careers without him.

Flex was just a sucker prep-school boy from Teaneck, and Stacks had allowed him to claim and represent for P-town. The rest of the group at least were from the hood—had lived in the inner city. The closest Flex came to Paterson was when he visited his cousin, Sasha. Whoever said women were more trouble that they were worth didn't lie. Hooking up with that little girl had been a mistake. She had been as disloyal as her punk cousin turned out to be. She was the reason he ended up in jail the first time. All those years of selling drugs and he had never caught a case. When some punk tried to step to Sasha right in front of him, showing blatant disrespect, Stacks had beat the man almost to death. The assault charges probably wouldn't have stuck if the head trauma hadn't paralyzed the man. Stacks had had to serve three years before he could get paroled for good behavior. When somebody sent the D.A. tapes of him consorting with known felons and giving another man a beat down at Body Bag, he'd been sent back to prison to serve the rest of his sentence. He knew that disloyal chump Flex was behind the tape, just couldn't prove it.

Loyalty was not to be taken lightly in his business, and even though Teddy could be a useless fat mess-up most of the time, he had remained loyal. However, making Stacks wait for a ride out of the hellhole that had been his life for the past nine years was not cool. What could be taking him so long?

By the time Teddy did show up, Stacks had taken to just sitting on the bench wishing that he hadn't given up smoking. Stacks opened the door to Teddy's luxury sedan, threw his bag in the back seat and jumped in the front seat.

For a played-out rapper, Teddy seemed to be doing okay for himself. That made Stacks all the more ready to up his own game and begin living his life the way he knew it was meant to be lived. He'd get his money right first, and then he'd take care of those disloyal punks. He could wait on his revenge because it was going to be so sweet that he would savor it all the more when he finally got it.

Stacks glared at Teddy as he leaned the car seat back into an almost lounging position. "It's about time!"

"Sorry, man. Traffic was a mutha." Shrugging, Teddy started up the car and pulled off.

His attitude was not apologetic enough for Stacks. Respect was key and Teddy seemed to be lacking it.

"Yeah, but, you should have accounted for that and left earlier, not keep me waiting out here like this."

"Yeah, I know. Sorry, man." Keeping his eyes on the road, Teddy seemed a little more sincere this time. So Stacks decided to let the lateness go, this time.

"So, what's good in the hood?"

Teddy shrugged. "Nothing, man. Everything is everything. We're still trying to hold it down at Body Bag. I'm sure your accountant and lawyer kept you up-to-date on that end."

"Yeah, I know most of the talent couldn't wait to defect. Barely let me get in jail good before they jumped ship. It's all good. They were dead weight anyway. We are going to get new talent and make Body Bag better than it used to be, definitely better than that wack Flex Time Records." It burned Stacks up that Flex Towns went from being a deejay to a mega producer and damn near superstar. It irritated him even more that Flex's label was the top hip-hop label when that place had belonged to Body Bag before he got sent back to jail.

When Stacks first landed in jail, The Real Deal was just finishing their demo. Once he was paroled, he was able to build his business back up quickly, even branching out into the music business by fronting a record label and signing The Real Deal as the first act. Getting caught for violating his parole and having to finish his sentence was a bad break. Coming back into the game after so much time away would be harder this time.

Teddy didn't make a comment in response.

"You hear from any of those cats lately? You still in contact with Flex?"

After a short pause Teddy turned and looked him in the eye. "Nah, man, Flex don't have time for people anymore. I holler at Louie sometimes, and Divine every now and then." He then turned his attention back to the road where Stacks felt it should have been in the first place, even though he appreciated a man who looked him in the eye when he spoke.

Stacks felt he could trust Teddy.

"Yeah, I peeped that TV special they had on that trick Dee. She had a kid and ain't told nobody. She could only run that kind of game on a chump punk like Flex." He laughed.

He couldn't stand Flex, and he'd never liked that trouble-making trick, Dee. She thought she was too good to sign to Body Bag. If she hadn't been messing around with Flex at the time, Stacks would have had the group make a couple of diss records about her.

When she signed with another label, the crew should have disowned her. Now she was being shown for the treacherous chick she was. Stacks felt that Flex deserved to be betrayed by the trick; now he'd know what it felt like.

Teddy nodded his head as he switched lanes. "I heard about that. Crazy."

"Yeah, it's crazy all right. Flex got a lot of shit coming to him. I know he was behind the D.A. getting those tapes of me consorting and the tape of me participating in that beat down at Body Bag, violating the terms of my parole. If I ever find out for sure that he was behind it, I'm taking him out. I might just take his punk behind out anyway, him and the rest of The Real Deal. They act like they was too good to holla at a brother while he was on lock down."

Shrugging, Teddy put his car on cruise control as they coasted down the highway. "Yeah, like I said, Flex is busy. He's a big time record mogul now."

"Busy soaking up all the shine that should have been mine," Stacks snapped.

Silent again, Teddy just stayed focused on the road.

"They still could have visited or wrote or something. Y'all wouldn't have had shit if it wasn't for me. Nobody would have even known your names. What did I get for my efforts?" Stacks didn't like showing that their betrayal bothered him, but it did, and he had a hard time holding it in.

Sitting in jail while the people you knew put you there prospered had a way of messing with your head. Then being a famous hip-hop label owner and having such a public case made it so that people were checking for him and ready to mess with him as soon as he walked up in the joint. He'd had to fight off a lot of unwanted attention and he hadn't always been successful. Someone was going to have to pay eventually for the things he went through in prison.

"To be fair, after what went down with Sasha, Flex and Divine weren't very happy at Body Bag. Sasha was Flex's only cousin, and Divine and Sasha grew up together. Divine's mom has a picture of Sasha and Divine as little kids in the tub together. That's how far they go back." Teddy turned to face him again and had a weird expression on his face, an expression that Stacks couldn't place, and made him a little uncomfortable.

Why was fat boy getting into the 'what happened to Sasha' story? That stuff was in the past and no one would ever be able to prove that he had anything to do with it. She was just a girl who was in the wrong place at the wrong time. Period. Stray bullets don't have names. That's just how the story goes.

"So what you saying? What? They ain't never been able to prove I had anything to do with Sasha's death. And they ain't never gonna be able to prove it. I know you ain't tripping like them?"

The expression on Teddy's face changed quickly. He shrugged and then laughed. "No, I'm just saying things got real ill, and they may still have hard feelings, that's all."

"Whatever. All I know is they some soft behind punks and Body Bag is better off without them. Word is bond. That Flex better watch his back. I never liked him, and I like him a whole lot less now. The brother got a lot more to lose than a cousin, so he better stay outta my way." Stacks leaned back and closed his eyes, tired of talking. *Let Teddy keep his fat self company on the ride back.*

Teddy didn't respond and Stacks thought that was okay. It was time to go about business, the business of destroying the competition and rebuilding his empire, both the legal and illegal parts. It was time to show them who was really the boss.

CHAPTER 12

"Hush"

Flex rang Deidre's doorbell with an air of certainty. She had given him a hard time about his plans for them the previous day, but he was determined to get her to see reason. He didn't want to spend the entire weekend trying to convince her that marriage was the best option for them and their daughter. The sooner she came to terms with her fate, the better.

"What are you doing here? Kayla's in school. I thought you were coming back on Friday afternoon when we leave?" There was barely a crack of an opening in the door, and Deidre's body filled in that space. Clearly, she wasn't planning to let him in.

He held up a bag of pastries and a cup holder with two cups of Jamaican Blue Mountain blend coffee that he'd picked up from a coffee shop on the way to her house. "I figured we could have some breakfast and maybe finish our discussion from last night. Do you still love chocolate croissants?"

Her eyes darted to the bag of pastries and then she stared at the cup holder. She gave him a weary glance before opening the door a little wider and letting him in.

She led him back into the kitchen and moved a stack of papers aside before sitting down. He sat in the chair opposite her and placed the pastries and coffee in the middle of her retro-style kitchen table. Taking one of the cups of coffee, she fished out her favorite pastry.

She didn't say anything as she nibbled and took sips of her coffee.

Letting his eyes wander, he found himself again examining his surroundings. She had made a nice cozy home for herself and their daughter. He could see why she wouldn't want to leave it. Just as cute on the inside as it was on the outside, Deidre's home almost made him want to move in with them. If he didn't have a business to run and obligations to maintain, he would have considered doing just that.

He drank his coffee in silence and tried to think of how to begin the conversation in a way that would get her to do exactly what he wanted. He noticed that she'd opted for a cute little outfit instead of the baggy nondescript clothing she'd had on the other day. The red, low cut short-sleeved t-shirt and denim skirt that came just above her knees showed just enough skin to make him wonder if her body would still feel the same under his hands. Her long hair was out of the ponytail holder and slightly curled at the ends. The style framed her face nicely and the sunlight from the kitchen window bounced off her golden highlights. Her lips had just enough color on them to make him think about kissing it off.

He shook his head. He had to maintain focus. The last thing he needed to do was to start developing a physical attraction to Deidre. She'd proved herself to be disloyal. The only thing he needed to focus on was his child and how to get her under his roof to give her the family he'd never had. Although he would never forget what Deidre did, he hoped he would one day be able to forgive her and look at her without her betrayal clouding what he saw.

He placed his coffee cup down and sighed. She glanced up, then quickly diverted her gaze.

Might as well start slow, he thought ruefully. "So, Deidre, I was wondering if you'd tell me a little more about our daughter. I'd really love to see some pictures of her when she was younger. I feel like I have a lot of catching up to do."

She eyed him tiredly. "I kept a scrapbook of her first five years. It's on the bookshelf in the den. I'll get it for you and you can look at it in there." Getting up from the table, she motioned with her shoulder for him to follow.

"I was hoping that you would look at it with me. You know, fill me in on the details that don't come out in the pictures. Give me more insight into what she was like then, what she's like now." It wasn't too much to ask, he figured. He'd missed out on a whole lot, and he had a lot of catching up to do.

She bit her lips and fiddled with her hands. "I do have these papers to grade, since it seems like I'll be spending the weekend in New York."

"Actually, we'll spend the weekend at my mansion in Englewood Cliffs."

Her eyes rolled in an exaggerated manner and she shook her head. "Great, Jersey! Can't tell you how excited I am to go back there." She waved her hands over her head in mock enthusiasm and started walking out of the kitchen.

Flex followed close behind her. He knew that Deidre couldn't make it away from Bergen County, New Jersey, quick enough when they finished high school and from what he could tell, she hadn't been back there in a long while. It couldn't be helped, however. The slower pace of Jersey would provide a better backdrop for him getting to know his child. So, Deidre was just going to have to deal. He realized the battle for Deidre's cooperation was going to be an uphill one at best.

Once they were in the den she pulled out a large pink and yellow scrapbook and a huge burgundy photo album and sat down on the kente cloth-covered futon. He admired the colorful art that hung on the walls of her den. She had some nice pieces throughout the house, but the den held a lot of colorful, vibrant art. There was even some graffiti art on screen; he noticed a print of Lady Pink's *Brick Lady*.

He sat down next to her and felt her take a sharp intake of breath when his thigh touched hers. If he were feeling gentlemanly, he would have given her a little more space.

He reasoned that he didn't really have time for space. So he moved a little closer to her and smiled when she gulped. *Playing fair went away when she lied and kept my kid a secret.* He rested his arm on the futon behind her and sat back.

"So, let's take a look at those pictures, shall we?"

She leaned back carefully, clearly trying to avoid contact with the back of the futon and his arm and then opened the scrapbook. The first picture in the scrapbook was a picture of Deidre holding Kayla as a newborn. Underneath were letters spelling out, *Just in from the delivery room.*

It was his turn to gulp. Deidre looked beautiful. She was probably the only woman he knew who could look that gorgeous after just giving birth. He swallowed because his mouth was, all of a sudden, dry.

"The labor and delivery wasn't that bad. I was only in labor for a little over five hours and once she started coming, she just popped on out. She was more than ready to be here." Deidre was talking low, and she kept her eyes on the picture.

Flex wished that she would look at him. He wanted to see her eyes as she remembered giving birth to their child. He could imagine all the emotion he would find in them. She was never able to keep her feelings out of her facial expression, especially her eyes.

She swallowed and continued. "I named her Kayla for her two grandmothers. It's a combination of your mom's name, Kay, and the first two letters of my mom's name. I wanted her to have something of both of them."

Flex had figured as much when he found out his daughter's name, but it was something else hearing her voice it.

She turned the page and gave more feedback and history. The more she did, the more he uneasy he became. He'd missed so much—too much. And it hadn't had to be that way. Why couldn't she have just trusted him, and trusted that he was doing the right thing, even though she couldn't fully understand his actions? He knew that he would have given her the benefit of the doubt back then. He loved her that much. She obviously hadn't felt the same way.

When she got to the end of the scrapbook, she put the big burgundy photo album on his lap. "The rest is just random photos, school pictures, silly stuff. You can look at them now, and maybe Kayla can share some memories with you later." She got up and started to walk away.

Not about to let her run away again, Flex grabbed her arm and pulled her back down on the futon. He turned her to face him and cupped his hand under her chin.

"Fred—"

"No, just listen to me for a minute. I think we need to set some things straight. First of all, I think that you have done a wonderful job raising our daughter. She seems happy, healthy, and very well adjusted. I want to thank you for that. She really is a beautiful child." He paused for a moment to let the words sink in because he truly wanted her to know that he appreciated the love she'd given their child.

"But I need you to understand, Deidre, that now that I know about my daughter, I won't let anyone or anything stop me from being there for her, being a father to her. I want you both in my life. So you will move back to the East Coast to live with me. We can either live in the city or in Jersey, but we *will* live together. It's the only way that I can be sure that the two of you are safe."

He watched her eyes closely and when he saw the resignation settle he almost wanted to change his mind. He didn't want to bully her into doing his will. He also didn't want to pick up the phone one day and hear that something had happened to her or Kayla because some idiot was trying to get at him.

"Okay, I'll consider relocating to the East Coast, but I think it's best if Kayla and I maintain our own residence. Kayla can visit back and forth between us, but I think it would be best for us to live under separate roofs."

Flex shook his head. *She just didn't get it.* "No, Sweetness, you will live with me. We will live under the same roof, as a family."

Urgh! Sweetness! Why on earth is he picking this moment to call me Sweetness? Can't he just keep his attitude and keep calling me Deidre?

Deidre swallowed and inched away from him on the futon. The man was obviously a whole lot more dangerous than she'd originally thought, calling her Sweetness and whatnot. *What am I supposed to do with that? I have never had any defenses for his soulful chocolate-brown gaze combined with his seductive voice calling me Sweetness. Never.* Just the sound of his voice calling her by the loving nickname sent a soft, sweet sensation through her chest.

"*Fredrick*, for the record, while I totally understand your desire to have us all under the same roof like one big happy family, I have to say that it will be a bit difficult to pull off. Based on the way things ended between us, I honestly cannot say that this is something that I would even want." *Liar, liar, pants on fire*, a small voice in the back of her head chanted. *You know you want him.*

"Then let's revisit the past and clear the air once and for all, hmm? You seem to be under the impression that I was being unfaithful before you left for good. Right?"

"Yes. When you weren't touring with The Real Deal, you were out partying with them and Stacks all the time. I know how those guys, especially Stacks, rolled when they were on the road or at a party. A trick is a trick is a trick, right?"

"You know what they were like because you were with us on the road sometimes and you went to parties with us, so you know how I was too. You know that the only woman I ever had eyes for was you. Even when the groupies came around, I never played you out like that." He let his hand caress her cheek as he held her in his gaze.

"When I was there, of course, but toward the end, after Sasha got shot, you didn't want me hanging out. Honestly, I didn't want to hang out. The night I left our apartment was the night you got really scary and damn near violent because I wanted to go with you guys to the Zanzibar."

"That was because I knew that things were about to get ugly and I didn't want Stacks to have anyone to lash out at but me. I had been hanging with him more than usual to get the information I needed to send him back to prison. I wanted him to go down for what he did to Sasha. I got him violating his parole on the assault sentence he caught just before we went to college. If you recall, he was arrested that night."

"I know. None of that changes you yelling at me and shaking me. You frightened me, and for the first time ever, I felt like I used to feel when my father was going at it with my mom. I couldn't stay with you after that. I honestly don't think I can live under the same roof with you now. I don't want my child growing up in fear, hearing her father yell at and belittle her mother. Seeing him hit her mother."

Flex leaped from the futon and ran his hand across his head before he turned his pleading eyes on her. "You know I would never lay a finger on you, Sweetness. I would chop off my hands first. You gotta know that."

She'd thought she did know that. That was why she had been so shaken when it happened. She sighed. "On some level I do know that. On other levels I don't. When we first started hanging out, I never would have imagined you losing your temper and screaming on me the way you did. It did happen, however. So, I really don't know if I can make the conscious decision to move in with you and risk Kayla having the same rotten childhood I did."

He sat back down and put his hand on hers. "She won't. I can promise you that. I got counseling and had some anger management training after you left. I knew that I had messed up really bad, and I knew that if I ever got the chance to make it right that I needed to be ready. I'm ready, Sweetness. Give me a chance. Give us a chance."

Counseling? I've heard that one before. Even though my father's counseling apparently saved their marriage, I've never been a believer. But thinking about the man that Flex had become made her wonder. She had noticed a change in him—a calm. It made Deidre think back to the Flex she knew back then. She truly believed that *that* Flex would not be on her futon trying to woo her to move in with him so that he could give his daughter a two-parent family. *That* Flex would be throwing a fit and demanding that she bring her behind back to the East Coast yesterday and make sure she had his child with him.

"We'll see, Fredrick."

He gave her a sexy, lopsided grin and inched closer on the futon. "And another thing, Sweetness, what does a brother have to do to get you to call him Flex? Fredrick is my old man, baby, not me."

She couldn't help groaning then, because the sly devil knew exactly what he had to do to get her to call him *Flex*. In the throes of passion she could never stop herself from calling him what he always was to her in her head anyway. Memories of her screaming out 'Flex' made the heat rise from the pit of her stomach to the nape of her neck. Her eyes squinted slightly as she studied her new threat packaged as her old love. *Oh yes, this brother is more dangerous than I ever could have imagined.*

CHAPTER 13

"Old Times Sake"

The flight to Newark airport in Flex's private jet had Kayla beyond excited and talking a mile a minute. The limousine ride to Flex's home in Englewood Cliffs was proving to be even more exhilarating for the child. So much so that Deidre fought the green monster prancing around in her head.

Flex couldn't help it that he was rich and perfect. Who knew that at heart Kayla was such a daddy's girl? *The turncoat,* Deidre thought as she stared out the window, taking in the less-than-picturesque view of northern New Jersey. Factories and tenements, tenements and factories. The northern part of the state apparently left it to the southern part of the state to uphold the nickname Garden State. Even though she would *always* be a Jersey girl at heart, she was not ready to come home yet. She certainly didn't want to come home like this, forced, kicking and screaming.

Oh how I miss my nice smog-free city of lakes, she mourned. After moving with her baby to Minneapolis to get her MFA from the University of Minnesota, Deidre had felt settled and safe for the first time in her life. It had been hard, but she managed to finish her degree and build quite a stable life for herself and Kayla. She just had to steel herself and make sure that she didn't allow Flex and his grand plans for a shotgun wedding twelve years too late to ruin everything.

Busy thinking, she missed most of Flex and Kayla's conversation.

"So, Mom, what do you think about that?" Kayla had a grin so wide on her face that Deidre could swear she could see every tooth and every piece of dental work.

Deidre couldn't help smiling at her daughter. It was wonderful to see Kayla so happy, even if she wasn't the cause. "Think about what, Kayla?"

"About having all of my grandparents over this weekend, so I can see Grandmommy and Granddad and meet my other grandfather. I hope he likes me."

Pulling Kayla into a quick embrace and mussing her hair, Flex assured their daughter, "Oh, he's going to love you. Ever since he found out about you earlier this week he has wanted to meet you. He almost shoved his way on this trip with me. I convinced him that it would probably be best for me to meet you alone first."

Deidre realized that her mouth was open and she hadn't said a word. She was all for Kayla meeting Judge Fredrick Towns II. The man was wonderful and she really liked him, even missed him sometimes.

However, having Dr. Howard James in the mix did not set right with her at all. She wasn't sure if she could deal with the level of drama that a meeting between herself and the good doctor would no doubt bring into the equation.

While he'd never laid a hand on her or even raised his voice very much when she was growing up, Deidre had lived in constant fear of her father. Even when she rebelled in school she did so because she wanted to break away from the fear that trapped her. Each time she hoped it would make Lana decide to leave him again. In her mind, if she somehow got him to lash out at her instead of Lana, she would know his wrath firsthand and it wouldn't have the power to paralyze her. She would be able to do something besides run and hide in her bedroom or in the closet if he ever hit Lana again.

For some reason, he never took the bait. She reasoned the counseling must have done him some good, but she never fully trusted him. He kept his distance from her once she and Lana moved back in with him when she was fourteen. When she finally gave up her acting out because it had ended up with her at Teaneck High, she was on the straight and narrow—until she met Flex.

"I don't know if it will be such a good idea to invite Grandmommy and Granddad. Maybe we should just leave this weekend for you to meet your Granddad Towns. He has never met you, and your other grandparents have had you for years." Plastering a smile on her face, even though she felt like doing anything but, Deidre reached out and fixed the bang on Kayla's head that Flex had mussed.

"I really want to see Grandmommy, too. I miss her," Kayla pouted.

"I didn't say that you couldn't see her. I just said that maybe this trip we should focus on getting you all introduced to your other grandfather, Judge Towns, that's all. He's a wonderful man. You're really going to enjoy spending time with him." Deidre maintained eye contact with Kayla as she spoke.

Flex cleared his throat and spoke. "I think that having everyone around might not be such a bad idea. This is a celebration and the entire family should be included." His tone had the unmistakable air of finality to it.

Deidre glanced up and shot Flex a harsh stare. *Oh, who asked you for your two cents?* "Fine, if you guys are all gung-ho, far be it from me to be the wet blanket. Let's make a party of it. Why not invite the world?" Being sarcastic seemed her only ammunition against the Flex and Kayla double team. Not very good ammo, but her only ammo nonetheless, so she decided to use what she had. *Why did they even ask my opinion if their minds were made up?*

"The entire world is a bit of an exaggeration. Your mom and dad deserve to be there as much as my dad. When was the last time you even set foot in Jersey?" Flex had picked up on her sarcasm, and it was clear from his tone he didn't like it. "I bet nothing could have dragged you here when you were hiding out and keeping Kayla a secret in Minneapolis. They probably want to see you and Kayla this weekend also. It would be mean to keep them out of the celebration."

"Yeah, it would be kinda mean, Mom." Kayla nodded her head up and down.

Considering herself sufficiently chastised, she gave in. "Fine."

"Great, I'll get some people to plan a small dinner celebration at my house for tomorrow evening. Should I have them contact your folks, or will you contact them?"

"Oh, I'll call my mom and let her know. I was planning on calling her and letting her know that we were in the area, you know. I was even planning to spend some time with her, while you got to know Kayla better. I wasn't going to just breeze in and out of town without seeing my mother." Deidre would move heaven and earth for Lana James if she could. There were only two things that she wouldn't do for the woman. The first thing was out of her hands now, since Flex knew about Kayla, and the second had to do with Deidre and her father making peace. She didn't see that happening anytime in the foreseeable future.

"Now we can all see your mom. I haven't seen her in years. It'll be nice to see her again." Flex smiled, and she tried to decide if he was being smug because he'd gotten his way or if he was just genuinely happy.

Since she couldn't tell, she just mumbled, "Yes, lovely."

Flex frowned. Things were not going as planned. From the minute they got on his jet, he'd sensed extreme irritation coming from Deidre. She seemed to be more than a little aggravated by every word that came out of his mouth. So he spent the time talking with and getting to know his daughter.

He thought that having Deidre's family around for part of the weekend might put her more at ease, but apparently since the idea came from him, it wasn't suitable either. He knew she might have some apprehension about Dr. James being there. From what he knew about their relationship, the two weren't really that close.

He'd just thought that by the time she reached her thirties the two of them would have reached an uneasy state of peace, the way that he and his father had. That clearly wasn't the case.

He was at a loss as to what to do to bring Deidre to a state of ease. He wanted her to relax. Once she was relaxed, he would be able to start his plans to get her to see reason and realize that marrying him was the best thing for her and Kayla.

The marriage plan seemed more and more like a long shot, and he realized that he'd be lucky to get the stubborn woman even to move in with him again. She was difficult beyond comprehension, and he wondered how he ever dealt with it in his shorter-tempered days.

Apparently not well, he thought, *or else she would still be with me and I wouldn't have missed the first twelve years of my daughter's life.*

He turned his attention back to the one person in the limo who seemed to be captivated by his every word: Kayla.

"So what do you want to do this weekend, besides see your grandparents? We could go to an amusement park. We could go shopping. I'm open to do whatever your little heart desires."

"Do you think it's wise to go to an amusement park or a mall? Those places are highly populated and we wouldn't want Kayla bumrushed by your adoring fans, now would we?" Gazing out the window, Deidre didn't even turn around as she spoke.

Although he knew that highly populated areas were probably not the best place for them to go, especially with Stacks out of jail, it irked him that Deidre was being so flippant. "I could always rent the amusement park for a day. Then we could have the entire place to ourselves and Kayla wouldn't have to worry about being bum-rushed by anyone."

When she turned to face him, the look on Deidre's face was priceless. Flex thought the way her mouth fell open and no words came out was one for the record books. He had never known the woman to be speechless.

"Maybe next time, Dad. I think I'd like to get a tour of Flex Time Records if possible, though. I've never been inside a real record company, and I would love to see what the inside of a studio looks like."

He couldn't believe that his daughter had just called him Dad. He turned to Deidre to see if he was the only one who'd heard it, and her jaw had dropped even lower. Although still speechless, her eyes spoke volumes. She was more shocked by the fact that Kayla had called him Dad than he was. Since her eyes also told on her emotions, he also saw a hint of fear. That bothered him, but he would address it later. Somehow, he had to make her understand that she had nothing to fear when it cam to him being a part of their lives. He wasn't trying to take Kayla away from her. He only wanted to make some room in their unit for him.

When she finally blinked and swallowed, he assumed that she was going to be all right. He turned back to Kayla.

"I think a tour of Flex Time Records is definitely doable, sweetie pie. I happen to know the guy in charge, and I can get us in with no problem. As for the inside of a recording studio, how about several? I have a recording studio built into the lower level of my home. You can see the three studios at Flex Time to boot."

"This is *so-oo cool!* I can't wait to tell Lily that I saw a real studio. She's going to flip!" Kayla bounced up and down as she spoke and his heart flip-flopped.

Flex still felt the frog in his throat as he tried to respond to his daughter's excitement. He'd had no idea that he would react so strongly to Kayla calling him Dad for the first time, but there it was.

"Maybe, if we have some time, you can get on the microphone and show me some of those skills you say you have."

The gasp that he heard come out of Deidre's mouth let him know that he had gone a little too far in his excitement. He glanced over at her and saw that she was shooting him a lethal look.

"That would be *beyond cool!* Lily will be so jealous to hear that I rocked the mike in a real studio. We'll have to tape it because she would not believe it at all. *Oh. My. God.* You are the *best* dad *ever*. Mommy, did you hear that? I'm going to make a recording!"

"Yes, Kayla, I heard that." Deidre turned and started looking out the window.

Flex basked in the glow of Kayla's approval and being the best dad ever, but he knew that it had cost him major cool points with Deidre.

CHAPTER 14

"I'll Be There For You/You're All I Need To Get By"

Still fuming the next day at the small dinner party, Deidre did her best to keep a fair amount of distance between herself and her father. She blamed Flex for her discomfort. Not only was she forced to face the man she would have gladly not seen again anytime soon, but she also had to figure out a way to lay down the law about Kayla getting on the microphone and possibly recording, knowing it would crush her baby's dreams. She didn't like being the wet blanket to Flex's super-cool-dad routine. One of them had to be the responsible adult, though.

"So, baby, how's everything going so far? Fredrick and Kayla both seem happy. He seems totally smitten with her, and she with him." Lana rubbed Deidre's back as she spoke, and it momentarily soothed her irritability.

Deidre glanced across the room to where Kayla was busy being the center of attention with her two grandfathers and Flex. "Yeah, I'm an unwanted third wheel."

Lana's hand stilled on Deidre's back and she shook her head as she spoke. "Mmm, mmm, mmm, I never thought I'd see the day."

"You never thought you'd see the day when what?"

"When my child let the green-eyed monster take over. You're jealous of Fredrick and Kayla's relationship!" Lana shook her head again in mock disappointment. "I guess I should blame myself. I should have had other children. Then you wouldn't be an only child and you would know how to share."

"Oh brother, give me a break, Mom. I know how to share. I've shared Kayla with you since the day she was born. I'm perfectly fine sharing Kayla's affections with her father."

Deidre eyed the designer opulence of the room they were standing in, and thought about the private jet and limo that had brought them to Flex's gorgeous red-brick colonial mansion, It stood on gated property in the exclusive Englewood Cliffs neighborhood, which was known for being a retreat for stars and other VIPs who wanted to be close to New York City but still maintain a sense of being away from it all. The mansion was huge and even had a 30-foot pool out back. He had a movie room with real theatre seating and a state-of-the-art studio in the basement. The suave ultra-modern furniture looked as if it had come right out of the pages of one of those decorating magazines. He even had servants. It wasn't even his only house! He had a penthouse in the city, a beach house in Miami, a spot in the Hamptons, as well as on the Vineyard, and who knew what else. How many homes did one man need? *Talk about conspicuous consumption*, Deidre thought. *How is my little cottage supposed to compete with all of this?*

The penchant for material things that Flex had apparently picked up since she left him was unsettling. In her opinion, such an intense focus on material things was not good and wouldn't set a positive example for Kayla. That was part of the reason she didn't let Kayla listen to a lot of contemporary rap music. The emphasis on *bling-bling*, money, cars, and sex just didn't represent the kind of values she wanted for her child.

"I'm just sick of him throwing his wealth and his record company and studio around. You would think I'm the bad guy, just because I want my child to grow up not obsessed with material things. I want her to get an education before she gets all caught up in the dream of being a superstar rapper. I mean, really, what if she can't rap anyway?"

Lana started smiling from ear to ear and her voice filled with pride. "Oh, she can rap. My grandbaby can rap! She's good. It must be in her blood."

"Oh, not you too, Mom! Tell me you haven't been encouraging my child to rap? No wonder it's been so hard to get her to focus on other things besides being the next child rapper to make it big." Deidre sighed and shook her head.

It wasn't as if she wanted to crush her child's dreams, but she knew what it was like being a woman trying to make it in the testosterone-filled space of rap music and hip-hop culture. She wanted her daughter to be fully grown and ready to handle herself in that space. If Kayla happened to develop other interests in the meantime that took her away from hip-hop, all the better.

"If you're listening to her rap and telling her that she's going to make it big, then no wonder she's still holding out hope. Having a super-producer and hip-hop mogul for a dad will only push her further into the dream. Do you see what I'm up against?" She threw up her hands in disgust.

"I really don't see what the big deal is. So she becomes a rapper. You were one. Her dad's a producer. Maybe it's as much a part of her as it was a part you all. I mean, I have to say that I was a bit clueless when you were a senior in college and became the rap gangtress, mack-momma rapper down with a bunch of gangsta rappers called The Real Deal Niggas." Lana shook her head and Deidre knew she was remembering her own arguments against Deidre taking time away from her studies to do shows and to perform lyrics that went against every virtue of womanhood she'd tried to instill in her.

"I rolled with the flavor, as you kids like to say, and it wasn't half bad. You should listen to Kayla and then explain your views on why you think it's best that she waits." Lana patted Deidre's back.

She should have known that Lana would throw her own history in her face. There was really no talking to a doting grandmother anyway. Lana James was about as useless in this scenario as Flex the *super-cool* father was. Neither of them seemed to be able to tell Kayla no.

Realizing that she wasn't going to get anywhere with Lana, Deidre took a deep breath. "Fine, Mom, I'm going to take this all into consideration." *Not!*

She walked away from Lana only to walk right into the man that she had been successfully dodging all night.

"Muffin." Dr. James shoved his hands in his pockets nervously as he stood in front of her.

"Hey, Dad." Deidre folded her arms across her chest and readied herself for whatever the good doctor had in store.

"It's good to see you and Kayla. Thanks for inviting your mother and me to share in this occasion." He turned and glanced back at Kayla with what appeared to be adoration. "She's growing up so fast. I feel like I don't get to see her nearly as much as I would like too."

"Yeah, well, time does fly. They do grow up quickly." Deidre aimlessly looked around the room for something to do that would pull her away from the uncomfortable moment. Finding nothing, she crossed her arms and let out a sigh instead.

"Flex was telling me that he's trying to get you to move back to the East Coast, and that he wants to do the right thing and marry you." Dr. James removed his hands from his pocket and then, as if he didn't know what to do with them next, put them back in his pocket.

Deidre shot Flex an evil glance and then looked her father in the eye. "Oh, he did, did he?"

"Yes, and I think it's a good idea, Muffin. I know that your mother misses you terribly and if you were closer, she would be able to see you and Kayla more frequently." He chuckled nervously. "I'd also like to see the two of you more. I know that part of the reason that you've stayed away is because of me, but I hope that if you move back closer to home we can work on some of that."

The conversation was not going where she expected it to go, and she had no idea how to respond to the kinder-gentler dad reaching out to her. "Why work on things, Dad? The past is the past. I'm fine with our relationship the way it is, really."

Dr. James took a deep breath and a sad look came across his face. "I don't know if I believe you, Muffin. Because if that were true, you would be able to look at the way Fredrick is with his daughter and the way he looks at you and see it for what it is. You would be able to take the plunge, do the right thing and take him up on his offer."

Deidre smarted. This was a conversation that she did not want to have, especially not with him. "What goes on between Flex and me is between us. Trust me, I don't need you to tell me about doing the right thing." *Like it's the right thing to beat your wife and terrorize the household.* "Thanks for your input; however, it is unwanted."

"Muffin, you know I got help. I didn't push things when you and your mom moved back home because I wanted you to deal with things in your own time. I think it's time now for you and me to deal with the past and put it behind us. Your mother and I have long since worked through—"

"Oh for Christ's sake, can we not have this conversation right now? I mean, really, I *do not* want to have this conversation with you, *at all.* What went on between the two of you and how you deal with your relationship is between the two of you." Although some things were just plain unforgivable in her mind, Deidre had long ago realized that it wasn't her place to say whether Lana should forgive what her husband had done to her. She drew the line when it came to working on her own relationship with the man.

"I think if we—"

She had to cut him off. Her throat was starting to constrict and her heart was pounding against her ribcage. The shortness of breath would come along at any moment. If she let him go on, she wouldn't be able to breathe.

"No!" She turned to leave just as Flex walked over to them.

"Hey, thought I'd come over and see what you two are over here chatting about." Flex put his arm around her waist and pulled her close. She was surprised at how easily his touch calmed her and made her feel safe.

"I was just telling my daughter that I'm happy to see her and I hope to see more of her and my grandchild, that's all."

Deidre watched as her father put his hands in his pants pocket and walked away. She let out a sigh of relief and exhaled the breath she wasn't even aware she'd been holding.

Flex had observed the increasingly heated conversation from across the room where he was chatting with Mrs. James and Kayla. He didn't know why he'd felt the need to intervene, but he didn't like seeing Deidre upset, never had.

SWEET SENSATION

Watching Dr. James walk sadly away, he started to think it was a bad idea getting everyone together. Maybe the past was just too much to overcome.

"You okay?" he asked once he pulled his eyes away from Dr. James.

"I'm fine." Deidre sighed and twisted her neck as if it ached.

Flex moved his hands from her waist to her neck and started massaging her shoulders. When she didn't complain, he kept going.

"So, when are you two going to do the right thing and get married?"

Flex's moment of tranquility with Deidre came to a halt when Judge Fredrick Towns II walked up.

Judge Towns was nothing if not blunt and to the point. That had been a major point of contention between Flex and his father years earlier, and at that moment Flex found himself strangely close to revisiting those contentious times again.

"Dad, this is not the time to have this conversation. Also, this is between me and Deidre." He continued to massage Deidre's neck and hoped that his father picked up his not so subtle expression warning him to back off.

"Well, I think it's the perfect time to have this conversation. The entire family is here, and we've all been denied a chance to grow and get to know one another as family because of whatever you did to make Deidre decide she couldn't trust you to be a father to your child." Judge Towns took a moment to shake his head before he finished speaking. "I told you all your wild, menace-to-society antics were going to come back and bite you in the behind one day. Just look, you barely know your own child."

"I don't think that's a fair assessment, Judge Towns." Deidre placed her hand on Flex's hand, which still rubbed her neck. "I think that in the few short days Flex has known Kayla, he has a better relationship and a stronger tie with her than some fathers and children who spend years living in the same house."

Shocked, Flex stared at Deidre. He hadn't expected her to go to bat for him the way she had in the old days when she had his back and he had hers. The fact that she did warmed something in his heart that he thought had gone away a long time ago. He smiled as a warm tingly sensation sweeter than anything he had ever known spread across his chest.

"Well, Deidre, while that may indeed be true, the fact still remains that the two of you brought a child into this world, and the two of you need to do the right thing by that child, my grandchild, and make a formal commitment to one another." Judge Towns never backed down from an argument. That was why he'd been such a brilliant trial lawyer and made a name for himself all over the East Coast.

"Do you really think that marriage is the only answer? I don't." Deidre tilted her head to the side and folded her arms across her chest. "I think it's an antiquated solution to a situation that is not uncommon and can be worked out in any number of ways."

"I realize that you kids are from a different generation, and that nowadays it's cool to have baby mamas and baby daddys and so on and so forth, but you also need to be aware of appearances and what is best in terms of the progression of the race.

"Now the two of you grew up with more benefits then a lot of young African Americans. You are both college educated and poised to be a credit to your race. Flex, you're in the public eye as a successful black man. If you do not marry the mother of your child, it sends a message to the rest of the world about African Americans and black families. You have a chance to take a stance and do the right thing. At the end of the day, it is not just about you."

Although Flex agreed with almost all of what his father said, the reason he wanted to do the right thing for Deidre and Kayla was not for the rest of world or to be a credit to his race.

"At the end of the day, Dad, it's just about us. I want to marry Deidre, but she needs time to make her decision. I plan to work on getting her to say yes to me, but we don't need you or anyone else telling us what we ought to be doing."

Judge Towns shook his head in disagreement. "Flex, you have become a role model for lots of other young black people and you need to be cognizant of that."

"I realize the weight that my position in the public eye carries, Dad, but I will not sacrifice my relationship with my family to fit some public image. Deidre and I will do what is best for us." Flex was used to standing his ground, no matter how hard Judge Towns pushed. It was the only way the two men had been able to build a somewhat easygoing relationship after all the years of butting heads.

"Fine, but I really think you need to make some sort of a public statement, and acknowledge at least that had you known about the pregnancy, you would have married Deidre years ago, and that marriage is in your plans in the near future," Judge Towns offered grudgingly.

Flex shook his head. He knew that Judge Towns was also worried about his own public image as the man who raised Flex. The last thing he wanted to do was inadvertently tarnish his father's image, but he had to play things just right if he was going to win Deidre over. Standing there with her, he realized that he wanted to do so more than anything else he'd ever wanted.

"We will decide what, if any, public announcements we want to make, Dad. Thanks for your concern."

"Fine. I'm going to go and chat with the Jameses. I'm sure they are of the same mindset as I. We all really just want what's best for Kayla— oh, and the two of you of course."

"Of course."

Deidre and Flex spoke the words in unison and it shocked Flex to his core.

They looked at one another and grinned. It was so much like the old days he had to struggle not to break out in a fit of laughter.

Judge Towns shook his head before walking away, clearly irritated with the two of them.

Flex sat down on the sofa and pulled Deidre down with him.

"Must be the night of the crazy opinionated dads, huh?" he said jokingly.

"Be careful, *Pops*, that can include you too. You are a dad, and you do have some *crazy* opinions that you just happen to share with the other two crazies."

Flex laughed. He did agree with both Dr. James and his father, but when the chips fell he backed Deidre. That apparently hadn't changed. He didn't know what to make of it. "True. True. I suppose you're right. Call me crazy, but I do think we should get married."

"Call me stubborn, because I will not marry you simply because we share a child." She shrugged.

"That wouldn't be the only reason, of course."

"No?" she asked incredulously.

"No, of course not," he assured.

"What other reasons could there possibly be?"

"There is the fact that you are intensely, overwhelmingly, attracted to my handsome looks and sex appeal."

Deidre burst out laughing.

If he weren't so happy to finally see a smile on her face, he would have been insulted by her gut-busting, tears-in-the-eyes laughter. Only partially joking, he did think she was as deeply attracted to him as he was to her and he certainly thought he was handsome and had sex appeal.

When she finally stopped laughing she sat upright and wiped the tears from her eyes. "Okay, are those the only reasons?"

Flex frowned and then smirked. "No, there is also the fact that we make a pretty damn good team. I think deep down you know and have always known that I've got your back when the chips are down and I believe that you have mine."

Her face became all of a sudden serious. "That's no reason to get married. We can still be there for one another and not be husband and wife. It's just a part of sharing a child. We can be cool with sharing the part of each other's life that includes raising Kayla, and that's it."

"Okay, I can see it will take more convincing." He tilted his head and studied her carefully. He could tell that she still had feelings for him. She was good at hiding them, but she wasn't that good. Her beautiful golden brown eyes still bespoke every emotion and he saw the attraction smoldering in them. He hated to have to use her attraction against her, but when it came to her safety and the safety of their child, the gloves came off.

Kayla came over and squeezed between them on the sofa. "It's okay, Dad, we'll work on convincing her together. She's a tough one."

Flex smiled as he mussed Kayla's hair.

Deidre rolled her eyes and got up from the sofa. "I will not be bullied or coerced into marriage by anyone in this room. So save your energy and put it into something you have a chance at doing."

Flex smiled. He liked a good challenge. *Let the games begin.*

CHAPTER 15

"Lost Ones"

Stacks stood in front of Sasha's gravesite fighting the urge to kick in the headstone. Messing around with that chick had been one of his biggest mistakes. He'd ended up in jail the first time because of her, and he knew it was because of her cousin's vendetta that the D.A. got those tapes.

She'd actually thought she could just leave him and make her move on Divine. She'd tried to deny that she was leaving him for Divine, but that pretty boy had been sniffing around her just a little too much. He couldn't have that. That was not going to work for him, and . . . accidents happen.

Unfortunately, her death upset Flex and Divine and they couldn't get past it. He would have had them smoked too, but The Real Deal was hot and making him a gang of loot. Plus, Flex had pretended that he was still down. Couldn't shake the dude for a while. He'd been almost like a second shadow. Flex had hung around Stacks so tight that he neglected everything else, including his own lady, Dee.

Stacks had had a lot of time while he served out the rest of his sentence to think about Flex's actions during those last days. Nobody liked a snitch, and if he ever found out that Flex was one, ever got concrete proof, that would be the end for Flex.

Flex was too slick, too crafty. Now Flex Time Records was the hottest record label and putting out all the hits, while Body Bag couldn't buy a hit. All the players had changed during the time he was locked up, so even his illegal dealings were struggling. It was like someone was working hard at blocking every advance he tried to make.

He blamed Flex.

"What are you doing here?"

Well, well, well, if it isn't Flex's buddy and Sasha's true love, Divine.

"What's up, Divine? What's good?"

Divine just placed fresh flowers on Sasha's grave and gave him a once-over. The punk wouldn't have even tried that kind of disrespect back in the day. It was all Stacks could do to remain calm.

Stacks bit back the response he wanted to give and played it cool, figuring he'd be able to get some information out of Divine about that chump, Flex. "She was my lady, man. I'm just here to pay my respects. You know, since a brother was on lockdown, he couldn't visit her grave on a regular basis."

"I think it's disrespectful for you to even visit, and I'm sure her family, in fact, I know her family would feel the same way." Divine turned up his lips and took a posture that Stacks could only read as a threat.

Blatant disrespect! Who does this punk think he's dealing with? "Oh, so now you speak for the family? Ain't that something? Listen, partner, just mind your business and everything will be cool. You can't stop me from visiting the grave of my woman and neither can her family. Not even that super-producer chump Flex, so you can just chill."

Even when Stacks checked him, Divine didn't change his stance. Stacks had to calm himself because Divine was still standing there like he was about to do something, not backing down at all. That would never have happened before Stacks got sent back upstate, and it made him want to do someone bodily harm.

Divine brushed some nonexistent lint off his shoulders and Stacks couldn't help noticing the designer threads the man was wearing. Apparently everyone was doing well except for Stacks, and that irritated him all the more.

Divine looked at him and chuckled before he spoke. "Yeah, Flex is doing well for himself in spite of the way you played the group and the bogus deals you gave us. He's even taking care of the crew. He knows the meaning of loyalty."

"Loyalty! None of you know the meaning of the word. If it weren't for me there would have never been a Real Deal. How do you repay me? Y'all didn't even come or holler or write or nothing when I was in jail." Stacks stopped himself before he moved to push Divine. Starting a fight at the graveyard with no backup wouldn't have been a smart thing to do. He had to be strategic about the way he went after those punks, he planned to go after every single one of them. The only one who was relatively safe was Teddy. Thinking of Teddy made Stacks even angrier. Flex didn't take care of the crew; he only looked out for himself and Divine.

"Yeah, Flex looks after crew all right. Tell that to Teddy or that cock-eyed fool Louie. He's not looking after them. Far as I can tell, you and Flex are the only members of The Real Deal still living large." Stacks hacked and spit. "Don't think I don't know that Flex had something to do with me getting sent back to finish my bid. But that's okay. Every man will have his day, and from what I hear, Flex has a lot to lose these days. How is that trick Dee, by the way? And the little one? A girl, right?" Stacks laughed.

Divine's shoulders puffed up even more. Stacks couldn't believe the amount of balls the guy was showing.

"Teddy made his stance clear when he stayed on at Body Bag. You can't save people that don't want to be saved. Louie is doing his own thing and building his own production company. We're still cool. He knows he always has a home at Flex Time. If Teddy ever gets tired of kissing your behind, he's got a home with us as well." Divine paused, looked him in the eye and sneered. "Oh, and the last thing you want to go on record doing is threatening Flex's family, Stacks. He is not the same guy you *think* you used to punk." His expression turned threatening. "Truth be told, he never was. You might have got away with whatever you did to Sasha, but you don't want to mess with Dee and let Flex get wind of it."

Laughing it off, even though the whole conversation had him on edge, Stacks managed to speak through a tight jaw. "Oh, you giving out advice now? Flex does not put fear in my heart, son. You got the wrong somebody."

Divine just gave a sarcastic laugh. "You wanna go to war? Then go to war. Leave the women out of it. You don't want to go there."

"Yeah, since you all on the Flex bandwagon, then you just tell that punk to watch his back, and while you're at it, you might want to watch your back too. Since you so cool with Louie, tell him to keep one of them cock-eyes on his narrow behind as well."

Divine's slanted his eyes and then he smirked. "Right. I'll come back to visit when it's a little less crowded here."

It was all Stacks could do not to pull out his piece and cap Divine. All the exchange showed him was the level of disrespect that had been allowed to grow and fester since he'd been out of the game.

Flex was going to have to be hit and hit hard, but he was trying to wait until either Body Bag or his drug business or both were back on top before he went after him. Seeing Divine let Stacks know that a message had to be sent to Flex. Flex and his whole Flex Time crew were in violation—committing fouls all over the place. He'd have to make some phone calls, but one of those Real Deal punks was going down. Maybe not the one he wanted to hit, but someone was going to get hit.

If Stacks could hold off at least until he built up his holdings, he would be able to handle Flex properly once and for all. Holding out with the amount of disrespect in the air would be a struggle. What he needed to do was figure out a way to send a message to Flex without having Flex feel the need to retaliate before Stacks was ready for him. Either way, those punks in The Real Deal had to be schooled quickly.

CHAPTER 16

"It's Bigger Than Hip-Hop"

"Are you sure?" Flex ran his hand across his head as he listened to Divine relay his conversation with Stacks at Sasha's gravesite. He'd just dropped Kayla off at the Jameses' home. Deidre had decided at the last minute not to accompany Kayla for the weekend. So, Kayla and Lana had come up with a plan to help him woo Deidre, and he was on his way to Minneapolis to carry it out. When Divine sent him an urgent text message about Stacks, he made a pit stop at Divine's townhouse on the way to the airport.

"Yeah, man. Teddy was right. Dude is losing it, slowly but surely. We're going to have to be on point because he's not acting like a rational person. He looked crazy as hell standing there. I kept my hands on my piece, because I thought he might try something stupid and I was going to have to smoke him."

Not good news. Deidre still wouldn't agree to move in with him, and with Stacks acting like a lunatic he needed her and Kayla where he could protect them.

As they sat in Divine's den with a music video on the wide screen playing softly in the background, Flex leaned back in the black leather sofa and studied his friend closely.

"I want at least two more men inside at Body Bag. I don't care if they can only get in the mailroom. We need more eyes and ears over there."

Firm and assured, Divine nodded his head. "Flex, Teddy has it covered. He wants to bring Stacks down as much as we do, maybe more so."

Frowning, Flex leaned forward. "Why? Because his solo album flopped? Man, this is so much bigger than his doomed solo career. He should have left Body Bag when we did."

Divine sighed. "He didn't leave Body Bag because he wanted proof that Stacks either killed Sasha or had her killed."

"What? Why is he so concerned about that? Sasha was my cousin. She was your best friend. I know she hung around the crew a lot, but she was dating Stacks." Flex waved his hand dismissively. "Why is Teddy so concerned about that? Besides, I tried that route. I hung out with that scumbag for a whole year, and the most I could do was gather evidence of his parole violations. Stacks wouldn't slip up and admit it. Teddy is just wasting his time."

"Whether he's wasting his time or not, that's why he's stayed on at Body Bag. That's why he's become Stack's shadow. He has his own agenda. He'll give us information and help us as long as it doesn't mess with his plan. He wants to make Stacks pay for what he did to Sasha, and he's willing to stay close to Stacks' side to make that happen."

Divine seemed so sure about Teddy that Flex wanted to believe him, but he couldn't fathom why Teddy, of all people, would be so concerned about what happened to Sasha. He also didn't want to sit there and argue with Divine about it.

"Fine, whatever, all that means is we really need to see about getting more men on the inside. If Teddy had to worry about keeping his cover to get what he wants or helping us, he is going to keep his cover. And I can tell you right now, he's not going to get Stacks to confess a thing."

"Yeah, but what if he did? What if, after all this time, we got proof that Stacks was behind that drive-by. That Sasha's death didn't have anything to do with people hating him, but with him trying to control her?" Divine's eyes lit up with the hope that Flex had long since given up. The only thing Flex wanted now was to make sure that Stacks didn't hurt anyone else he loved.

While he had given up hope of finding proof, if he ever did somehow prove that Stacks had something to do with what happened to his cousin, he knew without a doubt what he would do.

"I'd kill him myself."

Divine nodded and Flex could tell by his expression that, if proof of Stacks' involvement were ever found, he would have to get in line behind Divine for revenge.

"That's exactly how Teddy feels."

Flex shrugged. "Well, good luck to him. I've got to focus on getting Deidre and Kayla in my house for good."

As if happy for a lighter topic, Divine laughed. "Dang, I thought you would have had her down the aisle by now. What's the holdup?"

Not taking kindly to his friend's laughter, especially at his expense, Flex frowned. "The holdup is she is very stubborn."

"Wow, I'll bet this is new for you. Finally, a woman who isn't doing what you say when you say. Must be tough, huh?" Divine put his feet up on the black lacquer coffee table and crossed his arms across his chest.

"Man, shut up! Deidre will come around. If I had all the time in the world, I would let her see the light in her own good time. Unfortunately, since we have a lunatic to consider, I'll have to give her a little push in the right direction. The most important thing is that she and Kayla are safe, not to mention that Rick and Frank are ready to leave the Midwest for good."

Divine chuckled. "Good luck with that. I think that if you just came clean and cut all this crap about 'doing the right thing' and 'making sure they are protected,' and admitted that you're still in love with the girl and you're now double hit because you have fallen in love with your daughter, too, you'd be able to convince Deidre to marry your behind. I don't blame her for holding out and standing her ground."

He gave Divine a pointed look. The man was getting a little too happy. "Deidre and I have a lot of things to work out before we'll be able to discuss feelings. Love requires trust. She doesn't trust me. I don't know if I could ever really trust her again either."

"Then leave her alone. Make sure she's protected the same way you are doing it now. Pay child support. Continue to get to know your daughter and leave Dee alone. If you can't admit you love her, then you need to step away."

"It's bigger than all that crap, Divine." Considering what Divine had said about Stacks, stepping away from Deidre was not an option. He knew he wanted Deidre and Kayla in his life. He wanted Deidre as his wife. Even though he did not want to admit to himself all the reasons why, he knew that much was true. "What's wrong with wanting to do the right thing and marry the mother of my child?"

"Nothing is wrong with that, *if* she wants to marry you. What's wrong is you punking out and trying to play it like you're not hella attracted to Dee and you're just 'doing what's right.'"

Divine smirked and chuckled again before he finished speaking. "Marrying Dee would not be a hardship for you. I can tell by the way your eyes light up when you talk about her or whenever anyone mentions her name. You've got it bad. I'm just being a good friend and letting you know before it bites you on the behind."

"Whatever. Nothing is going to bite me on the behind because I can handle this. I mean, yes, I'm attracted to Deidre. She's sexy, sweet, all the things I fell in love with years ago. That was a long time ago, however. That was before she had my baby and didn't tell me about it."

Divine just twisted his lips incredulously and shook his head.

Flex was about to say more to convince his friend when he heard something in the background that made him pause.

"Turn up the TV," he said, feeling his voice shake.

Divine reached for the remote and turned up the television. The news reporter broke news that made both men go still.

"Rapper Louie 'Loose Eye' Jones was gunned down in a recording studio in Brooklyn today. The murder occurred sometime between five and six o'clock, and so far there are no witnesses. The police are looking to talk to anyone who may have information leading to the arrest of . . ."

"Shit!" Divine turned down the television. "I know he had something to do with it. He threatened all of us, man."

Flex just stared at the screen. He hadn't spoken to Louie in months. Louie decided to strike out on his own after never really finding his niche at Flex Time Records, but they had remained friends. He'd always figured they would reconnect eventually. Everyone in the group was kind of doing their own thing and life just got in the way. Now the man was dead, and they would never get a chance to reaffirm their friendship.

They would never find out who killed Louie. Flex knew that as sure as he knew his name. 'Another rapper slain,' had become almost a cliché. He knew that the police would have about as much luck finding out who killed Louie as they had finding out who killed all the other rappers that had been murdered.

He also knew that Stacks was behind it somehow. Even though Flex had made sure that Stacks' business connections and money were shaky at best, Stacks had somehow found a way to get to Louie. Flex knew without a doubt that he had to make sure Stacks could not get to the other people he cared about.

After moments of stunned, contemplative silence, Flex finally found the words. "Stacks is behind this, and we need to make sure this is the last person he hurts. I need those extra men inside at Body Bag. I need to step up my game and be ready for anything Stacks comes up with. Teddy can't give us all the information we need, especially if Stacks is unstable. There's no telling when or how the man will strike out. His funds are virtually non-existent and still he made a move on Louie."

Divine sighed. "Probably because Louie was off on his own and not connected to us in the same way. I shouldn't have pissed him—"

"It's not your fault, man. We just have to be prepared and be proactive. This cannot happen again." Flex stood up. He had to make it to Minneapolis and make sure that one former rap princess and current spoken word artist realized that she needed to be with him where she was safe.

"I agree with you on that." Divine stood up.

They gave each other pounds and Flex continued his trek to the Midwest. Getting Deidre to move in with him had just become urgent, and he wasn't going to take no for an answer this time.

CHAPTER 17

"Bonita Applebum"

Wooing Deidre was going to take a cunning craftiness that rivaled anything he had ever done in the music business. She was determined to resist his advances and her feelings for him. If it weren't so utterly irritating, it would have been funny.

He liked a challenge as much as anyone else. However, Deidre was a step beyond challenge. Over a month had passed since she and Kayla they spent the weekend at his mansion in Jersey, and Deidre had yet to agree to move in with him, let alone marry him.

She'd been very nice about letting Kayla come and visit him on the weekends, and he was getting to know his daughter. The last two weekends Deidre had found something else to do, or she'd said she was too busy to come along with Kayla.

When Kayla and Lana suggested that he go back to Minneapolis to catch Deidre at a poetry open mike, he'd jumped at the chance. Both Kayla and Lana thought it would be a good idea for him to go and hear her, then take her out afterward. He just hoped they were right, and he hoped that she hadn't yet heard about what happened to Louie.

The coffee house where the open mike was taking place was a small black-owned coffee house on Lake Street in Minneapolis. He thought its name was cool—*Coffee, Black*. The logo outside was a hip-looking cartoon of a sister with locs drinking from a steaming mug. The relaxing atmosphere of the establishment came through in the smooth earth tones on the walls and the plush sofas in rusts and browns. The sofas provided extra seating for those who didn't want to drink their lattes and cappuccinos at the tables or the bar.

The place was a bit more crowded than he expected it to be. He didn't even see Deidre at first, but then he noticed her sitting up front sipping something hot from a big brown mug with the coffee shop's name and logo on it.

He took a seat in the back, along with one of his bodyguards. He searched the room and saw that Rick was in the back pretending to be reading a magazine. He hoped that he would be able to get Deidre to see the light soon. She was fairly observant, and she would be able to make Rick eventually.

Thinking of his own presence in the small coffee shop, Flex hoped that the backpack crowd that frequented these kinds of venues could care less about having a rap producer like himself in the mix if they recognized him. He had a feeling, though, that he didn't have to worry about getting swarmed by adoring fans.

Once the open mike got started, he began to regret coming. Listening to poetry was bad enough, but listening to bad poetry was torture. It was worse than listening to bad rap, in his opinion, because at least if you had bad lyrics there was still a chance that you could get some banging beats to compensate for them.

The closest thing to having beats came when one guy had another man banging on some African drums while he read. It was almost as if every one had seen the movie *Love Jones* and said, "Hey, that's cool, I think I'll write a poem and read it so that people will see how deep I am and snap their fingers in appreciation when I'm done."

When the host finally called Deidre's name, Flex smiled and breathed a sigh of relief, hoping that he would be able to get her to leave soon after she read. He didn't want to sit through another bad poem.

"Good evening, everyone. How are y'all doing tonight?" Deidre gazed out into the crowd and smiled her dazzling smile.

Flex was taken by how positively the audience responded to just her greeting. It was as if they, like him, had been waiting for Deidre to grace the stage.

"I'm not going to read a lot tonight, just two poems," she stated.

"Oh, come on sis, I know you're gonna give us more than that," a man called out.

"Yeah, you can do more than two!" a woman added.

"No, just two tonight. I promise to read more next time. These two poems came to me as I was thinking about what's going on in hip-hop today." She paused and took a breath. "Now, don't get me wrong. Quiet as it's kept, I still love me some hip-hop. Every now and then, I'll play some and reminisce on back in the day when hip-hop and I were really in love, when I saw its promise and everything was all good."

"I hear you, girl. I used to love him, too!" a young sister with long locs tied up in an elaborate scarf made a sly reference to the Common Sense's song about hip-hop, "I Used to Love H.E.R." She snapped her fingers from side to side.

"Yeah, some of y'all know what I'm talking about. When I was young and dumb, it didn't matter if things got a little wild between us. 'Cause I could hang, you know. But when you grow up and you're trying to raise babies, especially girl babies, you have to check yourself."

"Before you wreck yourself!" another man called out.

Flex let his eyes move across the room and he noticed that the audience was captivated, even though Deidre hadn't said a word of poetry yet. The way they responded to her was unlike the response for any of the other poets. She still had it; that was certain.

"Yeah, I know y'all know what I'm talking about. Even the fellas know. That's good, because we need the brothers to get it. We need female and male soldiers to be a part of this. It's hard loving hip-hop as a woman when hip-hop doesn't always love you. It's hard raising your girl child, hoping that you can give her the strength to combat the woman-hating crap that passes for music, especially when you loved that culture yourself. But I'm gonna stop preaching now because y'all came to hear some poetry."

"Girl, you go 'head!" a younger man with a bald head and wire-rimmed glasses encouraged.

"Preach, sister! Tell it! Let them know!" the sister with the locs shouted.

Deidre smiled so brightly that her happiness gleamed in her eyes. She looked just as happy as she used to before she did a show or when she was in the studio recording or in a free-style battle. Seeing her so elated sent a jolting sensation through his veins.

"So I listen to what gets played on the radio these days and what passes for music, and I wonder what has happened to the culture I loved and the promise of the music. The rampant materialism, the focus on money, girls, and cars, all of that is just such a waste of lyrics and a waste, quite frankly, of good beats. I know we weren't given back the booming bass of the drum so that we could hear some of the things that we hear. I often wonder if there is anything left to love. So, the first poem I'm going to read for you all is titled, 'Word.' I want to dedicate this poem to the memory of a friend who was murdered today. Another senseless life lost to the violence that is killing off some of our most creative minds and lyricists."

Flex sighed. She knew about Louie and, based on her little opening, she already had a finger pointed at whom to blame. The very music and culture that he was still very much a part of. He leaned forward to listen to her poem.

When I first heard
brothers on the block saying word
I got excited
I sensed we would be getting our power back again
There is power in the word
the strength of NOMMO
was going to take us home
But when I tell you of this new coming strength
all you can say is
Word!
I try to get you excited
I tell you about the Griots
the storytellers of the motherland
telling history in ceremonial detail
I told you about the power of slaves and ex-colored men

using the word to tell their narratives
to illustrate incidents in their lives
to punch holes in that peculiar institution
And all you can say is word?
In the'70s the word was spoken and black was beautiful again
We'd lost the knowledge
of our beauty for so long
And all it needed was to be spoken into existence
We spoke it and there was power
Black Power
I tell you this and you, awed by history I suppose, simply say, word . . .
I mean the word is supposed to be more powerful than that
The word is supposed to take us back
The word and the drum they are with us again
We have the word in rap
and the drum in the boom-bap
But no one seems to be using them in the way they were meant to be used
They don't uplift, inspire, or even engage
And I complain to you and all you can mutter is word
WORD
I know that you know that word is bond
Word is life
In the beginning was the word
God spoke it and created day and night
"In the beginning was the word
the word was with God
and the word was God
He was with God in the beginning"
There is power in the word
And don't look at me or even fix your mouth to say word, but
Be word enact word
Be word enact word
Be word enact . . .
Word

People actually got up out of their seats and gave Deidre a standing ovation. Flex felt a smile widen across his face, and he clapped extra hard. He'd always known she had skills, and he'd seen her rock many a hip-hop crowd. There was something about seeing her in this element that made him realize all the more just how talented she really was. She spoke her words with such rhythm and flavor that he could have sworn he heard music, but there was no music playing. The way her body swayed as she spoke left him captivated. He couldn't take his eyes off her and it amazed him that the people around him seemed to be experiencing the same thing.

"Okay, thank you, guys, for real. I feel the love and it really means a lot to me. It means a lot to me because I know that if y'all really felt that poem then I can still have hope for hip-hop. The last poem I'm going to do is also about hip-hop. I wrote this poem because I was missing those days when we used to have real deejays who really knew how to spin a record. I guess I was yearning for the golden era of hip-hop when the deejay and the emcee went together like peanut butter and jelly, hot butter on popcorn. Y'all remember the deejay and those days?"

"Hey Mister Deejay, you can get it started!" the sister with the locs called out.

"Last night a deejay saved my life!" the older black woman added. Both women giggled and the audience joined in on the laughter.

Deidre laughed also. "Y'all feel me! I was at a party a while back and the deejay was playing CDs. What's up with that? How you gonna be a deejay without vinyl? Anyway, I digress. Let me give you this poem so I can sit down. The title of this poem is, 'Where Have All the Deejays Gone? With a special shout out to those not mentioned by name.'"

Not to be on some ole nostalgic tip
but where have all the deejays gone?
Back in the day you couldn't be a fly emcee unless your deejay
was as nice as you
Nowadays you can't be a platinum selling artist
without a track from a super producer

SWEET SENSATION

And I'm not making a value statement
it is what it is
all I wanna know is where have all the deejays gone?
because back in the day
the right deejay could break an emcee off
something proper
like slowing down the beat
or bringing in a dope scratch
just when the emcee is about to
break it down
switching records like only a
true mix master
a real beat blaster
could
where have all the deejays gone?
I'm not longing for some yesterday long forgotten
though sometimes I do get a little misty-eyed
for the days when you knew what deejay went with what crew
you know like
Grandmaster Flash and the Furious Five
Run DMC and Jam Master Jay
Sweet Tee and Jazzy Joyce
Gang Starr and Premier
Pete Rock and CL Smooth
Salt-N-Pepa and Spinderella
Marley Marl and Dimples Dee
and then Roxanne Shante
and then MC Shan
Tribe Called Quest and Ali Shaheed Muhammad
DJ Jazzy Jeff and the Fresh Prince
Scott La Rock and KRS-One
and I won't even get started on the commercialization of the mix tape
because I know by now you have got to be feeling me
I'm just asking

where have all the deejays gone?
because you know wherever they are
there has got to be a fly ass party going on

The crowd cheered and whistled as Deidre left the microphone and some fans approached her with chapbooks to sign. Taking a deep breath he sat back in his seat. He noticed that even Tommy, his body-guard, couldn't take his eyes of Deidre. The man had nodded his head the entire time he listened to her performance. Flex caught his eye and Tommy blinked as if coming out of a daze. Flex realized the man looked how he himself felt. *Blown away.*

It wasn't just the fact that she was stellar, but also the things she'd said. It was clear to him that she still had love for the culture that had brought them together. He wondered, however, if she had enough love for hip-hop to get together with him when, based on what he gathered from her poems, he was a part of everything that was wrong with it.

Louie's death and her feelings about hip-hop made him think about her resistance in a new light. While he had a lot to think about, he also knew that in the end, if he wanted her safe, he had to find a way to get her to move past her inhibitions.

He made his way to her table in the front of the coffee house.

"You were fantastic, Sweetness. I really enjoyed your poetry."

Deidre looked up, startled. The last person she expected to see in the coffee house during open mike was standing right in front of her.

"Hey. What are you doing here? Better yet, where is our daughter?"

"I let Kayla spend the night with your mom in Jersey. They both seemed to think it would be a good idea for me to come here and check out your reading, then maybe take you out for a bite to eat and show you what charming and pleasant company I am." He pulled out a chair and sat down, all the while keeping his gaze firmly locked with hers.

Deidre couldn't help laughing. Even though she was tired of the nonstop pressure that everyone was putting her under, seeing Flex in his mack-daddy-woo-her-mode brought out the comedy in an otherwise stressful situation. She was sure the brother had never had to work so hard to get a woman's attention in his life. Just thinking about the way she'd fallen over backwards to impress him in the early days of their relationship let her know that she wasn't entirely immune to his antics.

This time, however, she was resolved to resist, or to at least go down fighting. Hearing about Louie's death today strengthened her resolve that she was right to want to keep her distance from the world Flex inhabited. As much as she still loved hip-hop, things had changed.

The funny thing was, before hearing about Louie, her resistance had almost run thin. She had been so close to throwing up her hands and agreeing to at least move in with Flex, it wasn't funny. The only way she could be sure to hold out was not to see him. If she was around him for any stretch of time and he started calling her Sweetness, and rubbing her back or sitting really close, all bets were off.

"Now why are you laughing at a brother? I'm trying to be sincere and show you how I feel and you're laughing. That's just cold, Sweetness." He placed his hand over his heart in mock hurt.

"Oh, poor baby. I'm sorry." She feigned concern.

"If you're really sorry, let's go grab a bite to eat, and then you can really make it up to me."

"Yeah, right. I don't think so. There isn't that much sorry in the world."

Flex clutched his heart again. "You're killing me, Sweetness. You're killing me. You mean, I came all the way here after dropping Kayla off with your mom, and you won't even go out to dinner with me before I go all the way back?"

Squinting her eyes, she contemplated his offer. Dinner probably wouldn't hurt, and he had traveled an awful long way . . . "Of course I'll have dinner with you. Make no mistake, however. That's all I'll be having with you."

He gave her a sexy grin and clutched her hand in his. "Let's go then. Do you know any place really good? What are you in the mood for?"

When he touched her hand, she felt a shiver and her heartbeat skipped a beat. "That Puerto Rican restaurant that I love is in this neighborhood, on Lyndale. We could always go there."

"Fine, let's go." He stood then, still holding on to her hand.

A warm and sweet tingly sensation pulsed up her arm and down her spine as she got up and followed him out of the coffee shop.

CHAPTER 18

"My Place"

She hadn't expected to have such a lovely time at dinner. Flex hadn't mentioned her moving in with him once. He had been witty and charming and they'd had random conversations about everything from politics to hip-hop.

Deidre realized something she had been denying the entire time she was separated from Flex; she'd missed her best friend. She'd missed the late-night conversations they had after making love when they were in college, before The Real Deal got signed and Flex took off touring.

She'd missed the way he listened to her, really listened to her, in ways that no one ever had before or after.

They were sitting in her den having an after-dinner nightcap before he headed back to Jersey to spend the rest of the weekend with Kayla, and he was sharing his thoughts on her poems.

"I really liked the deejay poem, of course, even though it sliced me like a double-edged sword." He gave her a sideways glance before continuing.

"It felt like you were dissing the super producers that make the hip-hop hits nowadays and, as a former deejay who is now a producer, I felt torn listening to it. It really is all about evolution, though, when you think about it. Rap has always drawn on technology. From the sampling to the way the turntable was turned into an instrument, the technological advancement was always there. Now we have producers doing things with sound that we couldn't have imagined ten or fifteen years ago, let alone in the mid-seventies when things were jumping off in the South Bronx. I think that hip-hop has evolved and it will continue to evolve. Who knows, one day we may not even have producers."

Deidre couldn't help smiling. If she'd known Flex was in the audience she probably would have picked another poem. If she ever became a famous poet and some graduate student wrote a thesis about her life and poetry, she shuddered to think about the chapter that would discuss her relationship with Flex Towns and that deejay poem. Since she wasn't ready to start analyzing that connection herself, she opted to take the conversation in another direction.

"Yeah, I think it's cool that the culture has evolved. I mean, I didn't expect people to still be rapping, hip-hop-hippin'-to-the-hippin'-the-hip-hip-the-hop for the next twenty years. At the same time, I listen to the music now and I hear so much focus on material things and violence." She paused, thought about Flex's many homes, cars and limos, and hoped that he didn't take offense. She didn't mean it as a comment on his lifestyle. She really did see it as a drawback in the culture.

"It's like it's worse than that gangsta rap stuff we did back in the day, because at least gangsta rap *pretended* to be about something, depending on what group you listened too. It wasn't as banal as some of this stuff that's all about the money you have and the car you drive and killing this one and having sex with so many women. Okay, some of that was gangsta rap too, but you know what I mean." She'd never thought she'd see the day when she had anything good to say about gangsta rap, but she had long since learned to never say never. For all the drama that gangsta rap had brought to her life, being involved with it had given her insight into herself.

Flex laughed at that and she smiled. "Okay, so you are open to change. You just don't like the changes that have happened?"

"I guess I just always felt like the music could be doing more, like it had so much potential. Even when I was performing, *especially* when I was performing. Do you remember those rhymes I used to come up with—the ones that were really pro-woman and about something?" She shook her head. Although she wasn't ashamed of her image back then, she often wished she had been allowed to do the music she wanted to do.

"You remember what my label thought about those pro-woman rhymes. How they wanted me to keep making those same songs that painted me as the bad trick down with The Real Deal. I guess I got tired of it all sooner than I thought I would. I wanted to grow, and I felt stifled."

Flex leaned back on the futon and then glanced up at her. "Did you feel stifled in our relationship as well?"

Her eyes widened and she felt her back straighten. "Whoa, how did we go from talking about my feelings about hip-hop to our relationship?"

His eyes narrowed and his tone became dead serious. "Oh, come on, Sweetness, the two have been intertwined from the beginning. If we're going to have any kind of a future, which I hope by now you realize I really want, then we will have to work out how they are connected eventually."

Deidre thought about what he said and she couldn't get around how true his words were. She was going to have to finally really deal with everything in the past that she had been running from and how it was all connected.

Does it have to be tonight? she wondered. Taking a deep breath, she braved Flex's penetrating gaze.

"In a lot of ways I think I blamed you and our relationship for my stint as Sweet Dee, because it was a whole lot easier than blaming myself. It's funny how you can rewrite history in your mind." She laughed nervously and continued.

"Through the years, I have done a lovely job of convincing myself that if I hadn't been so head over heels where you were concerned, I would never have rapped about half the things I did back then. I was a former debutante, a graduate of one of the most prestigious colleges for black women in the country, and had taken a vow to uphold the ideals of my fine sorority, for goodness sake. I think I'm still unofficially blacklisted from the Zetas, by the way." She let out a nervous chuckle.

Smiling, she remembered that when she decided to pledge Zeta during their sophomore year in college, Flex pledged Sigma even though he had no interest in pledging a fraternity. He told her later that he knew that since Zeta and Sigma were brother and sister organizations and often had pledging activities together, he would be able to watch and make sure no one hurt her or came at her inappropriately. His overprotective nature had annoyed her at the time, but she found herself missing it while they were apart.

"When I really think about it, I see that a part of me liked being that bad girl, Sweet Dee, and rapping about turning guys out and busting caps, and being fly but dangerous. The lyrics were wack and didn't really say much, but the persona—yo, I have to admit Sweet Dee was something else!"

Flex smiled. "Is that why you performed at the *Source Awards* with Lil' Niece and Sexy T? You wanted to be a bad girl again?"

"I don't know why I performed. I think on some level I knew that their cover of 'Turn 'Em Out' was going to start people wondering what ever happened to Sweet Dee. I think that I wanted to show people that Sweet Dee was still here and she was still the baddest. So when they called and asked me to perform the hook that they sampled from the original, I was cool. What better way to show the world that I'm still here?

"I didn't think about the consequences at the time. Like the fact that my students might see it and put two and two together, or that people would be curious enough to want to find out more."

She still kicked herself for not being smarter about the repercussions of performing at the *Source Awards*. She was just lucky that she was teaching at a community college and most of her students were non-traditional. That semester she'd taught three evening courses with students who were mostly older and employed during the day. They had no idea who Sweet Dee was, what the *Source Awards* were, and could care less.

"When I saw you at the *Source Awards*, I was speechless. I wanted to take you home and never let you get away again." Flex placed his hand on her thigh.

She swallowed and gazed at the strong hand before daring to speak.

"Yeah, right. You seem to forget I saw that knock-out that you were with. I doubt that you gave me a second thought after I walked away."

"You were on my mind the entire night, Sweetness. When I won the award for best producer, when I celebrated after, I was thinking about you. Your performance was spectacular. You blew everyone away." Sincerity shined so brightly in his eyes she had to blink.

"Thanks, Flex." *Shoot, I meant Fredrick!*

"What? She called me Flex for the first time in how many years? I don't believe it. Maybe there is a chance in hell that I'll be able to get you to marry me after all."

"Oh, don't go reading too much into things and getting them all twisted. My calling you Flex is no big deal. It is your name, isn't it?"

He placed his finger on his chin and a mock serious expression crossed his face. "A name that about fifteen years ago, you said you would never call me again if you could help it. Because, let me see if I remember this correctly, you wanted me to be able to clearly distinguish you from all the groupies and hoochie mamas that hung around The Real Deal." He broke into a smile and his gaze softened.

"Truth be told, Sweetness, you didn't need to call me anything different to distinguish yourself from them. You already had something that none of them ever had a chance of getting, my heart."

Deidre closed her eyes. *Why does he have to be all sweet and charming? It's much harder to resist him when he's like this.* "That was a long time ago. No do-overs."

"Says who? Who says we can't have a second chance to get it right, to do it right? Huh? I'll be the first to admit that I messed up big time by not letting you know every day how much you meant to me. There should have been no room for doubt, no matter what was going on at the time. You should have known that you could trust me, that you could trust us. I want a chance to get it right. Come on, Sweetness, you owe me one."

"I do not!"

"Oh yes, you do. You didn't give us a chance back then, and I missed out on the first twelve years of Kayla's life. You've got to give me a chance now, just on general principle. You owe me that much."

His serious tone and steadfast expression showed just how much he clearly believed what he was saying. Deidre closed her eyes and then opened them again, as if doing so would give her some way to combat what she had fondly deemed Flex-Speak—*when you know your answer is the right answer and the only answer worth pursuing.*

"What does giving you a chance entail? I am not going to marry you based on 'I owe you.'"

"Why not?" he asked incredulously.

"Because that's not a good enough reason to get married. When I tie the knot, *if* I ever tie the knot, I want it to be because I'm in love and he's in love with me and we can't imagine living without one another." She folded her hands across her chest.

"How do you expect to realize that if you keep running?" Removing his hand from its resting spot on her thigh, he rubbed his head.

Outraged, Deidre sat up straight and glowered at him. "I most certainly am not running."

"Oh yes, you are. You're running a marathon away from your feelings, and mine." He cocked his head to the side in a manner that suggested he dared her to prove him wrong.

"I am not. I'm just being cautious. Someone has to maintain a level head. There is a lot more at stake here then just our feelings. If we got married and it didn't work out, it could have an impact on Kayla."

"Oh no, you don't. You cannot use our daughter as an excuse for you to dodge your feelings. I won't allow it."

Deidre got up from the futon and put her hands on her hips. "Using my daughter to dodge my feelings? I'm doing nothing of the sort."

"Oh yes, you are. Stop trying to act all dignified and indignant. You know as well as I do what you're doing." He smiled and softened his look and his tone. "So if you won't marry me right now, give me the summer to woo you and make you see that I'm the only man for you and that we should be together."

Laughing sarcastically, she sat back down on the futon. "*Wow,* you really think can do all that in *one* summer?"

Flex shook his head and grinned his devil-may-care-grin. "Oh, yeah, in fact once you move in with me I plan to have my ring on your finger within a matter of weeks. We'll be married by the end of the summer."

Deidre raised one eyebrow and frowned. "Move in with you? Who said anything about moving in with you?"

"How else am I supposed to woo you, Sweetness? If you don't move in with me, then you'll continue running and hiding the way you've been doing. We can't have that, now can we? That wouldn't be fair to the process. If you can resist our feelings while living under the same roof with me, then I'll have no choice but to give up on us. You'd be right. If you're too chicken to give it a fair chance, then—"

"I'm not chicken. I just thought it would be easier on you to not have to come face to face with the failure of your little plans each and every day." She shrugged, trying to show bravery in the face of the fear that was creeping under her skin. She couldn't move in with Flex.

"I'm right, *Fredrick*, it is too late for us. If you want to make it harder on yourself, though, who am I to try and protect you? Fine, I'll move in with you." *What! What are you doing, fool? What about Louie? The violence. The danger. Your heart!*

"Oh, so we're back to Fredrick when we were making so much progress. That's okay. I'll have you calling me Flex yet."

Deidre felt the heat of passion rising in her cheeks at the thought. Wasn't that exactly what she was afraid of?

"So, Sweetness, do you want to pack a few things for yourself for the weekend? We might as well start now. You can come back with me this weekend. Next week when Kayla is done with school, the two of you can join me for the summer."

Deidre lifted herself from the futon and wondered how she'd gone from blissful resistance to dreaded captivity in a manner of minutes.

Flex allowed himself a nice long look at Deidre's retreating backside, secure in the knowledge that her days of running from him were almost over.

CHAPTER 19

"Kissing You"

Sure, it seemed like a fantastic and gutsy idea at the time, but she was starting to question the wisdom of taking Flex up on his challenge. Agreeing to live in the same house with that man had to have been the craziest thing she'd ever done. Every time he was within a few feet of her, a sweet sensation spread from her heart to the tips of her toes. She wasn't going to be able to resist him much longer. She didn't think she wanted to.

They had gone to Louie's funeral and, after attending it and seeing how a life with so much promise was wasted, she felt more than ever that she needed to resist Flex, but didn't have the strength to do it. Sitting in the living room of Flex's mansion she tried to figure out a way to gather the strength she was going to need.

"Hey." The word was whispered in her ear and sent a tingling shock down her back.

Only one person could have such an impact on her with just one word, so she didn't even bother turning around. She did look up when Flex joined her on the sleek, modern, slate-gray sofa that was designed more for style than sitting in her opinion. She missed her comfy futon and plush cream sofas in Minneapolis.

"What's up, Sweetness? You're being awfully quiet in here. What's going on in that head of yours?"

She sighed. "Nothing. Just thinking."

"Oh, no. Danger, black woman thinking." Slapping his hand on his knee, Flex laughed at his own joke.

Deidre smirked. "Ha, ha, ha. That's the problem with male/female relationships today. You guys can't handle a woman in full control of her own mind and being."

SWEET SENSATION

Flex leaned back and cocked his head. "Or you women are too scared to give up control for just a little while and let someone else handle things, or, God forbid, share control."

"So, you would like to take on some of my burden? Share control and help me with some of the issues that have been troubling my wee-little-woman-mind?" she asked sarcastically.

"I'd love to. I'd be honored to. I'm begging you to let me." His tone was just as sarcastic.

"Are you sure? It's not something easy. It's a very difficult and very serious matter."

"Lay it on me, Sweetness." He winked.

Licking her lips, she wondered if she could really just lay it on him. Like saying, *Well, Flex, I'm finding that I'm becoming too attracted to you for my own good. I'm feeling the overwhelming urge to run as if my life depended on it. Would you mind terribly if I just took my scared behind on back to Minneapolis where the threat of falling head over heels in love with you can be carefully staved off by a nice dose of seclusion and cold weather?*

She always tried to be upfront and real with people, keeping their child hidden for twelve years notwithstanding. He did claim to want to know what was on her mind.

"Here's the thing: I sincerely believe that me living under the same roof as you is not going to work out for anyone's benefit. I can, however, see how important it is for us to be in the same area at least. So, I'll put my cottage on the market and let the community college know that I won't be back next year. I'm thinking that I'll find a small place here in North Jersey and look into some adjunct teaching at either Bergen County or Passaic County Community College. Once I find a place, I figure I'll just move in as soon as possible." Okay, it wasn't exactly what she'd been thinking, but it would give her a way out. That would help solve her dilemma.

"So, in a nutshell, you're sitting here thinking about running from me? Wow, I never thought I'd see the day when that fierce brave girl who took on a basement full of guys and gave them more than a piece of her mind, would turn into such a wimp." Flex shook his head in disgust.

"First, you ran instead of letting me know we were going to have our child. Now you feel the attraction between us and you're running again. The contradictions in your personality are really baffling."

Deidre swallowed. The only problem with trying to shield your feelings from a person who knew you as well as Flex seemed to know her was that it seldom worked. "What makes you think I'm running from anything?"

"Oh, let me see. Could it be the fact that *you are running*?" he snapped.

"I am not running!"

"You are so running." His eyes slanted in aggravation and he ran his hand across his head. "I have a question for you. Do you really think that by moving out of this house you will be safe from your feelings? That distance will make it easier to forget about what you feel?"

Well, if he wants to lay all the cards on the table, then I'll just lay them out. "It makes it safer. It allows me a clarity and a presence of mind that, I'm sorry, is lacking when I am living in such close proximity to you."

"You say that as if you really believe that I wouldn't be in your home every chance I got." He laughed.

The look on her face must have given away the fact that that was exactly what she thought.

"Oh, Sweetness, you are even more misguided than I thought. Do you think this is some sort of a game and if you make it a little difficult for me then I'll just give up?"

A troubling smile came over his face and she felt her heart drop.

"Oh, you do think that, don't you? I wonder what would give you that impression? When have you *ever* known me not to go after what I want? I want us to be a family, Sweetness. I want you. I have *always* wanted you." He paused, letting his words sink in.

"You are in my sights and I have tunnel vision where you're concerned. You could move anywhere your little heart desires and that wouldn't change. I'll be coming after you and I *will* continue to come after you until I have you right where I want you."

No amount of swallowing could have soothed the dryness that settled in her mouth and throat, but swallow away she did.

The sincerity in his eyes and the gravity of what he was saying were not lost on her. The old Motown tune, "Nowhere to Run" ran through her head and she would have laughed if it wasn't so pathetic.

You knew the brother was dangerous when you moved in here. Now it's time to face the music.

"I think you're making more out of this than you really need to. It's not about me running." *It's about me sprinting as fast as I can.* "It's about us finding a livable, workable situation that is suitable to all of our needs. Our lifestyles are very different, but we share a child. I think that as soon as I can get my life on track here, I can set up a nice comfortable home for Kayla and myself. That way when we begin to share the parenting she'll feel that she has two safe, secure, and stable homes that she can count on."

He folded his arms across his chest and cocked his head to the side arrogantly. "I mean for her to have one with both of us in it. I won't rest until that happens. I see what's wrong here and trust me, I plan to rectify the situation as soon as possible." He leaned in close to her.

She blinked and started biting her lip. "What . . . what do you mean by that?"

"You have been given way too much free time to sit and plot and think about how you can make your escape. I have been remiss." He smiled seductively. "By allowing you the time to settle in and get used to living under the same roof with me, I gave you too much space. Don't worry. It won't happen again. I plan to fill your time and your space with nothing but examples of how good it can be between us."

"W-w-ell n-n-ow . . . Fred—"

The fingers that brushed her cheek halted her words. She told herself that she was only shutting her eyes for a moment to get her bearings, because it was damn hard to do so with Flex's gaze blazing into her soul. It was simultaneously dreamy and threatening, or was it threatening because it was so darn dreamy?

She opened her eyes and swallowed again. Opening her mouth to speak her piece, she was shocked when Flex's mouth covered hers.

His tongue entered her mouth so slowly, so methodically, that a part of her felt that she had all the time in the world to stop him, if only she wanted too. As her own tongue made its way out of her mouth and into his, she tried to remember all the reasons she wanted to move out, why she didn't want to open her heart to him again. She couldn't think of any.

The only thing she could think of was that his hands felt lovely caressing her breast.

The sweet laziness of their oral exploration was tripping up all her defenses. When Flex's teeth began a sensuous nibbling of her lower and then her upper lip, she couldn't contain the "ah" that escaped from her.

"You like that, huh?" He murmured the question just before he let his tongue began round two of its seductive torture.

"Mmm, mmm, hmmm." She couldn't believe he had her *humming* with just a kiss.

His hand went under her t-shirt and flicked across her belly. He moved his lips to her neck and her mouth was suddenly lonely. The tongue that started to flick her earlobe made her forget about her mouth for a second, until she realized that it was open and no sounds were coming out.

"I've missed kissing you, Sweetness," he murmured.

"I—I've missed kissing you too. But—but we really shouldn't be doing this, F—Flex . . . ahhhh." The line of reasoning she started out with such a good hold on went awry when he started to nibble on her throat.

"I love it when you call me Flex, Sweetness." The words were spoken just before his lips claimed hers again.

She realized that there was no stopping the merging of their mouths. She just had to ride it out and hope that whenever he stopped she could get enough distance to try to get him to see reason. Didn't he see that no good could come from restarting their relationship? Well . . . besides the kisses and other things that she was certain she would not allow between them if she could help it . . .

"*Wow!* Way to go, Mom and Dad! I think I need to give you guys some more time to be together without the kid in the way. Maybe I should go and spend some time at Grandmommy's house." The sound of Kayla's voice was barely enough to pull Deidre from her Flex-induced fog.

She pulled away from the kiss slowly and shook her head in a feeble attempt to get her bearings.

"Don't go getting any ideas, Kayla. This was just a one-time thing that shouldn't have happened. Your father and I do not need to be left alone."

Flex leaned back on the sofa and narrowed his gaze on her.

She cleared her throat and turned to Kayla again.

"So, Kayla, I was thinking that I would start looking—"

"Don't go there, Deidre." Flex shook his head even as he leaned back into a lazy, lounging position on the sofa.

"Don't go where? I simply want to tell Kayla about the plans I've made."

"I don't think it's a good idea. Plus, you promised me the summer. But, hey, if you want to chicken out on our deal and prove me right, then that's cool. I like being right. But you should know that backing out on our deal is not going to stop me from pursuing you. It's just going to make me even more persistent. You're not scared, are you?" He chuckled.

Even though she knew full well that Flex was practicing reverse psychology, she found it hard to back away from the challenge. Besides, it would make an even bigger statement if she did last the summer and was able to show him that the attraction was a mere figment of his imagination, that her resolve was strong and she knew what was best for everyone. She'd have to manage to trick herself into believing it first. But if she made it through the summer and was able to halt his advances, he'd see that there was no future for them and he'd have to just be content to share parenting under separate roofs.

"Well, fine, Fredrick. I was merely trying to give us a head start on the inevitable, but if you want to prolong things, who am I to stop you?" Deidre shrugged.

"Fine." He shot her a gaze that highlighted all his desire, and she swore she could see his mind working on plans to get everything he wanted.

"Fine," she managed to mumble as she found herself caught up in his stare.

Kayla started laughing. "Okay, that was a little weird, but whatever. Are we still going to have a movie night tonight? Mom, Dad got an advanced copy of that new action movie you wanted to see, because he did the soundtrack. We're going to watch it in the movie room downstairs."

"Yes, Sweetness, the first of many family nights to come," Flex said. His sexy, penetrating eyes were relentless.

Since Kayla had already given away the fact that she wanted to see the film, Deidre couldn't beg off by saying that she didn't want to see it. She certainly didn't want to look like the wimp Flex kept accusing her of being.

"That's wonderful. I can't wait to see it. I can't wait to hear what you've done with the soundtrack. So many soundtracks nowadays have nothing to do with the movie. Most of them make you wonder if the producer even read the treatment for the film, much less the script." Deidre forced a pleasant smile and rose from the sofa.

"I can't wait to hear the verdict." Flex stood up and laughed. "I'm sure you'll let me know if my soundtrack doesn't fit the film."

"Oh, I'll be sure to let you know."

Kayla looked back and forth between the two of them. "Okay, now you guys are acting *really* weird."

Deidre wrapped her arms around her daughter and led the way to the high-end multi-media room/home theatre that made her small den, futon, and 27-inch television in Minneapolis look like a playroom. "Let's just go watch the silly movie."

CHAPTER 20

"Mind Sex"

"So, tell me your deepest fantasy." Flex's voice, deep and dreamy, drew her into a place she dared not venture.

She blinked and swallowed before she answered, "M-my what?"

"Your deepest fantasy," He repeated.

"W-why would you want to know that?"

He looked at her with a hooded gaze that hinted this was just the tip of his efforts to seduce her. "Because I want to fulfill it."

"Why would you want to do that?"

"Because you make me want to."

"I make you want to?" Repeating every word he said was not working to halt his seduction, only working to make it more intense. So she wondered why she kept doing it.

"Yes. You make me want to."

She took a deep calming breath that did nothing to aid the furious pattering in her chest. "Tell me exactly how I'm doing that and I'll stop right now."

He smiled sexily. "I don't want you to stop."

Reaching over and smoothing away a stray piece of hair that didn't seem to want to stay put behind her headband, Flex made contact with her cheek ever so lightly.

Deidre let out a gush of air that felt as if it came from the bottom of her gut. It had been a week since the meeting of the lips and she had managed to stay clear of Flex for some time. It had worked until she got sucked into a scheme to have dinner in the city with him. She hadn't known that dinner would involve her, him, and the terrace of his penthouse.

The breathtaking view of New York City from the terrace and the breath-stealing man seated across from her, made it so that she couldn't get her bearings. Between the sinfully delicious meal and the soul-stirringly, seductive company, she figured it was only a matter of time before she hopped on the man and begged him to take her.

The fact was, she found it harder and harder to resist him or her feelings for him. If her feelings were just about lust, she might not have felt so overwhelmingly out of control. Lust she could handle easily: either she gave in or she didn't. The problem that made itself more and more prominent the longer she stayed around him was that her lust came with a whole lot more baggage than she wanted to carry at the moment. Feelings were coming into play and she found them hard to deal with.

"If you don't want to tell me yours, I'll tell you mine." He made the statement as if he were making some magnanimous offer.

"O-oh, that's okay, really." Show-me-yours and I'll-show-you-mines had gone the way of grade school. She was way too old to fall for that line.

"No, I want to share." Again he made the gesture, as if offering the greatest act of kindness known to man.

She shivered, and it had nothing to do with the soft summer breeze wafting through the city.

"This night air is a bit chilly. How about we go inside for a nightcap and I'll let you know my deepest fantasy." Holding out his hand, he waited for her to get up and place her hand in his.

When her fingers touched his, it felt as if a bolt of electricity charged through her. The bolt would have been fine if it hadn't traveled her body only to land in her heart. They walked back in from the terrace and got settled in the living room.

Being nestled on the sofa with him was not making the highly charged feeling go away. If anything it became more intensified.

The glass of red wine helped to settle her a little bit.

"So, let's see, where were we? Oh yes, my deepest fantasy. Where shall I start?" His arm rested behind her head on the sofa and he leaned back. "I guess I've had this recurring fantasy since the day you walked out of my life."

"Really, what of? My head on a silver platter?" Hoping her half-hearted attempt at a joke would get them away from what seemed to be a highly arousing situation, she laughed nervously.

Chuckling, Flex took a sip of his wine before continuing. "No, I had no reason to want your head on a platter. I thought you left because I'd messed things up." He paused. "That's reality; back to fantasy. So, anyway, from the moment you left, I have always thought about what it would be like if you came back to me. I often dreamed about it."

Deidre gave in. "Okay. So what does this dream me do when she comes back?"

"Oh, the dream varies a bit but the majority of the time it's a rainy night and I'm at my home in Jersey and there's loud knock at the door that wakes me from my sleep. I go downstairs to open the door—"

"Okay, interjection. You have a doorbell and servants." Deidre laughed nervously. "I have yet to see you answer the door. This *must* be a dream."

"Hush, don't interrupt the flow." Flex furrowed his brow as if in deep concentration. "Anyway, I get to the door and there you are soaking wet and wearing one of those sexy black trench coats. As soon as I open the door, you fall into my arms and start apologizing for leaving me and begging me to forgive you and take you back."

A laugh that sounded like a snort escaped her mouth. She had to interrupt him to let him know how much of a fantasy that was.

Waiting until she finished laughing, Flex continued. "Anyway, like I said, you're soaked. So I wrap my arms around you and lead you to the den. I start a fire and go to get you some towels so that you can dry off. When I get back you've taken off the trench coat and you're standing by the fire in a black lace bra and panty number with thigh-high stockings and a garter belt, like a walking Penny's Personals advertisement."

Snorting a laugh again, Deidre responded, "Sounds like a Hookers of Hollywood ad to me."

Flex raised his eyebrow and cocked his head in warning. "If you don't remain quiet and let me finish telling you about my dream, then I'm going to have to find something better to do with that mouth of yours."

The thought of the things he could do made her swallow in a desperate search for moisture.

As if assured that she'd heeded his warning, he smiled and continued. "So, anyway, you're standing by the fire shivering, looking vulnerable and sexy as all get out. So I walk over and wrap one of those huge Egyptian cotton bath sheets around you and rub you to help dry you off and warm you up. Once you're somewhat warm, we move over to the sofa and sit. I take a smaller towel and rub your hair dry. You thank me for being so kind to you after you left me without giving me the benefit of the doubt."

"Huh—" Deidre started to interject her two cents when Flex narrowed his eyes.

"Watch that mouth, Sweetness . . . Anyway, like I was *saying*, you thank me for being so kind in spite of how horribly you treated me and you gaze at me with those beautiful golden-brown eyes that I have always gotten lost in and I'm speechless."

Laughing, Deidre shook her head. "Umm, did slutty-me happen to say why she was at your front door in her drawers in the pouring rain?"

"No more warnings, Sweetness." Flex bent his head and covered her lips in one swoop. She didn't have a chance to back away and when their lips connected she found that she didn't want to. His embrace almost made her feel as if she were sitting in front of a fire in nothing but her underwear. It made her feel sexy as all get out.

When he lifted his head he smiled the sweetest smile she'd ever seen. "Now hush, woman, and let me finish my fantasy. It's a guy fantasy; therefore 'Dream Sweetness' doesn't need a reason to show up at my door in sexy lingerie.

"So, as I was saying before, you give me this sexy and seductive look and I'm lost. It takes me a minute before I can think of something to say. Finally, I tell you that you don't have to thank me for being kind, that I've often dreamed of getting a chance to see you again, to hold you again. And you say that you've thought about me and dreamed about me as well. You want us to start over because you have never loved a man the way that you love me. And you have never had a better lover than me. Of course this makes me happy—"

"Well, of course," Deidre noted, her voice dripping with sarcasm.

The warning glance that Flex shot her made her button her lips quickly.

"So anyway, as I said, I'm happy. Of course, I need to do something to express my happiness. Your lips are looking so inviting, much like they are right now. So of course, I can't resist. I kiss you." He leaned forward and planted his lips again.

This time the kiss was slow and exploratory. It started out with teasing pecks and nibbles and deepened to a demanding and insistent pull that lured not only her mouth but also her soul. She couldn't catch her breath.

She allowed herself to savor the taste of his teasing tongue and mused on how accurate his dream was. She had never had another man make her feel the way he made her feel.

It went so much deeper than the teenage love thing. She had always felt that when she'd found him she had also found the other part of her soul. That was why she was so scared to give the relationship a second chance.

She didn't think she could stand losing her soul mate twice in one lifetime. Walking away from him had been the hardest thing she ever did, and she didn't think she could do it again. She pulled away from the kiss and inhaled deeply.

"Okay, I didn't interrupt you that time. What was the kiss for?" She tried to look irritated, but that was hard to do when she had been so thoroughly and deliciously kissed.

He winked. "The kiss was because you were sitting there looking so beautiful and trying so hard to resist what you were feeling. You distracted me just by sitting there."

"Yeah, right, finish your story."

Smiling he teased, "Oh, so you can't wait to hear more. May I ask why? Are you planning to help make my deepest fantasy come true?"

"Yeah, right, in your dreams, buddy. Finish the story."

"Anyway, I kiss you. You kiss me back. It's like our lips never forgot the taste and feel of each other. We each crave more and more. Nothing can stop this kiss. Before I know it I'm kissing you on your neck. My lips caress your breasts, that ticklish spot on the back of your knees, your inner thighs and—"

Deidre found her hand traveling upward and clasped it to her neck just in time to halt the fanning she wanted to do. Fanning would have clued Flex in to just what an impact his dream was having on her.

She made another attempt at lightening the sexually intense mood. "Wow, for this to be your fantasy, you're certainly doing a lot of the servicing. I would think that a woman in soaking wet lingerie would be the one showering kisses."

"Since this is my fantasy, *not* yours, you can save the commentary," He said, then smiled seductively. "Why can't my deepest fantasy be pleasuring you until you can't take anymore, until you're speaking in tongues and calling out my name. 'Flex, oh, Flex, Flex!' I personally think it would be heaven on earth, a fantasy I'd *definitely* like to see come true."

Her hand lifted. In spite of her previous efforts, she sat there fanning her neck. She got up from the chair. "I think we should leave the fantasies alone now."

"But I'm not finished. I didn't even get to the part where—"

"Honestly, I think we've had a long enough visit in fantasy land. It's time to get back to reality." She paced the floor a moment before turning to him. "So here's the thing. I think that we need to set up some clear boundaries so that we don't delude ourselves into thinking that we can really have a second shot at this. Things happen for a reason, and I think we need to make peace with the past and move on. We don't have a future as a couple.

"We do have a future as parents to a wonderful girl child who is going to require both of us to keep her on the right path. She is our child and judging from my teenage years and yours, we have one hell of a time coming up in a few years."

Laughing, Flex scratched his head. "Hmm, I hadn't thought of that. You know, my father used to threaten me by saying that my kids would give me back ten times the hell I gave him. You don't think that old wives tale is true, do you?"

Deidre hoped to God it wasn't. Between the two of them, they'd probably be dealing with a demon-teen. "I don't know. If it is, we need to be ready."

"All the more reason for us to face the future as a united team, as a married couple." He tilted his head as if he had proven the world's greatest point.

Talk about a one-track mind! "Not really. Don't you see, if we got married for all the wrong reasons we would be bringing a third person into the mix. The teenage years are rough enough without having to deal with parents who shouldn't be together."

Flex sighed. "We won't be your parents, Sweetness."

"I didn't say that. I just—"

"You're scared. You've gotta stop running." His gaze was pleading and she wished for a moment that she were woman enough to answer his plea.

Crossing her arms over her chest, she closed her eyes for a moment before focusing an intense gaze on him. "I'm not scared. Do you love me?"

The silence that followed her question was telling. Deidre almost regretted asking it. If he lied and said he did love her, it would be just as bad as if he told the truth and said he didn't.

In her mind, there was no way Flex could possibly love her.

"I care about you more than you know. I honestly don't think the love I once felt for you ever went away. Is it the same? No. Can it be the same? I don't know. I think this is bigger than the question of whether I love you." He paused and stood up so that he was standing right in front of her. "We share a child. I want to do the right thing and give you and our child the home, the life you both deserve, and all of myself that I have to offer. After keeping Kayla away for twelve years, I think you should at least give me a chance to see if my way works."

She didn't think that hearing that he no longer loved her would hurt as much as it did, but there it was. The sharp pain trailing through her chest made her want to close her eyes and curl up into a tight ball. *Game face time.*

She did the best she could to meet his penetrating gaze without flinching. "You see, Fredrick, we really have two very different approaches. I don't think we can meld them without somebody getting hurt." *Somebody like me.*

"When and if I ever get married, I want to marry a man who wants to marry me because he loves me. Because he can't think of anyone else he'd rather have or anything else he would rather do. I didn't tell you that I was pregnant because we were having such a bad time in our relationship that I really did think it would be only a matter of time before we broke up. The last thing I wanted then was for you to stay with me for the baby's sake.

"I wouldn't have been able to bear it at all. That would have been too much like my parents. I really can't bear it now either. Your wanting to marry me because of Kayla goes against everything I want for my life. So, can we please find a way to compromise? A way that gives us the space we need to move forward in the best way possible?"

"Sweetness, I wish that I could so that. It's more than just me wanting to marry you because of Kayla. That is a big part of it, but only a part. That fantasy that I started telling you about was real. I have dreamed of the two of us together again for some time." He placed his hands on her shoulders and slowly massaged her. "There is an attraction between us. I can feel it and I know you do too. In fact, if you can look me in the eye and tell me that in all these years you have not dreamed of the two of us reunited, that you are not attracted to me right now, then I will leave you alone. We can do things your way."

Steeling herself, she prepared to look him dead in the eye and tell him once and for all what she needed to tell him to protect her heart. When their eyes meet, however, she found that she couldn't say the words she needed to say. Even though she credited herself with being able to weave a good tale when forced to, she couldn't tell Flex that she had never dreamed of the two of them together again. The man had haunted her dreams from the time she met him and all through the time they were apart.

If the moisture that flooded her panties after listening to just that small bit of his deepest fantasy was any indication, she was still very attracted to the man. So, she found herself just staring at him, grasping for words that wouldn't come.

"I'll take your silence as your answer and your agreement that there is something between us that needs to be explored."

"Okay, maybe you're right. Maybe there is something between us that needs further investigation," she offered ruefully. "I would think that this is the kind of thing we would examine before taking a trip down the aisle. I also think that we need to explore it as best we can without involving Kayla. If we find that things really are over between us, I don't want Kayla to get her hopes up for a relationship that's not going to happen."

"Fair enough. So what does this mean? That we are officially secretly dating?"

"I guess so. This will require discretion. I don't want Kayla hurt by this." She did not want Kayla to experience the same things she herself had experienced as a child.

"Trust me, Sweetness. There are two people in this world that I would rather cut out my heart than hurt, and that's you and Kayla." He cocked his head and smiled. "So, you wanna hear the rest of my fantasy?"

Deidre leaned back in the sofa and sighed. *What's a girl to do?* "Fine. Finish your tawdry little tale, and then maybe, if you're good, I'll tell you mine!"

CHAPTER 21

"Sweetest Thing"

Secretly dating the mother of your child, who happened to be living in your home, was harder than Flex imagined it would be. If they hadn't been trying to protect their daughter's feelings, it might have been a little easier, but not much. The more he tried to woo Deidre and tell himself that it was because he wanted to do the right thing and protect her, the more he realized that his feelings went way beyond those somewhat innocent urges. He desired her in ways he'd thought were long gone. Feelings he'd thought were buried came bubbling up when he least expected them. Even more, he found himself wishing and hoping that she was experiencing the same wellspring of emotions— that he wasn't alone. He needed Deidre to trust in him and their relationship more than he wanted to admit.

To say that he was happy that she couldn't bring herself to lie about how she felt about him would be a huge understatement. Even though they hadn't had many more *secret* dates since the dinner at his penthouse, he found himself hopeful about the amount of progress they had been able to make. They both could have gone on ignoring their attraction for some time; they'd done so for several years while they were apart. They were both on the same page in that regard. That was a plus in his view.

While he hadn't expected her love question and knew that his answer wasn't perfect, he had told the truth. He still had feelings for her that hadn't gone away. He wanted to investigate what those feelings were. In hindsight, examining them before they jumped the broom was probably a good idea. He wanted to do the right thing by Deidre and Kayla, and hoped that their exploration would lead them both to the right decision, whatever that was.

They'd managed to get Lana to watch Kayla for the weekend and they planned to spend the weekend together at his beach house in Miami. Waiting at JFK airport for the limo to show up from Jersey with her in it had him pacing the floor. He almost rang her cell phone to find out if she'd changed her mind. Then the limo pulled up. When she stepped out, his heart stopped.

Dressed in a stunning yellow halter-style dress and sexy, strappy brown leather sandals, she took his breath away. Her golden-brown hair was swept up off her shoulders with soft tendrils curling away from the elaborate French twist she wore. The soft touch of her makeup allowed her true beauty to shine.

He walked over to the limo, grabbed her bag and her hand. The weekend together could have a huge impact on the rest of their lives and the pressure was even more pronounced.

Once they were seated in the jet, he tried to gauge her feelings, to get a sense of whether she was having any regrets. When it was clear that he wouldn't be able to tell just by observing her, he decided to ask.

After clearing his throat, he spoke. "So, are you still cool about the trip and us getting away this weekend?"

She looked up hesitantly and then smiled a shaky smile. "As cool as I'll ever be. I thought about canceling and spending the weekend with Kayla and Mom, but I didn't want to give you another opportunity to call me a chicken." Nervous laughter followed her response.

"You know I would have," he teased her lightheartedly, even though her apprehension concerned him.

"Trust me, I know," she offered ruefully. "So, I'm here. I'm nervous. I'm wondering every five seconds if we're doing the right thing by exploring our attraction and our feelings, but I'm here."

"What more can a man possibly ask for, a willing participant." Deciding to keep the mood light and hoping it would make her more comfortable, he winked at her.

She smiled and let out a soft hiss of air before speaking. "*Willing*, hmmm. I suppose we can go with that for now. So what are your plans for this weekend? I hope they're low key. The last thing we need is the press and the paparazzi speculating on whether or not Flex Towns and Sweet Dee are having a relationship."

"They're already speculating about that. You are living in my house." Having long since gotten used to the workings of the public eye, Flex shrugged.

The news reporting about their so-called relationship had hit all the gossip rags, and most of the entertainment shows were speculating. Between his so-called relationship with Deidre and the on-again off-again reporting on the murder of Louie that mentioned The Real Deal, the reporting on him and his record company had become almost old news.

"Yes, but that kind of speculation doesn't harm Kayla, because she knows that already. She's under the impression that we're living with you for the summer until I find a place in Jersey. She sees us every day. She knows I sleep in one room and you sleep in another." Her chin lifted in determination. "If the paparazzi got some pictures of us together, walking along the beach, or having dinner at some trendy spot in Miami, that would give Kayla other things to think about. So, I think we should keep a low profile."

"The beach area surrounding my home is somewhat secluded. The paparazzi would have a hard time breaching it. That's why I purchased the property." Wanting the weekend to be so magical that she would consider at least coming clean about their relationship to their daughter, Flex offered, "I thought we would spend sometime on the beach. Maybe at night."

Deidre just shook her head. "Somewhat secluded and secluded are two very different things." Then she focused those golden-brown eyes on him, and his heart almost melted because her desire was as plain as day. "But maybe a moonlight walk on the beach would be cool. I think we should spend most of our time in your beach house, safe from prying eyes."

"My father used to tell me that everything you do in the dark will eventually come into the light, Sweetness." They couldn't hide forever. She had to know that. He didn't want them to hide a minute longer. The feeling shocked him somewhat, but it also felt right.

"People, including Kayla, are going to find out eventually," he added.

"I just want to be a little more sure before Kayla finds out. So, I think it's best that we just take things slow as far as public displays go." A saucy grin spread across her face and she planted those golden browns on him again. "In private, well, that's a completely different story."

Holding her gaze he murmured, "Umm, that last sentence holds some promise."

"It's meant to. In fact, I've been doing a little thinking about that fantasy of yours." She crossed her legs seductively and leaned forward in her seat.

Even though he cleared his throat before he spoke, his voice still sounded strained and choked to his ears. "You don't say?"

"Yes. I've thought long and hard about it. I really think that the fantasy can be improved upon."

"Really?"

"Yes. I'm thinking that while the sexy lingerie under the trench coat is a good fantasy," she paused and placed her finger on her chin in mock consideration, "complete nudity is even better."

"Really?" Flex couldn't help loosening the top button on his shirt.

"Mmm, hmm. I know you really believe that paying homage to my body with your lips until I beg for mercy is the ultimate fantasy. I just think that a reciprocal lip fest would take your fantasy over the top." Flicking her tongue briefly over her top lip before biting her teeth slightly on her lower lip, she paused for effect. The effect was not lost on him; he lurched forward slightly.

She smiled and continued. "I've really thought about it. I believe that my lips would feel left out if they didn't get to kiss you in that ticklish spot behind your ears. My tongue would not stand for not being able to lick up and down your chest and taste the sweet salty flavor of your sweat. And if I couldn't—"

"Okay, I get the idea, Sweetness. Maybe my fantasy could use some touching up here and there. However, if you don't want to be the first woman to christen this jet into the mile high club, you need to change the subject. Fast."

Leaning back in her seat, she crossed her arms and smiled. "Oh, not so much fun with the shoe on the other foot, huh? Okay, I'll change the subject."

"Thank you." He knew for sure he wouldn't have been able to stand another moment of her teasing seduction. He also knew that turnabout was fair play, and he had a long weekend to make sure that she got exactly what was coming to her.

The first order of business in order to make it a memorable weekend was to somehow show her that he still knew her better than any one, that in many ways he'd never really left what they'd shared. If he could do that, then she would trust what they were feeling enough go with it and push it further.

In addition to having plenty of chocolate croissants and Jamaican Blue Mountain coffee on hand for breakfast, he'd also stocked up on her favorite perfumes, bath salts, and scented candles. He hadn't forgotten her fondness for freesia. He made sure her bathroom was stocked with body splash, candles, oils, and lotions in that scent. It soon permeated everything in the beach house. He only hoped that he could endure the things that the combination of the fresh floral scent and her natural delicate smells did to him.

It also helped that Miami had restaurants that catered every kind of Caribbean food he could imagine. The first night he gave her a taste of the Puerto Rican food she loved.

The second night they shared her other favorite food, Jamaican food. The curried chicken and rice and peas had just the right amount of kick. Sure that the spicy tangy foods did something magical to their erogenous zones, he could barely contain himself as he watched her enjoy each bite. The expression on her face alone was more than enough to make him happy.

They'd finished the evening the night before with a walk on the beach that ended with a heavy make-out session and the two of them sleeping in their separate bedrooms.

He decided that he really didn't care whether they took things further this weekend. He'd waited years to have Deidre back in his life. He could wait a little longer to have her in his bed. She was more than worth the wait.

"This is the best Jamaican food I've ever had. Thanks for remembering how much I love my island delicacies." Deidre used her napkin to gently pat her mouth. "That Cuban barbeque with *mojo* sauce and those *mojitas* we had for lunch were excellent also. It's really hard to get any kind of Caribbean flavor in Minneapolis."

Flex smiled. He really didn't have anything against Middle America. That part of the country bought a lot of his music, according to *SoundScan*. He just couldn't see living there. "I'll bet. I can't see how someone with your fiery taste buds lasted in that place for twelve years."

"Trust me, tasting the rice and peas and washing them down with this champagne cola has me wondering the same thing. Thanks for making this weekend special, Flex."

He locked eyes with her and took pleasure in her wide-eyed realization she had just called him Flex. "Damn, the food is so good it has you calling me Flex? I'll have to hire the chef from that restaurant to come and cook for you every day."

The red tinge that highlighted her cheeks made him laugh. She could be so shy sometimes. He supposed that she was always a little more reserved than he was, but he also knew that she had a wild side. "So, would you like to cap the evening with another walk on the beach? We could burn off some of those calories from that curried chicken."

"Oh, I don't know. I think we could think of other more interesting ways to burn off those calories." Her saucy grin was back.

He took the twinkle in her golden brown eyes as an open invitation. "Word?" he asked, just after taking a sip of water. The look in her eyes—the feelings he saw highlighted there—made him hotter than the Jamaican curry.

"Word!" She nodded her head in the affirmative and then tilted her head sassily.

Laughing and thinking of her poem, he had to be sure that she was really saying what he thought she was saying.

"So, are you really sure you want to take this to the next level?"

"As sure as I'll ever be. Plus, when we get back to Jersey, who knows when we'll have another free moment to, ah . . ." Pausing, she licked her lips. "Explore things between us."

"Yes, but we don't have to go faster or further than you're ready to go just because we won't have the chance to be alone at home." A small voice in the back of his head screamed to be heard over his carefully reasoned approach. *Shut up, man! Stop trying to ruin this for us, she's ready!*

"I know, and trust me, at least on this part." She cast her eyes down for a moment, breaking their gaze. Then she looked up brazenly. "We are not going faster than I want to go. In fact, I had us in the bedroom ten minutes ago."

CHAPTER 22

"Into You"

If she could ever get enough of his kisses, she might not be in the amount of trouble she currently found herself in. Not only were his lips addictive, his kisses went straight to her heart in a way that nothing else ever did. In deep trouble, she had no idea how she was going to get out of it.

"Are you sure?" He stopped kissing her for a moment and voiced the words against her neck as if pausing to compose himself and struggling to do so.

Am I sure? Geez, I don't know. Let me see. She thought the words to herself in an effort to gain some sense and reason in a space where clearly sense and reason had long since vacated.

She swallowed and closed her eyes. "I'm sure."

He kissed her then, his mouth scorching. The heat of his kiss made her knees give and she stumbled. He moved her closer to the big four-poster bed and stopped.

His dark brown eyes held her captive in a penetrating gaze that she swore saw more of her than she ever wanted to reveal. Her own eyes always gave away more of her feelings than she wanted. Sometimes that was a curse, and sometimes it was a blessing. She couldn't figure out what it was at that moment. She only knew that if her eyes were showing him half of what she was feeling, she really was in trouble.

"Do you trust me, Sweetness?"

Deidre studied his face carefully. His soulful brown eyes told her all she needed to know. They told her everything she should have already known, everything she should have trusted in all those years ago. *This man will never intentionally hurt me. I can trust him.*

"I trust you."

"Good." He kissed her on the forehead. "'Cause we are going to try a little experiment."

"An experiment?" Her eyes widened at his suddenly mischievous grin.

"Yes. I promise you'll enjoy it."

Taking a step back, he slowly began to undress her. The garments fell to the floor with ease. His fingers left goose bumps on her skin.

Once she was fully unclothed, he simply looked at her. She wasn't self-conscious about her body. She knew that the thirty-five-year-old her had filled out a bit more than the twenty-two-year-old, especially after having a child. For the most part, she really liked the changes in her body. The fuller breasts and slightly wider hips made her feel like a woman. But as she stood there for what seemed like an eternity, she began to wonder if a man who had dated a string of supermodels, an occasional actress, R&B singer, and that young beautiful girl she'd seen him with at the *Source Awards,* who had to be at least ten years his junior, could appreciate her unadorned and un-enhanced grown woman's body.

"So does the exercise in trust involve me standing here naked and you watching?" she asked nervously.

He smiled and kissed her; his tongue traced a path along her lips and moved to her neck before he stopped.

Placing his arms around her neck, he stopped and took a deep shuddering breath. "I'm getting ahead of myself."

"I-I think you were doing just fine."

He pulled away and the playful, mischievous look came back to his face. "No, I need to put a few more things into place. Stay right there. Don't move. I'll be right back."

She squinted as she studied his face, trying to figure out exactly what he was up to. "Okay."

He left her bedroom and she sat on the bed to wait. Not that there was any chance of her losing the desire to make mad passionate love with him. If she were honest with herself, she would admit that she'd wanted to do that since the day he showed up on her doorstep.

When he came back into the room she looked up to find him shaking his head in mock disappointment.

"You moved," he admonished.

"I sat down," she corrected.

"Yes, but you were supposed to stay still." He walked over to the bed. "Never mind. Stand up."

As he walked over, she noticed that he was carrying an array of colorful silk scarves in his hands. "What are those for?"

A glimmer of amusement trailed across his eyes and he smiled. "They're for our little experiment. Turn around."

Seeing him so playful and excited did something to her inside. She felt a tiny fluttering sensation in her belly as she obeyed and turned to face the bed. "Hmmm, alrighty then."

When he tied one of the silk scarves around her eyes, she took a deep breath. *Taking this trust thing a little far, I see, or rather, don't see. Hmm.* She let out a nervous giggle as the silk tickled her nose and she tried to get used to the sudden darkness.

He turned her to face him again and she took a deep breath. She heard him swallow before he spoke.

"So, we're going to see if I still know all the ways to make your body sing."

She felt his hand caress her cheek and the flutter in her stomach picked up pace.

Flex's deep voice continued. "It's all on me. You don't have to do a thing. In fact . . ." He placed her on the bed and lifted her hands above her head. "Your hands are pretty much tied in this exercise."

He tied her hands above her head.

Umm. Kinky. Hmm. "I see you picked up some new tricks."

His lips brushed across hers and she felt her lower lip quiver. "No, Sweetness, more like I've been waiting for just the right person to share another one of my fantasies with."

"Hmm. Okay. So, I'm all tied up with no place to go." She laughed and tried to move her arms. There was more than enough slack and the scarf wasn't tight at all. Clearly he'd tied the scarf holding her hands together to another scarf that was tied to the headboard.

"Okay, so now what?"

"Now we begin. Sit back relax and enjoy."

"Right . . . ahh."

His lips began their voyage on her neck and the goose bumps returned. Not being able to see seemed to heighten the experience.

"Now if I remember correctly, Sweetness, you really love it when I do this." His fingers latched onto one of her nipples and gently squeezed while his other hand caressed and massaged her other breast. Then his mouth joined the massaging hand and his teeth teased her other nipple.

She swallowed and took short, calming breaths. "Ahhh . . . yes . . . I-I still like that a lot."

The sweet torture seemed to go on forever. By the time his fingers found her core, her hips had already started to rise and she writhed wantonly on the bed.

His lips left her breast and she felt the absence immediately.

His hands continued to move seductively all over her body and she sighed. With his fingers deftly maneuvering the innermost part of her, she soon lost track of the number of times she came—the number of times she screamed out his name. All she had to do was lie there and feel the pleasure he was giving her. But she couldn't help twitching and pulling on the scarves. She wanted to touch, too.

"No hands, Sweetness, just enjoy." His voice was a seductive whisper.

"But I want to touch you," she complained even as the voice in her head told her to shut up and take the pleasure ride.

"Soon," was all she heard before she felt his head between her thighs and her mind ceased to think properly.

That man's tongue and fingers should be outlawed, was all she could think just before an earth shattering orgasm shook her to the core. "Oh. God. Flex!"

He didn't seem to pay her any mind. His tongue on assault, he worked her over thoroughly. Alternating between thrusting deeply and flicking teasingly, he had her in a frenzied and delusional state. When his mouth finally left her, she wished that she could curl up and recuperate.

She tried to listen to the sounds around her. *Didn't I hear somewhere that when one of your senses is limited your others kick in overtime? Was that a zipper? Yes, lord, that was a zipper.* The sound of ripping plastic became very distinct. *Condom? Good.*

The bed shifted when his weight came down on it. She felt his hands near her head and then she could see again. Smiling up at him she noticed the intensity of his gaze and was sucked in even further. She couldn't look away and didn't want to. If things didn't work out between them this time, it would be hell getting over him again. She didn't know if her heart would be able to stand it.

His lips connected with hers as his arms reached up and freed her of her silky restraints.

Her hands immediately went into a frenzied exploration of his body. The taste of herself on his lips and on his tongue did something extra to her desire. She put her hand behind his neck and pulled his head closer, deepening the kiss. She then let her hands glide down his back and took her time toying with each muscle along the way.

His hands lifted her hips slightly before he entered her and, for a minute, time stood still.

Flex had to pause when he entered her. She felt almost as tight as she'd felt the first time they'd made love, her first time. How could that be?

"Oh, baby, you're so tight." He paused and gazed at her, trying to gather himself. "Has it been a long time?"

She bit her lower lip. It seemed as if she wasn't going to respond. "You can sort of say that."

"Yeah? How long?" He slowly eased out and back in, wanting her to adjust to him again.

"Oh, about thirteen years or so."

He stopped then.

The reality of what that meant was not lost on him. He'd been her first lover. She hadn't been with anyone since they broke up. He kissed her and let his tongue take over her mouth, because he was at a loss for words. When he lifted his head, he just gazed at her.

She smiled and slowly rolled her hips, taking him deeper inside her with each move. "Umm, are you going to let that stop you? What? Are you afraid that you won't be able to compete with my last lover?"

He blinked, realizing that she had him in a daze. "Sweetness, we are definitely going to have to find something better to do with that mouth of yours."

"We've got all night, Flex. Maybe we can find some other uses for those silk scarves of yours." She winked at him and squeezed his firm behind with her now free hands. "I think my mouth wants to do a little tasting."

"Brazen, aren't you." He moved faster, thrusting deeper inside of her. He could feel himself stretching her and filling her.

"Yeah, Flex—" Her words got lost in a soft murmuring sound that escaped her lips.

He picked up momentum and rode her body as if he would never get the chance to again.

She wrapped her legs around his waist and held on for the ride.

He couldn't stop looking in her eyes. What he thought he saw there as he went deeper and deeper into her shook him to his core. Her eyes were saying things he knew she was not ready to face. He didn't know if he was ready to face them.

"Oh, Flex. Oh, my God."

"Yes, come on, baby. One more time for me. Come for me, Sweetness."

"Flex," she moaned, her voice a barely distinguishable whimper.

"Sweetness, you are sincerely my weakness, girl. I adore you, baby."

He went to town then, thrusting as if his life depended on it. He felt a jolt shoot through him just as she tightened on him like a vice, clenching and draining him. They reached completion together that time. But the night was still young.

CHAPTER 23

"All I See"

Zig-zig zap
Zig-zig-zig zap
Zig-zig zap
Zig-zig-ziggy zap zap

Cutting and scratching on the turntables always helped Flex to clear his head; and he had a lot of things running around in his head that needed sorting. The weekend with Deidre in Miami went better than he had expected. The problem was, he didn't know how he felt about that. Frankly, he couldn't wrap his mind around the impact she was having on him. It went so much further than chemistry. His emotions were involved and becoming increasingly so the more time he spent with her.

That, combined with trying to keep tabs on Stacks and make sure that no one else close to him got hurt, left Flex feeling open and vulnerable. He needed to make sure that Deidre and Kayla were protected and he needed a clear head to do that. Time spent thinking about whether or not he was in a relationship with Deidre was breaking his focus.

She still wouldn't agree to be upfront about their relationship with their daughter. He was getting tired of sneaking a hug here or a kiss there. He understood that she didn't want their daughter to get hurt if things didn't work between them, but what he couldn't understand was why, after everything that had happened between them, she didn't have more faith.

So he found himself in his basement studio practicing the turntable skills that he hardly ever got a chance to use anymore and trying to figure out the exact extent of his feelings for Deidre.

"What's up, Dad?"

Looking up, he saw his daughter enter the studio. "Hey, Kayla." He stepped from behind the turntables.

"Hey, don't stop. I like hearing you cut it up." She flopped down on the small leather loveseat he kept in the soundproof room.

He walked over to her and mussed her hair. "Yeah, what do you know about cutting it up? That was way before your time, kiddo."

"You guys keep sleeping on Kayla-Kay. I told y'all I'm the truth in this hip-hop game. It's in my blood, yo." She moved her hands in an old school, hip-hop manner, striking a b-girl stance.

He had to laugh at that. The girl was truly something else. He'd let her get on the microphone in the studio a couple of times, and she did have skills. Like most little kid emcees though, she didn't have much real life experience to rap about. She could string some pretty interesting phrases together, however.

He agreed with Deidre. Kayla shouldn't pursue any kind of career in entertainment until she was older, had gotten some life experience, and hopefully, an education. "Well, I can't wait until you finish college and your first album drops, so we can all see just how much hip-hop is in your blood."

"That's cold, Dad. Cold. I had such high hopes." Kayla shook her head in a defeated manner. "I see you've been pulled into Mom's way of thinking."

He leaned back on the loveseat. "If by pulled into Mom's way of thinking you mean I believe you should be focused on getting an education and then having a career, I guess you're right."

"Thank goodness, maybe she'll listen to you," a voice echoed from the doorway.

Flex looked up to see that Deidre had joined them in the studio.

"I was looking all over this huge place for the two of you. I should've known that you would be down here." Sitting on the arm of the loveseat next to Kayla, Deidre caught his eye and smiled.

Not able to help himself, he winked. "Yes. Our daughter was just informing me that hip-hop is in her blood."

Deidre chuckled softly and fixed the mussed hair on Kayla's head. "Good. If it's in your blood, then it won't go anywhere, and it will still be there when you finish school."

Kayla brushed Deidre's hand away. "Oh, man."

"Oh, man," Deidre teased. "It's not so bad. I didn't record my first album until my senior year of college. Your father was a junior in college when he first recorded an album."

"No offense, Mom, but, I don't think the world should have to wait for me to finish school to be blessed with my skills. Ask Dad. I'll blow all the little kids and some of the adults rapping today out of the water."

Deidre's eyes widened in mock amazement, and she exclaimed, "Good, then you'll only get better."

"How do you know? You won't even listen to me," Kayla mumbled.

The sullen look on Kayla's little face tugged at Flex's heart. "You should listen to her, Deidre. She has a nice little flow."

"Little flow? Little flow?" Kayla turned to face him. "Oh, Dad. I can't believe you dissed me."

"I'm not dissing you. Come on." He jumped up and walked back over to the turntables. "What beat do you want to flow over? I'll hook it up on the turntables. You can free-style for your mom."

Kayla eyes went up in her head and she pouted. "Well, I don't know with my *little flow* and all . . ."

"Okay, I'm willing to listen this once. So let's see what you've got, Kayla." Deidre moved and took his vacated spot on the loveseat.

"You sure, Mom?" The excitement in Kayla's voice vibrated throughout the room. It was clear she really wanted Deidre to hear her rap.

"Yeah, I'm sure." Deidre smiled.

"I will if you free-style with me. I know. Let's have a free-style battle!" Kayla bounced up and down in the seat.

"What?" Deidre's head spun and she did a double take. "Child, please, you really do not want to battle me. Don't you know? I made other female emcees cry at the mike when they tried to battle me. I left guys trembling. You really don't want to go there."

Smiling, Flex offered in what he hoped was a nonchalant tone, "I think it would be interesting to see you two come off the dome in a free-style battle."

"Yeah, Mom." Kayla tugged on Deidre's arm as she got up from the loveseat. "Come on. I know you're not too chicken to battle little twelve-year-old me."

Deidre halfheartedly pulled her arm away as she got up from the loveseat herself. "I most certainly am not. I was trying to spare you. But, like they say, you can't save 'em if they don't want to be saved." She brushed imaginary lint off her shoulder and gave Kayla a menacing look.

"Cool. Give us a beat, Dad."

Flex smiled. *This will definitely take my mind off my worries.* "Old school? New? What?"

"It doesn't matter." His two girls spoke the words in unison.

He went into his crate of records and decided to go with some old school break beats for the first round. Going back and forth between "Big Beat" and "Breaking Bells," he finally decided to go with the classic "Big Beat." When he put the records on the turntable and the beat started, Deidre smiled.

"Nice choice, Mr. Deejay. I don't think the little one knows anything about 'Big Beat.' Takes some years to sincerely appreciate the boom-bap." Deidre waved her hand in Kayla's direction. "I'll tell you what Kayla, why don't you go first since you're in such a hurry to share your talent with the world."

Kayla walked over tentatively, and Flex hoped that she didn't freeze. After getting to know his daughter better, he realized that the most important thing in the world to her was having Deidre hear her and validate her talent. But he hadn't expected her to suggest a free-style battle.

"That's cool," Kayla said.

Flex brought the beat back and keep it going, adding a cut or a scratch for effect as Kayla took the microphone.

"Yeah, yeah, unh." Kayla moved back and forth as her hand clutched the microphone. Then she started to flow.

Waited for this day
Just about all my life
For Sweet Dee to see me bless the mike
That day is here and I have to say
It's time to step aside for Kayla-kay
Don't mean to disrespect
Not trying to be rude
I got 'nough love for that ole school
The next generation is aimed
and ready to get on the grind
Making me wait won't stop my shine
So cut a kid some slack and just grant your blessings
Consider this free-style your very first lesson

Flex smiled, added an extra scratch, and spoke into the microphone that he kept by the turntables. "Kayla-kay. Next up, Sweet Dee."

Deidre took the microphone from Kayla and shook her head. "Okay. All right, Kayla-kay. I see you. Now check it."

That's so cute
You waited your whole life
But it's clear you still don't know what to do with the mike
Don't worry, baby, the lesson you can save
Mommy is gonna school ya and be sure you make the grade
Making you wait isn't about stopping your shine
When you step out into the world,
kid, you're representing mine
Can't have Sweet Dee's kid be wack
Can't have it be said mother's child can't rap
You gotta go to school, live your life and that's a fact
Kayla-Kay?
What kind of emcee name is that?
Don't sweat it, though
I'll help you with it

Next time you pick up the mike
Make sure you know what to do with it

Flex faded out the beat and brought in "Heartbeat" to slow it down. He noticed Deidre glance at him and smile when the new beat started. He was glad she remembered her first free-style battle as much as he did. "Sweet Dee. Kayla-Kay, you got next."

Kayla took the microphone and studied Deidre carefully. "Yeah. Unh. One, two, check it."

That's what I get for trying to cut you some slack
'Cause it's been a loooo-ng time since you tried to rap
Now I see that you took the kind for the weak
That's okay 'cause my first rhyme was a sneak peek
Of all the talent I have stored
I'm glad you finished up, cause I was getting kinda bored

Flex laughed when Kayla faked a yawn. "Woo-wee." He scratched and brought the beat back in as Kayla continued.

You went there and dissed my name
but that don't faze me
Rapper's haven't been Sweet
since the days of Kool Mo Dee
but it's cool 'cause the throwback is back in style
Matter of fact
I think I saw your name in that retro pile

Flex faded out the beat and brought it back. "Wooooo-weeeee, Sweet Dee?"

Deidre cut her eyes at him and took the microphone from Kayla.

All right deejay, enough with the ad lib
Sounding like Diddy on some ole we won't stop tip
I'm gonna finish this free-style up

SWEET SENSATION

I acknowledge you Kayla-Kay,
You got skills
Now what?
How many little kid rappers do we still hear about?
Like child TV stars they become has-beens and washed out
Keep on writing and rapping
and since you're a kid have fun
But before all of that make sure your homework is done
Because at the end of the day
While you've shown you have skills
You will finish college before inking any deals

"Aww, Mommy!" Kayla threw her hands up in the air.

"That's right." Deidre hugged Kayla and smiled.

Flex came from behind the turntables and walked over to the most important women in his life. "Hey, what was with that Diddy reference? How you gonna diss the deejay? That's not right."

Rushing toward the door, Kayla squealed, "That was so cool. I can't wait to tell Lily that I battled Sweet Dee and won."

"Hey, you didn't win," Deidre snapped.

Kayla turned around and smiled. "Okay, it was a tie."

"Whatever!" Deidre tilted her head and folded her arms across her chest.

Kayla threw up her hands. "You said I have skills."

"Yes, you have skills, my darling daughter. But you *did not* beat Sweet Dee in a free-style battle." Deidre smiled "Since you are my child and any talent you have is thanks to me and my good genes—"

Flex cleared his throat.

She glanced at him and smirked. "My good genes and your father's good genes, then I'm willing to call it a draw."

Kayla shrugged. "Cool. I'm going to call Lily in Minneapolis. Can she come and visit us for a week?"

"Sure, I'll call her mom and we'll work something out."

"This is the best day of my life!" Kayla dashed from the room leaving Flex alone with Deidre.

"So you still got it going on, a little something-something," Flex said as he pulled her down on the loveseat with him.

"Please, I'm so rusty it's not even funny. Kayla, however, did a great job coming off the top of her head like that." Deidre smiled and rested her head on his shoulder. "She really is pretty talented, and her little flow isn't half bad either. Her voice is kind of squeaky, but she is only twelve."

"Yeah, she's something," Flex agreed.

She lifted her head and gazed up at him. "I still want her to wait until she's at least finished with high school before she starts trying to make a career out of it. Maybe women rappers will have clothes on again by then."

"Things do evolve and change in hip-hop on a regular basis, so by then who knows what it will look like."

Deidre did a half snort, half laugh. "Judging by the sexism that has always been a part of the music, that part of it may not be moving far."

"So why don't you do something about it?" Flex had been thinking a lot about the poems she read at *Coffee, Black* and their conversation about the music and the culture.

"Like what?" Deidre shook her head. "I'm not involved with it on that level anymore."

"Yes, but you obviously have a lot of opinions about it." The more he spoke the more he thought he might just be on to something that could not only bring Deidre back into the culture she loved, but also give them the second chance to work together and be together. "So, why not help make a change? Anyone can complain."

"Like what?"

"How about coming to work at Flex Time Records?"

"Work at Flex Time? Doing what?" She sat up and turned to face him.

"I don't know. I was thinking of breaking off into the spoken word and nuevo soul that, at least in some ways to me, seems to be bringing some of the old school flavor back." He shrugged. He hadn't really thought it out much. It had just come to him.

"Yes. That doesn't mean I should be the one heading it up." Shaking her head, she rested it back on his shoulder.

He draped his arm over her shoulder and caressed her cheek with his hand. "You have very definite ideas and criticisms about the state of the music and the culture. I'm giving you a chance to do something about them."

"Do you think I could?" She tilted her head and gazed at him.

"I wouldn't be offering you a job if I didn't. Who knows? You might just be vital in the new direction at Flex Time." *As well as vital in the new direction of my life . . .*

"Wow. I'd miss teaching, but this could be fun. It would mean that I wouldn't have to look for a teaching gig." She actually seemed to be getting excited.

"Right."

"I'm sure working for a big time record label I'll be able to afford an really nice place for Kayla and myself to live." She snuggled in closely to him and he felt his heart flip-flop. "How much is the pay anyhow?"

Flex shook his head and pulled her fully into his arms so that she was on his lap. "We have not decided that you will be moving anywhere. We'll talk about the pay later." He kissed her.

"Umm . . . well, I hope you don't think you can pay me with soul-stirring kisses, seduction, and sex." She broke away momentarily. "Because I expect all of those anyway."

"Right. So are you ready to tell Kayla that we are going to work this thing out between us and be a family?"

She pulled away. "Not yet, but soon. Let's see how it goes between us. Okay?"

Trying not to let his disappointment show too much, he simply nodded.

CHAPTER 24

"If Headz Only Knew"

"I'm telling you, Lily, I wish you could have been here last week." Kayla flopped down on the huge sleigh bed in the bedroom that Flex said she could decorate any way she wanted to. They'd just picked her best friend up from the airport. She couldn't wait for all the fun they were going to have. She didn't know any kids in New York or New Jersey, so having her best friend spend the week with her was a treat. Even though Lily was a year older, they had been friends ever since they were in Brownie Scouts together.

"Battling my mom on the microphone was off the chain. I think she was going easy on me. It's cool though, 'cause one day she's going to have to give me my props."

Lily flopped down on the bed next to her and they both stared up at the ceiling. "I can't believe I missed that. In Minneapolis, she wouldn't even listen to us rap. What changed?"

"I don't know. We were just all in my dad's studio downstairs and the next thing I knew my dad was telling her I had a nice little flow—"

Lily sucked her teeth, sat up on the bed, and interrupted Kayla's story. "*Little* flow? What's up with that?"

Kayla sat up too. "I know, right! Anyway, like I was saying, they are both going to see how fresh my *little* flow is when we get somebody to offer us a record deal."

The two slapped hands in agreement and giggled.

"Yo," Lily exclaimed. "I heard on Music Television that Stacks Carter is out of jail and looking to build Body Bag Records back up."

"That was the label The Real Deal started on back in the day. That Stacks guy looks kinda scary." Kayla shook her head.

Lily jumped up and started dancing around. "Yeah, but he's looking for new talent since all his artists left when he got sent away."

Frowning, Kayla shrugged. "Maybe they left for a reason."

"Don't be all scared. I thought you wanted to prove to your folks that we could get a deal? I'm telling you, there haven't been any kid female emcees. We have to strike while we're still kids. Once we hit fourteen and up, we won't be a novelty. I'm pretty sure they had a few teenage girls rock it. I'm pushing it, because I'm thirteen already. I'm telling you, we can blow up!"

"Or by messing around with Stacks and Body Bag we can get blown up." Kayla rolled her eyes. Although her parents never spoke to her about Stacks or Body Bag Records, she sort of had a feeling that if they ever told her anything, it wouldn't be good.

"Oh, come on Kayla-Kay." Lily flopped back on the bed and coaxed. "It's perfect timing with me being here this week while he's having open auditions. All we have to do is find a way to get into New York City."

Kayla thought for a second. If she got someone to offer her a record deal, then maybe her parents would see that she really was good. Then they would let her and Lily record at Flex Time instead. "Well, Dad said he'd take us to Flex Time Records so you could see the place and get to see a real studio like I did."

Lily jumped up. She started dancing around, doing the moves they used to practice when they were making up routines for their rap duo. "Perfect. Now all we have to do is figure out a way to sneak away and get to Body Bag Records!"

"I don't know how we'll be able to do that. We're only kids." Even though the thought of getting a record deal excited her, she knew that there was no way her parents were going to let her go gallivanting around the city. "It's not like they're going to let us go wandering around New York City. Plus, what are we going to do? Get up there and audition with no music? We don't have anything to use."

Lily ran over to her bag and pulled out a CD. "My silly brother gave me some of his best tracks to give to your dad. You know he thinks he's going to be the next Swizz Beats and stuff. Anyway, *our* track is on here!"

Kayla smiled as she remembered them sneaking into Lily's brother's room and practicing to his beats while he was out. They had a really nice dance routine and rhymes to go with one of his tracks. She almost felt as if they could pull it off. "Still, we wouldn't be able to get them to let us go out into the city alone. That will never happen. Between my mother and father, I'm on lockdown."

"Lighten up. I'm telling you, Kayla, this is destiny. I can feel it. It has to work." Lily's voice became all of a sudden sad. "Otherwise, I'll be in Minneapolis for good when you move here. We'll never see each other again. Who would I run my raps by? Who will watch videos on Music Television with me? Who will I sneak and listen to Patrick's CDs with? I'll tell you who. Nobody!"

"Yeah, but—" Kayla started to speak only to be interrupted by Lily.

"No, Kayla. Ever since I saw the special they did on Stacks and Body Bag Records, I knew it was a sign. If we get him to offer us a deal, my mom will have to move to the East Coast. Right? Then we can still be best friends."

Lily looked so happy that Kayla felt she should at least go along with her.

"We'll still be best friends no matter where we live."

Frowning, Lily simply mumbled, "You say that now, but I know that after a few months of living here in this big old mansion, and meeting all those famous people you will meet now that you're Flex Towns' daughter, you'll forget all about our friendship."

"I will not!"

Lily sucked her teeth. "Yes, you will."

"No, I won't. Besides, it's not like I don't want us to get a record deal. I'm just not sure that we should go after Body Bag Records." Kayla didn't want to start off their week together angry. She had so many cool things planned for them to enjoy together. "I heard that a producer got beat up in the studios there. I heard that somebody might have actually been killed in the offices there. That Stacks might have done it."

"Oh, come on. If he killed somebody, he wouldn't be out of jail now. He would have stayed in jail a lot longer, don't you think? Those are just rumors." Lily huffed and sucked her teeth.

"You know how they spread stuff like that to build hype about the label and make people think that people actually leave Body Bag Records *in* body bags. It's all publicity." Lily laughed and tugged Kayla's arm. "Oh, come on. Even if you don't want to do it, you should audition with me. This could be my one big shot. When else will I have a chance to be in New York City with a record label holding open auditions? We have to give it a shot."

"I don't know—" Kayla hedged.

"If you were really my best friend you would at least try." Lily rolled her eyes and folded her arms across her chest.

"I am your best friend." Kayla couldn't help pouting. "My mother will kill me if we get caught."

"So, we won't get caught, then," Lily assured.

"If you say so."

"I know so." Lily sat up again. "Are you in?"

"I guess."

"Pinky swear that you'll do it." Lily held out her pinky finger and waited patiently.

Reluctantly, Kayla latched her pinky with Lily's and hoped that they would be so busy doing all the fun things she had planned that they wouldn't have any time to go to any stupid audition. "Okay, okay."

CHAPTER 25

"I Need Love"

With Kayla's little friend visiting from Minneapolis for the week, Flex found that he and Deidre were able to enjoy more stolen moments together. The only problem was, the more time they spent together, the more irritated he became that she was not willing to trust in what was happening between them and tell Kayla the truth. He felt that he was opening himself up to her and she was holding back, waiting for things to go wrong so she could run away again.

On a surface level she behaved as if she were giving her all, willingly sharing her body and participating in the relationship. Then she would pull back, never really going the full yard.

Initially he'd felt that her working at Flex Time Records would at least help them to bridge their different approach to the music and culture they both loved. If he was really honest with himself, he had to admit that he hadn't been happy for a while with the kind of music that his company had been putting out. The music business had lost its allure, and he hoped that the breath of fresh air, the motivation to do better that he felt when he heard her perform her poetry, would change his company for the better.

He hadn't banked on the fact that spending more time with her was going to make him want her more than he'd ever wanted her before. Not just physically, they had that. He also wanted her emotionally. He'd never thought he'd see the day when he'd be the one complaining about someone else being emotionally unavailable.

Spending the last twelve years mourning his lost relationship with Deidre and guarding his heart by not getting serious with another woman, he was now in the ironic position of feeling like the one hanging on, waiting for more, not sure it would ever come. *Not a good feeling.*

When Deidre walked into his office to go over the plans that she came up with for the new Spoken Word/Spoken Soul division of Flex Time, he could barely focus on what she was saying. The new division was important to him, and he wanted her on board. He also needed to know where her head was as far as they were concerned and if she was going to give them a chance.

"So, I'm thinking that we should start off looking for the underground poets, not the slam champions, or people who are already well known." Her excitement palpable, her eyes gleamed as she spoke. "I know most people would probably want to start by signing someone big who has appeared on the poetry jam, or who has toured the world and already has a following. There is so much talent out there, so many people waiting for that big break, that I think we could find our star and make them famous very easily."

He was surprised that she finally paused for air.

She grinned and continued, "So, I'm thinking that I'll go on a talent hunt. Starting in the States and haunting coffee shops and open mikes, I could begin as early as next month. If you wouldn't mind having Kayla stay with you while I'm on the road." She paused and bit her lip. "You travel a lot too. We'll have to alternate, maybe, to be sure that we are not both on the road at the same time—"

Flex couldn't believe it. He had mistakenly given her another way to run. "What? Are you planning to be gone that much?" he asked incredulously. "Do you really need to be gone that much? We have other employees. You can also hire folks to scout for talent. In fact, lo and behold, we actually already have people on the payroll to do just that."

"I know, but I thought that since I'd be heading up the division, I should make sure things are in place." She tilted her head, her excitement dissipated. "That is why you hired me. I mean—"

"I hired you to develop and run the division. Not to go off gallivanting across the country."

"What's your problem?" Deidre leaned back in her seat and stared at him.

"My problem is you can't seem to wait to get away from me," Flex snapped.

"That's not true. I'm just trying to do my job. You hired me to do this job. Now it seems you don't want me doing it." She started nibbling on her lip again, and it momentarily distracted him. Her little nervous habit had a painfully seductive quality.

"I do want you to do it." He ran his hand across his head in frustration. What did he want? Was he even ready to say it? "I just . . . I just think that at this stage in our relationship, we need to be thinking about spending more time together. I've cut back on my duties at Flex Time to be with you and Kayla this summer." He sighed.

Then he continued, "I'm sorry. The thought of you hitting the road is a little unsettling. I think we should inform Kayla that we're working things out between us."

Her back went ramrod straight then and her eyes widened. "Whoa, this is a bit much. I mean, we're still in the early stages. We have a lot to work through."

He stood up and walked over to where she was sitting. "No, Deidre. I think you have a lot to work through. You would gladly have us in limbo forever. Running around trying to hide our feelings from Kayla when she's long gone, off to college or, God forbid, off and married with children of her own. I can see it now, trying to sneak and kiss you so my grandkids won't get any ideas about grandma and grandpa being together."

Crossing her legs, she just shook her head. "Oh, come on. You're not being fair at all."

"Aren't I? I think I have it pegged right on the money." He sighed. "You're going to have to come to some sort of a decision, Sweetness. I can't go on like this. I need more."

She bit her lip again, and he fought the urge to pull her into his arms and kiss her.

"I'm really trying. What more do you need, Flex? I am trying."

"No, you're not, Sweetness. You're going through the motions and hoping I won't notice that you're holding back. You are holding back."

"I'm doing the best I can," she whispered as she gazed up at him with her beautiful golden brown eyes.

"I need more." Ready to admit his feelings and go for broke, he wanted her to be on the same page. He needed her to be able to say what he saw every time he looked in her eyes. Until she expressed it, she would continue to hold back and always be ready to run.

"That's rather selfish. Is it really all about your needs? I need more time. I need to be able to come to this relationship with a sense of security. I need to know that it will work out this time. I don't want us to be like my . . . oh my . . ."

Flex didn't say anything. He just gave her a knowing stare. Her mouth was wide open and a startling awareness shined brightly in her eyes, along with the beginnings of glistening tears.

Quickly, she jumped up from her chair and bolted from his office. He knew going after her would be pointless. Until she came to terms with all of her feelings, her love would never be his.

CHAPTER 26

"Bag Lady"

When Deidre ran from Flex's office, she had no idea where she was going. It wasn't until she found herself at her parents' doorsteps that she fully realized what she needed to do.

Her father opened the door before she had a chance to think better of her decision. Eyes wide with wonder and hope, Dr. James appeared genuinely shocked to see her. He opened the door widely and gestured for her to enter. Telling herself that she needed to finally confront her past, she came in.

"Let's sit in the family room, shall we?" A soft hesitant smile crossed Dr. James' face, and Deidre took a deep breath as she followed him.

Once they were seated in the family room, where she'd spent countless hours as a preteen watching music videos and listening to music, Deidre started to question the sanity of her coming there.

What could she and her father possibly have to discuss after all these years? How could she even begin to form the words to tell him that the things that had happened between him and her mother when she was around Kayla's age had left a mark on her soul that she had no idea how to erase? Was she even sure that talking to him would do any good, or give her the strength she lacked to finally trust the man she realized she'd never stopped loving? Would it be too little, too late for her and Flex anyhow?

"It's good to see you." He leaned forward in his seat and rubbed his hands nervously across his legs.

She focused her gaze on the man who had shaped so much of her life, and realized she hardly even knew him. Who was he, really?

Deidre got up from her seat, stared at the doorway, and sat back down. "I don't know why I'm here. I hardly expected you to be home. I just . . ."

"I'm glad you're here, Muffin."

Hearing the childhood nickname startled her for a moment. She remembered that he used to call her that all the time.

"Do you want something to drink? Some water? Tea? Soda? Anything?"

"No. I don't plan on staying long. I just wanted to . . . well . . . get some things off my chest." Taking a deep breath, she eyed him nervously. "To try to get to a point of closure so that I can hopefully move on."

A broad smile covered Dr. James' face. "So you and Flex are going to work it out. I'm glad. You know, when you first started dating him I thought, why is my daughter dating this ruffian?" He laughed comfortably and leaned back in his seat.

"I thought it was some form of teenage rebellion, like the rest of your antics, that you would eventually grow out of it and find a more suitable young man. Then the two of you went off to Atlanta for college and I worried about you getting pregnant before you even finished. You finished, thank God, and you got good grades. I was proud." He stopped and gazed at her.

Deidre tilted her head. Not knowing what to make of his rambling conversation, she just listened.

"Even though Flex was the last guy I would have ever picked for you, I was glad that he was in Atlanta looking out for you. I thought that maybe the both of you were going through a rebellious stage. That Flex was growing out of his as well. Then you both entered the music business. At the time, I thought that all of my hopes were dashed. I saw it as a waste." He let out a nervous laugh.

"When I look at the man that Fredrick has become, I know that I was wrong. He's a wonderful young man, Muffin. He'll make a fine husband. He's a wonderful father to Kayla."

Listening to her father drone on and on about what he thought and felt about her life caused the blood to boil and bubble under her skin. She found herself gritting her teeth and clutching the armrest on the sofa, her reaction to his observations too intense to be contained. Coming to see him was a bad idea. She stood up and headed toward the door. Then she turned and glared at him.

She took a deep breath and spoke through gritted teeth. "Do you not even realize that it's because of you that I can barely trust Flex enough to accept that he might be different from you? That he might not be a man so obsessed with his career that he will treat his family as a nuisance, at best an inconvenience. That he might not have the entire household living in a state of fear about disturbing his precious peace—"

Shaking his head vehemently, Dr. James interrupted her. "You were never an inconvenience. I never thought of my family as a nuisance. I might not have been the best at expressing it, but surely—"

Deidre sliced her arm through the air and cut him off. "It's my time to talk, Dad. I need you to understand what I felt like. From the time I can clearly remember until the time I was twelve and Mom finally packed up our things and left, I lived in a constant state of fear. I remember all the arguments. For years you simply yelled and made her cry. I remember being a kid and sitting with her once you left the room, telling her not to cry. Then I guess yelling wasn't enough. I remember the two times you hit her—"

"I'm sorry you—"

She shook her head and snapped, "My time to talk! For two years, I was happy. We didn't have much living on Mom's teaching salary, but I felt safe. The two years that Mom and I lived away from you were the happiest years of my entire childhood. Two years of happiness!" She took a deep breath and paused.

"When she told me that we were coming back here, that you had gotten help and things would be different, I wanted to run away. I *never* wanted to come back here. I told myself that this time, I'd be able to protect Mom, that I wouldn't let you hurt her again." She sank back down on the sofa.

Her father stood and walked over to her. When she glared at him, he simply put his hands in his pockets and stood there gazing softly at her.

"Muffin, I did get help. As soon as your mother left me and took you away, I got help. I went to counseling for a year, and your mom and I did couple's counseling for a year after that. I wanted to do everything I could to get my family back."

"Why couldn't you just leave us alone? Why didn't you just stay away? That's why I acted out. I kept hoping that it would make you show your true colors and then Mom and I could finally be free of you." Tears were running down her face, and she angrily wiped them away.

"By the time I got kicked out of St. Mary's, and Mom started me writing in that journal, I was tired of acting out. Then I met Flex. He was everything that you were not. When I think back on that year, I know that in a strange way, hooking up with Flex saved my life. It gave me someone and something to believe in. Flex and hip-hop gave me something else to channel my energies into. I was happy. For a little while, I was happy." She allowed her mind to process and acknowledge all her fears and own them.

"Then Flex's success and his pursuit of more success and his need to control everything made him more like you, at least the way I thought you were. That scared me."

"You won't be able to blame me forever, Muffin. At some point, you'll have to take responsibility, you know. I worked really hard to change the man that I had become—to make myself the man I should have always been for Lana and for you." Dr. James looked as if he were about to sit down beside Deidre on the sofa, but then he walked over to the window.

He continued to speak. "I always loved her, even when I wasn't showing it. When I met your mother, she was a college senior starting her student teaching, and I was an intern at the university hospital. I knew that she was a special woman even then. I had finally worked my way out of the cesspool that had been my life, and I was a doctor. I knew without a doubt that I had found the woman of my dreams. I wanted everything to be perfect. I wanted to be able to give Lana all the things that my own father and all the horrible men that my mom dated hadn't given my mother.

"I figured that once I established myself, your mom would have already taught for a while and be ready to settle down and be a wife and mother. I had it all mapped out perfectly. When your mom became pregnant with you, we got married sooner than I planned. I wasn't established yet, and we had to live on more of your mom's teaching salary than I ever intended. I found myself resenting her because I felt like less of a man. So I started lashing out in the only way I knew, the way I'd seen my own father and my mom's boyfriends lash out. I yelled at her and tried to make her feel as bad as I did. Even after I established myself and became a success, I still screamed and yelled. In my mind, she'd seen me fail. I worked harder and harder because I didn't want to let her see me like that again, not being able to fully provide. The pace was too stressful to keep up, and the stress made me move beyond verbal abuse. I never thought I would become like them . . ."

She heard his voice shake. "I heard you tell her once that your life would have been different if she hadn't gotten pregnant," Deidre whispered as the memory of that moment, and what it had done to her young mind, came to her.

He turned from the window and looked at her. "I'm sorry you heard that. I *never* regretted you. Muffin, you have to believe that. I love you. I know you probably don't remember this much, but when you were a little girl, you and I spent a lot of time together. I adored you—still do. I only wish we could get past the past."

Wiping her eyes, Deidre sighed. "That will take time. I have a lot to figure out."

"For what it's worth, Flex may be driven in his career and focused on protecting and shielding you and Kayla because he loves you so much, but those are the only similarities between us." He paused.

"I don't think Flex would ever put a hand on you in anger. He might lose his temper and yell. I think we're all prone to that every once and a while. But I can't imagine him being truly verbally abusive. I know I'm probably the last person you would take advice from about this, but your mom feels the same way. I sincerely believe that he would cut off his arm before he raised it against you."

"I know that," Deidre heard her voice respond and it felt as if she were outside of her body.

"So, will you give it a chance? I want you to be happy, Muffin. I know you think I don't know the first thing about you, but I've watched you closely all your life. Even when you left here, I kept myself apprised of your life and Kayla's life. I'm proud of you, and I will always be proud of you. I'll be even prouder once you face your fears." He walked over, and then sat beside her on the sofa.

"I don't want him to marry me because of Kayla and then regret it." She hadn't realized that she had spoken the words out loud until she heard her father's sharp intake of breath.

"I never regretted marrying your mom. I regretted not establishing myself first financially and not being able to give her all the things I thought you and she deserved. That was my foolishness and it led me to my biggest regret: not being the husband and father I should have been, and almost losing the love of my life." He sighed and continued, "And it led to losing my precious daughter. If I could go back in time, Muffin, you would know more than two years of happiness in your childhood."

Standing up, Deidre wiped her face again. "We can't go back, can we? We can only go forward."

"Yes, and I hope that we can go forward together and work things out. Seeing you and Kayla, knowing what I have been missing out on, pains me more than you could know." He stood up and awkwardly rubbed her shoulder for a moment.

She gazed at his hand, waiting for some kind of repulsion to set in. When it didn't come, she simply sighed. "We'll see, Dad."

Surprised that she felt a little bit lighter, she walked toward the door. She'd had no idea how much she had been carrying around all those years. Far from healed, she at least felt as if she could be in the same room with her father, maybe even have a civil conversation with him. What had happened between her parents had happened between them. What was happening between her and Flex needed to be removed from her parents' history. It wasn't fair to Flex. It wasn't fair to Kayla. It wasn't fair to the family they could possibly be if she overcome her past.

CHAPTER 27

"Real Love"

Driving back to Flex's mansion, so many thoughts ran through her mind that she had a hard time clearly seeing her way. Ready to own the fact that she loved Flex and she'd probably never stopped, she knew the reasons why she'd run. As unacceptable as she now knew them to be, she couldn't go back and change them.

The fact of the matter was that she was a different woman from the rapping girl he knew and loved. He himself had come a long way from the scrawny deejay that she fell in love with. Even though she took issue with what the youth culture they both once loved had become, and saw how record labels like Flex Time participated in corrupting both the youth and the culture, when she was really honest with herself, she had to admit she loved the self-assured, strong, professional man that Flex had become.

She wondered if they could disagree about the music he loved and produced and still be happy together. His giving her a job at Flex Time Records might well have been his way of trying to show her that he was open for dialogue and change. But if he were going to limit her being able to do her job, how open was he really being?

She could understand his not wanting her to travel too much if they were trying to build a relationship. His traveling and her lack of trust had added fuel to the fire of their break-up years ago. She just wanted to be able to meet him somewhere in the middle.

When she walked into Flex's home, she found him sitting in the living room.

"So you guys made it back from the city already?" Trying to keep her tone light—much lighter than she felt—she sat down on the sofa across from him.

Flex studied her so carefully, she almost felt a little self-conscious. "Yeah. Your mom stopped by Flex Time and picked up the girls. She's taking them to see a show on Broadway. Then they're going to spend the night with her, a girls' night out."

"Girls' night out? Without me? That's not fair." She faked a pout, knowing that she was more than happy to be home alone with Flex.

"Your mom thought we might enjoy some time alone." He leaned back, gazing at her intently. "So where did you go this afternoon?"

"I went to see my dad."

"Really?" he asked.

"Yep. We discussed a lot of things. While I don't think we're anywhere near a happy reconciliation, I can say that we are making progress." She sighed. "I now realize that even though what happened between my mom and dad had a huge impact on my life, it was their relationship. It was between them. Some things are unforgivable, but in a lot of ways it was never for me to forgive. Mom and Dad made their peace."

Flex got up, walked over to the sofa she was sitting on, and sat next to her. "Do you think that if they had included you in some ways, talked to you about what was going on, and let you have a say, that maybe you wouldn't have been so crushed by it all?"

"I don't know. I guess." She shrugged. It was hard to say what she would have felt if things had been different.

"You know, my dad said that he and my mom went through couple's counseling when they were spilt up. I do wonder what my relationship with my dad would have been like if they had made it family counseling and included me. I think my mom, and even my dad to an extent, tried to shield me from the problems they where having. Even though I saw the fights, they tried to sweep everything under the rug around me. So, I just ended up feeling helpless. It was *not* a good feeling."

"I bet." He placed his arm around her and she leaned into his embrace. It felt good to be in his strong arms.

"So, maybe if we really don't want to repeat the past, we should let our daughter know that we're a couple now; that we're working on our relationship and we intend to be together. We can see how she feels about that. That way she won't have to be in limbo wondering what's going on. It's her life too," he offered.

Deidre figured that Kayla would be pretty excited about a possible reconciliation between them. "I know. I guess talking to my dad was a good idea. I can at least see how to handle things with Kayla a little better." She tilted her head and gazed at him. "Although I have to ask, when did we decide that we were a couple?"

Flex pulled her into his arms and planted a soft kiss on her lips.

"Didn't you get the memo?" he teased.

She let her tongue trace his lower lip before responding. "No, that one must have slipped right past my desk."

"Take it from me. We are a couple. I have no intention of letting you out of my life again. I know we have things to work on, but I am dedicated to working them out. I am dedicated to you."

She closed her eyes and grinned. "Wow."

"Is that all you have to say, wow? You're the poet, surely you can be deeper than that?"

She laughed. "Double wow."

He kissed her again, hungrily this time. His lips caused a burning desire that shot from the pit of her stomach to the nape of her neck. The sweet sensation sent aftershocks rocketing through her body.

"Should we move this upstairs?" Once she pulled away, she managed to mumble the words, even though she was having significant trouble catching her breath.

"That might not be a bad idea." He pulled her into his arms. Together they walked up the stairs.

As they walked, he nibbled on her neck and ears. The teasing nips had her stumbling at several points and thanking God that Flex held her firmly in his arms.

His steps were sure even as he tortured her with his teeth, tongue, and lips. Once his hands started roaming up and down her body, she couldn't get to the bedroom quick enough.

They fell on the bed with a thud, and Flex covered her mouth quickly with a kiss. The heat that had started downstairs turned into an inferno.

"Mmm. Mmm. You are the best kisser, Flex. Honestly, the best kisser I have ever kissed."

"You're the only woman I want to kiss—ever." He let his tongue trace her mouth slowly.

She swallowed. "That's a long time, Flex. You know people change. We might find a few years from now that—"

He cut her off. "My feelings for you never changed, Sweetness, and I don't expect that they ever will. I was fooling myself when I thought that I was or ever could get over you. You're in my heart and soul, Sweetness. You have always been the best part of me, even when we weren't together. I promise you that I am never going to let that part of me go again."

His words struck something deep inside of her, and she realized it was because the magnitude of his feelings mirrored her own. She'd wanted to tell him for so long that she still cared deeply for him.

She let her hand roam his chest and paused over his heart. Her own heart skipped and stuttered as she felt his heart beat. Things had to work out between them because there was no way she wanted to live without him.

Her lips fluttered against his and she felt him let loose a shaky breath. "My feelings for you haven't changed either." *I still love you. Always have. Always will.* "I'm so happy you didn't give up and made me give us a chance. I know we have a little ways to go before things are right between us. I want us to make it, Flex. I want us to be a family." *Because the alternative, life without you, is unbearable.*

That she still didn't feel secure enough to share all her feelings with Flex bothered her somewhat. Knowing that she *could* feel and not be afraid was such a huge step for her, however. She'd lived in denial for so long that she had almost started to believe that she was better off on her own.

Flex's lips parted and his tongue thrust into her mouth. She gladly sucked it in, and then let her own tongue explore his mouth. Kissing Flex made her feel things in ways that no man had ever come close to duplicating.

When his hands started to undo her buttons and remove her clothing, she couldn't help aiding him in the task. The touch of his hands on her skin caused such an overwhelming sensation that she sighed in contentment just from the brush of his thumb on her nipple.

"You're so beautiful, Sweetness. Your skin is so soft to the touch. Your lips are so tasty." He closed his eyes and opened them. Then his gaze locked with hers.

"I want to touch you, Flex," she said as she removed his tie and then started to unbutton his shirt.

He helped her by standing and removing all his clothing, slowly, all the while holding her entranced in his hooded gaze. When he got back on the bed he kissed her. "How do you want to touch me, Sweetness?"

She let her hands trickle down his chest and stomach, stopping at his groin. Taking a moment to smile seductively, she bent her head and tasted him. His breath caught and she felt him shiver.

"Oh, Sweetness, you're killing me," he groaned.

His reaction to her caused her to work all the more vigorously. She gazed up for a moment and the look on his face made her shake with pleasure. Giving to the man she loved in such an intimate way shook her to her core.

"Oh, baby, baby, you have to . . ." Flex pulled her up and planted a wet, seductive kiss on her lips.

"Umm . . . Why did you stop me?"

"Because as sweet and skilled as your mouth is, I have other plans for a mutual release."

"That sounds . . . umm . . . that sounds good." She had to pause for a moment when his hands started to massage her breasts.

She let her hands roam his chest. "Who said I was done touching you?"

"You can touch as much as you want." His lips covered hers again and she opened to his kiss.

His kisses burned her from the outside in. Her body flushed with more excitement than she could ever have imagined. She knew it was because she had finally admitted, if only to herself, how much she had come to care for him, how much she loved him.

By the time he stopped and reached for protection, she was so far gone only the feel of him filling her, stretching her, completing her, could bring her back.

She loved him and she wondered if he could ever love her again. While they had both admitted that they still had feelings for one another and that their past feelings had not changed, that was a far cry from saying, *I love you.*

"Sweetness." He moved slowly, in and out, over and over, all the while gazing at her as if she were the most beautiful woman in the world.

Making love to the woman he loved had Flex shaken and sprung. His heart felt ten times lighter knowing that her feelings hadn't changed. Gazing down at her beautiful face and into her sweet golden-brown eyes made his heart melt. They both felt what he saw mirrored in her gaze.

As he moved his hips, she met him thrust for thrust. In their love-making, he felt connected, a team that could face anything. She wrapped her long, luscious legs around his waist and wiggled her hips so seductively he almost lost it.

With her, he felt that he could take on the world. His feelings of love for her connected with his body's responses. When she began to shake with more passion and he looked into her eyes and saw the love there, the rumbling inside his chest exploded at the same time as he felt her tighten around him spastically. He also felt a bolt shoot right from his gut to his toes.

Her orgasm sparked his own, and soon they were both crying out in pleasure.

"Flex. Oh, Flex," she murmured.

He smiled and kissed her passionately. "Sweetness, my Sweetness."

Flex watched Deidre as she slept and he couldn't help praying that things worked out this time. He loved her. While he hadn't said the words, he hoped that she could tell. The things he had said about his feelings never changing and the way he felt their spirits connect when they made love, all pointed to the overwhelming storm of emotions that existed between them, to their love.

He'd started out simply wanting to do the right thing and protect her and Kayla, no more no less. He'd felt that he should be married to the mother of his child and that they should give Kayla a two-parent family. He'd also known that the only way to ensure their safety was to keep them where he could watch over them.

While he still believed that, he now knew that what he shared with Deidre was so powerful, he couldn't imagine living without it. He just hoped that the next step, making her see the very real love between them, went a lot more smoothly than the other steps. He knew, no matter what, he was going to get her to see just that. He was going to have the woman he loved—the mother of his child—as his wife.

He pulled his sweet sleeping beauty closer and kissed her gently on the forehead before drifting off to sleep himself.

CHAPTER 28

"I Can"

Kayla tried to make up for the mistakes Lily was making, but it was hard to cover both parts of the routine. They'd managed to get Flex and Deidre to let them go for a second visit to Flex Time Records that coincided with the Body Bag open auditions. Kayla even managed to get Flex to let her give Lily the tour of Flex Time on her own.

After managing to sneak away from Flex Time and take a cab all the way to Body Bag, Lily was messing up the audition.

It was okay, because no one seemed to be watching Lily anyway. All eyes were on Kayla. Even Stacks Carter kept his focus on her. Busy trying to keep with the routine, and remember her part and Lily's, she couldn't really read his expression except to say that it sent a chill down her spine. She couldn't tell if he liked them or not. He didn't smile. He didn't frown. He just stared and whispered back and forth with some guy standing next to him.

When they finished, three men, including Stacks, walked up to them and Kayla noticed that the other men were clearing out the room.

Lily nudged her and grinned. "Look, Kayla, they are sending everyone else home. This could be it! We're going to get signed and become famous."

Watching the men rush everyone else out of the room, Kayla started to get an uneasy feeling. "I don't know, Lily. We weren't that good. We messed up a bit."

"Try to be more positive and smile," Lily said between clenched teeth.

"Well, well, well, this is a very interesting turn of events. I can't believe who I have here at my record company trying to get a deal."

Stacks' deep voice had a hard, mean edge, and it made the hair on Kayla's arms stand up.

The words he said, and the way he said them, gave her the feeling that things were about to go bad.

"Do your parents know you're here?" His steady gaze, and the way the other men stood there looking as if they were ready to pounce at any minute, made her grab hold of Lily's arm.

"My parents?" She had no idea how to answer that question.

"Yes. Your parents." Stacks glared at her and bit out his words.

"They can get here as soon as possible. We'll need them to okay the contracts, right? You want to sign us?" Lily jumped into the conversation after giving Kayla a glare that read, *You are messing this up.*

Lily might as well have said nothing. He barely gave her an irritated glance before turning to Kayla.

"Do Flex and Dee know that you are here?" he asked harshly.

Oh no, no, no. He knows who I am. He knows who my parents are. I should have never come here.

"Pardon me, sir?" Glancing around the room, Kayla wondered if she and Lily would be able to make it to the door without Stacks or his men catching them.

"What are you, stupid? Do that punk Flex and that trick Dee know that their daughter is here trying to be discovered?" he snapped. Then he turned to the men. "I would have to say no. Because I know that there is no way in hell her parents would let her come here for any reason, let alone to get a record deal. Since she just fell in my hands, I would have to say that today is my lucky day. Wouldn't you say so, fellas?"

"It would appear so, sir," The smaller of the two men said.

"Man, Stacks, she's a kid. Let her go. We have bigger things to be concerned with. I don't think you want to—" The bigger man started but Stacks cut him off.

"Teddy, shut up and stop being such a punk." Stacks turned his evil gaze to Kayla. "I mean, here I am trying to rebuild Body Bag after having to serve time. Time I had to serve because the cops somehow got wind of things that put me in violation of my parole. I can't prove it was that punk Flex who ratted me out, but I have my theories. I get out of jail and find Body Bag at the bottom while Flex Time Records is on top. Flex is stealing all the shine that should have been mine. Then his daughter shows up at my label looking for a deal. What's the matter? Daddy won't sign you?" he sneered.

Now that it was apparent that things were definitely bad, Kayla had no idea how to respond. Things could only get worse. She looked at the bigger man and realized who he was. Teddy used to be in The Real Deal with Flex. He didn't look as mean as Stacks, but he didn't look nice, either.

When she didn't answer Stacks, he became more irritated. "Listen, little girl, it's disrespectful not to respond when someone asks you a question. You're lucky. I'm not going to hold it against you. I see a future for you here at Body Bag Records. You might be just the gimmick I need to put Body Bag back on top. You're a pretty good rapper for a kid. There hasn't really been a little girl rapper yet to blow up the spot. Your lyrics would have to be harder, like your mother's used to be back in the day." A snarl came across his face when he mentioned Deidre. "The biggest gimmick, what I find just lovely about it all, is the fact that Flex Town's daughter will be rapping for my label."

Lily cleared her throat before speaking. "We're a group—"

Stacks cut her off sharply. "No one was speaking to you. I don't want to sign a female rap group."

"Well, her parents don't want her rapping until she finishes school." Lily's voice was almost pleading. "If you are really looking for a solo artist, I know my mom would come to New York and sign me—"

Waving his hand dismissively, Stacks snapped, "Shut up, little girl, or we'll have to shut you up."

He then turned his attention back to Kayla. "Now, back to business, and back to the beauty of the whole thing. I'm sure that as of right now only one of your parents has any legal say-so about what you can and cannot do. Once that parent realizes that your life kind of depends on her signing the contracts that will make you Body Bag's next solo artist, then she'll sign them. Dee may be a bitch, but she's not a stupid bitch."

Kayla couldn't believe he'd called her mother that. And she didn't like the mean look that came across his face whenever he said Deidre's name. What did he have against her parents? "My mom won't sign the contract. Why are you doing this?"

"Stacks, you know Dee won't sign any contracts with Body Bag. Why don't you just let the kids leave?" Teddy asked.

Stacks turned and glowered at Teddy for a moment, then turned his attention back to Kayla as if Teddy hadn't spoken a word. "Hey, you came here for a deal. Now that I'm offering you one, you want to be all ungrateful. You got a cell phone? Call your mother and tell her to get down here."

"Please, Mr.—" Kayla started.

He cut her off. "Get her on the phone, now. I'd hate for something to happen to your little friend here." The leer he gave Lily made Kayla tremble.

She dialed Deidre's cell phone with shaky fingers. The trouble that she would no doubt be in if she made it out of there alive did not hold a candle to the trouble she now knew without a doubt that she and Lily were in.

When Deidre answered, Kayla found that she could barely talk. Crying, her words came out in a tangled sob.

"Mom-my . . . Mom-my . . . I'm so-rry. I did something wrong and now we're in tro-uble. Mom-my—"

Stacks snatched the phone from her.

"Dee. Never could bring myself to call you Sweet Dee. Anyway, listen, I got your kid down here at Body Bag Records." He laughed his evil laugh and glanced at Kayla before continuing. "She's pretty good. I think I can make a star out of her. You know how we do it at Body Bag. Anyway, she's a minor, and I need you to get your ass down here to sign these contracts so we can get started making me a lot of money."

Deidre's heart stopped when she heard Stacks' voice. She hadn't known that she had a worst nightmare until she realized that her baby was in the same vicinity, let alone the same room, with that animal.

Trying to remain calm, she responded as forcefully as she could when her hands were shaking and she couldn't get past the quiver in her voice. "Stanley, you must know that there is really no way in hell I would ever sign a contract with you, let alone let my child sign with you."

"See, that's the beauty of it, Dee. You really don't have a choice. You can get down here, or see your child hurt. Now I know no mother wants to see her child hurt."

The unmistakable menace in his voice sent a chill down her spine.

"You better not touch a hair on her, you asshole."

"Now watch it with the name calling, bitch," he snapped. "I tell you. Between you and your ungrateful kid, I don't know which is worse."

"Just let her go, Stacks," Deidre pleaded.

"I'll tell you what. Since I don't have time to argue with you, I'll put it like this. You can bring your ass down here, or something bad can happen to these girls. You know if I let them go by themselves in the city, anything can happen. *Anything.* They might not even make it back once I turn them loose. We wouldn't want that, would we? Why don't you come on down and we can get things rolling with Body Bag's next solo artist."

"Listen, I'll come and we can talk. When I get there, I want the girls to be able to leave. I'll stay and we can discuss—" As her mind tried to work out a scenario where the girls would be safe and okay, Stacks cut her off.

"You don't have any room to negotiate here, Dee. I'm holding all the cards, all the ones that matter, anyway. Just get down here, and come alone. Don't bring Flex unless you want something bad to happen to him." The threat in his voice more than a hint, he hissed out Flex's name.

Deidre closed her eyes and swallowed hard. She didn't know what to do. She only knew that she had to get her child away from that maniac, Stanley Carter.

"Fine, Stanley—"

"It's Stacks, bitch. You see, that's your problem, you never had any respect."

Taking a deep breath she sighed. "Fine, Stacks. I'll be there shortly. Please don't do any—"

The dial tone interrupted her plea, and she closed her cell phone.

The trip from Flex Time Records to the Body Bag offices was relatively short. She took one of Flex's limos and told the driver to wait downstairs. She hoped to send the girls right down as soon as she got upstairs. She had no idea if she would be able to pull it off, but she knew she had to try.

There weren't a lot of people hanging around at Body Bag. Compared to the hustle and bustle at Flex Time Records, Body Bag appeared to be a ghost town. The secretary led her into Stacks' office and she saw the girls sitting there with Stacks, Teddy and some other man she didn't know.

"Well, glad you finally made it, Dee," Stacks sneered at her.

"Hello, Stan . . . Stacks. I would say that it is nice to see you, but . . ." She pasted a tight smile on her face.

"Hey, no need for false pleasantries." Stacks shrugged. "There's no love lost."

That was an extreme understatement, in her opinion.

"So listen, Stacks. I have a car waiting downstairs for the girls," Deidre hedged. "How about we let them leave, and you and I can talk about your next solo artist."

Stacks shot her a glare and then threatened, "I don't know. You might not be so willing to cooperate without your daughter here to keep you aware of what's important."

Deidre glanced at the girls. Both of them were huddled together and crying. The sight of them so terrified made her blood boil. "Oh, I'm well aware of what's important. But you need to know that I will not be able to cooperate until I know that my child is safe. So, I need you to let them go."

"No. Now shut up and listen for a change, bitch." He turned to Teddy. "You believe this? Coming in here regulating. Calling shots, like she's running things. That's always been her problem. Flex shoulda went upside her head a few times. I bet she wouldn't have pulled that keeping the kid a secret crap. That's some bullshit! And what does his punk ass do? Take you and the kid into his crib and start dating you. Punk ass."

"Could you please curb the language in front of my child?" Deidre snapped.

"Can you please shut up and sit down?" Stacks snapped back.

"Listen, Stacks, you have to know that there is no way in hell Flex is going to let his daughter become a Body Bag artist."

"I think she's right, man. We need to let Flex's little bitches go and get back to the business of rebuilding Body Bag." Teddy trained his eyes on her, and she thought she saw something unreadable in his gaze.

Stacks waved his hand dismissively. "That's not an option. I have a plan for the rebirth of Body Bag." He turned to Deidre. "I've got this pretty standard—standard for the way we do things at Body Bag—contract here, that you need to sign. I want to get the kid in the studio right away to capitalize on all the hoopla about her being Flex's kid. Of course that makes her recording for Body Bag all the more scandalous."

"Do you really want to use a cheap gimmick to sell records? What happened to going legit? You can't really believe that bullying me into signing a contract for Kayla is legit?" Deidre shook her head. The man had a crazed and dazed look in his eyes, and didn't even seem to be listening to her.

"Sam here is the lawyer for Body Bag, and he can serve as your lawyer too. You know how we do. Just have a seat and sign and then you can go. Just be sure to have her back here first thing in the morning. I'd hate to have to sue your ass for breach of contract. I want to get a single out quick. Something dissing Flex Time and Flex."

Deidre couldn't help shaking her head at that. "You must be crazy. I'm not signing anything."

The blow that came across her face took her completely by surprise and knocked her to the floor. She had never been punched in the face before. When Stacks hit her, her only thought was that she hoped she could get her child out unharmed.

Blood dripped from Deidre's nose and her mouth. Kayla was sobbing uncontrollably, as was Lily. The girls huddled closer together, visibly shaken.

Teddy helped her up, and she tried to get her bearings. She used the back of her hand to wipe her mouth. "Either you let us go now or—"

"Or what, Dee? You don't call the shots here, girl. Now sit down, shut up, and sign these papers."

"No."

He slapped her again, this time grabbing her hair before she hit the floor. As he pulled back his fist to hit her again, it ran through her head that she'd never wanted Kayla to have to see this kind of violence.

CHAPTER 29

"Down 4 U"

Things were hectic at Flex Time Records, so Flex gladly let Kayla show Lily around on her own. There were lots of eyes around the label, and he knew the girls would be safe.

When he got the call from Frank, who was supposed to be keeping tabs on Kayla, that told him otherwise, he couldn't get out of his office fast enough.

"What do you mean, Kayla is in Body Bag Records and hasn't come out? How the hell did she get there, and why the hell didn't you stop her from going in there?" he snapped as he blazed down the hall, motioning for several men in his crew to follow him.

"You told us that we should maintain our cover, that you didn't want Deidre and Kayla to know that you had hired bodyguards. You didn't want them to be unnecessarily worried. When Kayla left Flex Time, I kept my tab on the low, like you ordered." Frank's calm voice bringing back Flex's orders did nothing to stop the fear spreading across his soul.

If anything happened to his daughter . . .

"Then when I saw that she'd gone to Body Bag, I waited for her come out. Then when I saw just about everyone else come out but her, I thought I'd call and see how you wanted me to proceed. Things could get hectic, if you know what I mean."

Yeah, Flex knew what he meant. Even though he expected the man to guard Kayla with his life, he also expected him to have more sense than to bum-rush Body Bag without backup and without calling first to let him know what was going on. If Frank had gone in there Rambo-style and got himself killed, who would have been able to tell Flex where Kayla was, or that she was in danger? Knowing all of that, however, and being able to deal with the fact that his daughter was in the presence of that sick bastard, Stacks, while the man who was supposed to protect her stood downstairs waiting, were two very different things.

Out the door and in his limo, he listened to the bodyguard offer excuses. He had people on the inside at Body Bag watching Stacks, but he wasn't taking any chances when it came to his daughter. He took five of his guys with him because he truly had no idea what he was going to find once he made it to Body Bag.

The trouble between him and Stacks had been brewing for a long time. That's why he had bodyguards following Deidre and Kayla. That's why he wanted them near, so that he could protect them. If he couldn't protect them, if something happened to them, if he was responsible for the loss of another life because he failed, he knew he wouldn't be able to take it.

"Take me to 2020 Forty-ninth and Seventh. Quickly." The fact that both record labels had offices in midtown Manhattan and were fairly close to each other had never been a problem, especially when Stacks was in jail. But now the always hectic, bumper-to-bumper traffic was going to make traveling the several city blocks that separated Flex Time from Body Bag difficult, to say the least.

Flex turned his attention back to the man on the phone. "Okay, here's how we're going to play it. I'm bringing five guys with me. You hold tight and watch the building until we get there. You said the place was cleared out, right? So—"

Frank cut him off. "Ah, sir, Ms. James just went in. She looks upset."

"What the hell?" Flex ran his hand across his head in frustration. *What is Deidre doing there? Hell, what is Kayla doing there?* Things couldn't be going more wrong.

"Her bodyguard, Rick, is here too." It sounded as if Frank had moved away from his cell phone but Flex could still hear his conversation. "Yo, Rick, what's up? Why is Ms. James down here? Did you notice anything strange?" There was a pause and then Frank came back on the line. "Yeah, Flex, Rick didn't notice anything. You want us to go in there and get them out?"

Frank sounded more assured about going into Body Bag with another man as backup, but Flex wanted to be on-site to make sure nothing happened to either Deidre of Kayla.

"No. I'm a couple of blocks away and we have more backup, plus a man on the inside. We'll all go in together." *And Stacks better hope he hasn't laid a finger on my daughter or my woman.*

Once they reached Body Bag Records, Flex and his men wasted no time bursting past the shoddy two-man security team Stacks had at the lobby level and up the stairs to Stacks' office. They didn't bother to knock on the door. Pleasantries were far removed from anything Flex was feeling.

When he saw Stacks' hand in Deidre's hair, and the other hand pulled back about to strike her, he lost all sight of reality.

He didn't care if Stacks had a gun, or if the other men with him had guns. He knew that at least one of them should have had a gun, since he was paying him to keep tabs on Stacks, but he barely glanced at Teddy.

Flex rushed over to Stacks just as his fist struck Deidre in the face. Stacks let Deidre fall to the floor and turned to face Flex. Seeing him strike Deidre filled Flex with a blinding rage and an energy more intense than anything he had ever felt. He grabbed Stacks and let loose a series of punches. Stacks tried to block the blows, but Flex barreled through the blocks with punches until they both stumbled to the floor.

"You bastard! You put your hands on my woman! You got a death wish? Did you think I would let you pull some shit like that and not kill you?" Flex straddled Stacks' chest and blindly pummeled him in his face. The only thing he saw was a red haze. Enraged, he wouldn't have been aware of what he was doing except for the pain in his knuckles.

Someone tried to pull him off Stacks, and Flex swung at him.

"Come on, man. He ain't worth it. You gonna kill him, and then you gonna be in jail." It sounded like Teddy.

Flex couldn't stop.

He just saw Deidre's body on the floor, the blood on her face. He saw Sasha's body in the casket. He saw Louie dead and gone. Stacks had to be stopped and if he had to go to jail for getting rid of the bastard once and for all, then so be it.

"Daddy! Daddy, please stop. It's my fault. I shouldn't have come here. I'm sorry. Don't kill him. I don't want you to go to jail, Daddy! We need you. Please. We just found you. Please stop, Daddy."

Anger filled him even more, and his eyes narrowed as he struck Stacks with terrific force. He'd never thought he would be able to kill a man, especially not with his bare hands, but the thought that Kayla had had to see Deidre get hit . . . How many times? How many times did that bastard put his hands on Deidre? No way could he let that slide.

He'd tried to do the right thing and follow the law when Sasha was murdered. When he couldn't get proof that Stacks had anything to do with it, he'd found proof of Stacks' other dirty dealings and sent taped evidence to the police.

Stacks had had to go back to jail for parole violation. While it hadn't been a punishment for his role in Sasha's death, it was something.

He couldn't follow the law this time. He wasn't about to risk Deidre or Kayla.

He glared at Stacks' bloody face, ready to deal with him once and for all.

"Flex, stop." Deidre's weak voice managed to break through his haze in a way that the others hadn't.

He turned to look at her. She had managed to sit up. The entire left side of her face was bruised. Her lip was cut and blood was running from her nose. A black eye was already starting to form. She took a deep, seemingly painful breath. He wanted to go to her and hold her. And he wanted to make Stacks pay. He tore his gaze away from her and looked back at Stacks. When a sneer crossed Stacks' lips, Flex punched him again.

"Flex, if you beat him to death, you're no better than he is. Think of your daughter," Deidre snapped. Then her voice softened. "You want her to live with the memory of her father beating a man to death? You have to stop."

Flex shook his head. "I can stop now, but he won't stop until someone stops him."

"It's not your place, Flex. Let the law handle him," Deidre pleaded.

"Frank, get Ms. James, my daughter and her friend out of here. See that they make it back to Jersey." Holding off on his assault, Flex motioned for the bodyguard.

"I'm not leaving you here, Flex. Come with us." Deidre stood up on shaky legs.

The sight of what that bastard had done to her, the terror he had put her and Kayla through, made Flex's heart ache. "Go home, Deidre. Get our daughter out of here. Please."

Deidre had never seen Flex like that, and her heart pounded double time. His wild and raging eyes made him appear so close to the edge that she didn't know if he could come back. She had to find a way to reach him.

"Flex, you have to stop this now." She put all the inflection in her voice that she could muster. Her head rang, and it felt as if a herd of elephants had stampeded across her face.

"Sweetness, please, do not make this into a struggle between us. I have to handle things here. Don't worry about me. I'm going to take care of this and I'll see you both at home tonight. Okay?" Flex stood up, leaving a bloodied Stacks behind him.

Flex appeared to have calmed down. However, he was too calm. She liked the killer cool calmness even less.

Deidre sighed. He'd stopped his physical assault on Stacks, but to Deidre that only meant that they wouldn't have to watch Flex beat the man to death with his bare hands. It did not mean that, in the end, Flex wouldn't be responsible for the death of another man.

She wanted Stacks gone as much as the next person, but there were ways to handle it, legal ways. She could have pressed charges on Stacks. However, since Flex had taken it upon himself to beat him, Stacks could easily press charges against Flex.

"Deidre, I don't want to have Frank and Rick carry you out of here. You need to take the girls and leave! Now!"

Deidre jumped at the harsh tone of his voice. Making him see reason was not an option any longer, not when he was like that. She kept pleading with her eyes until he gestured with his eyes toward the door.

When she caught a look at Stacks on the floor pulling out a gun, she barely had a moment to push Flex out of the way. The shot that rang out was loud, but she couldn't hear anything but her own heartbeat.

CHAPTER 30

"Song Cry"

Teddy killed Stacks. Stacks had always seen Divine the pretty boy as a threat, and not the heavyset Teddy, but Teddy had it in for Stacks from the day the woman he loved died.

Even though Deidre had seen Teddy shoot Stacks, it was the image of Flex beating the man with such fury that she couldn't get out of her head. She knew without a doubt that Flex would have probably beaten the man to death. Even though she knew it was because Stacks had assaulted her, she couldn't get past the rage that had consumed Flex. No one had been able to get him to stop. It scared her.

She didn't think he would ever raise his hand to her or Kayla, but the fact that he even had the capacity for such violence was enough to give her pause. She knew that he'd fully intended to get rid of Stacks, but Teddy had beaten him to it.

Then there was the fact that the violence in his world had touched Kayla, the one thing she hadn't wanted to happen. So Deidre did the only thing she could do at the time. Once she'd answered the police's questions about what happened and sufficiently appeased the legal system, she packed up her child and went back to their nice, quiet home in Minneapolis. She was happy that, although she had resigned from her job, she hadn't yet sold her home, and they had a safe place to rest their heads.

The on-punishment-until-Deidre-thought-it-was-time-for-her to-be-off Kayla had taken to moping around the house and seldom spoke. The only time she became halfway animated was when Flex called. Luckily, that was at least twice a day.

Glad that the two had bonded, Deidre just hoped that Kayla would see that their moving back to Minneapolis didn't have to interrupt that. It warmed her heart that the father and daughter had managed to connect with one another in spite of what she had done to keep them apart when she was young and scared. Flex would always be Kayla's dad, and they could still have a relationship.

Deidre just wasn't ready to make the step that it would take to be all the way in Flex's world. If she could have thought of another way for them to be together, she would have. She still loved him more than words could express. Leaving him this time was the hardest thing she had ever had to do. She could almost see why Kayla was sulking; she felt like sulking herself.

"Mommy, come look at this!"

Deidre's heart swelled at the excitement she had heard in Kayla's voice. The child had spent their month away from Jersey on punishment and, on her first day off, she'd simply sat in front of the television not saying a word. Deidre figured the girl was simply overdosing because she had gone through TV withdrawal, but it bothered her that the first thing the kid did once she was off punishment was turn on the television. *What about going outside to play with other kids?*

Deidre went into the den to see what Kayla was yelling about. A program on Music Television was playing, and Deidre had to restrain herself from cursing. *What are the idiots reporting now?*

The blonde black Barbie who had broken the news about Kayla just a few months earlier was doing her pseudo reporting again. "In a move that shocked the recording industry, especially after the recent murder of Stanley 'Stacks' Carter, record label owner and super producer Flex Towns announced that he has sold his record label, Flex Time Records, to the major recording company Power House. He noted that he will still produce the occasional artist, but his full-time stint in the record business is over. We here at Music Television wonder if his recent change of heart has anything to do with his own heart and a certain former female rapper, Sweet Dee . . ."

Deidre sucked her teeth, grabbed the remote, and turned off the television.

"See, Mommy, he's willing to make a change and give it all up for us." Kayla pulled her gaze away from the now-silent television and turned to Deidre. "What are we going to do for him?"

"Kayla, it's not that simple. And who says that he's giving it all up for us? Maybe he's just tired of the music industry." Not about to have a conversation about her love life with her preteen daughter, Deidre finally realized what her mother must have gone through when making the decision to go through counseling and stick by the man who had stolen her heart. The recognition was unsettling, but she also felt a strange sense of peace and decided she would have a long-awaited talk with her mother based on her newfound understanding.

The way Kayla's lips twisted to the side would have found the child on punishment again on any other day, but since the child was missing Flex, Deidre let it pass.

When the doorbell rang, Deidre got up to answer it, thankful that she was getting a break before she got the urge to strangle Kayla.

Flex was standing at the door, no big bulky SUV limo, and no entourage of bodyguards, just Flex.

"Hey." The smile on his face and the soulful look in his eyes went straight to her heart.

"Hey." Deidre stood there with the door half open just staring at him. It took a moment for her to process the fact that he was actually at her doorstep.

"Can I come in?" Flex warily eyed the door, and then her. Seeing the unsure expression on his face snapped her out of her daze.

She moved to the side and held the door open wider. "Sure, come on in. Kayla will be happy to see you."

As if on cue, Kayla came running out of the back room and hugged Flex.

"Daddy, I'm so glad you're here. We just saw the announcement that you've sold Flex Time Records and you're getting out of the music business. It's all over the TV."

"Hey, precious." Flex kissed Kayla on the top of her head as he hugged her back. "It's true. I've decided to explore other career options."

Deidre could hardly believe what she was hearing. She barely believed it coming from the television, and she didn't know what to think hearing the words come out of Flex's mouth.

"You love music," was all she could manage to say.

"I love you and Kayla more." His deep gaze cut through to her soul.

Torn between wanting to run into his arms and run in the opposite direction, she opted instead to talk. "I think we have a lot to talk about and get past."

Nodding his head in agreement, he kept those eyes locked on her. "That's why I'm here."

She took a deep breath and gnawed at her lower lip as she studied him. "Well, it won't be cut and dried, Flex. We have a lot of issues to surpass."

"No time like the present to start," he offered, along with a shaky smile.

Deidre sighed. "Why don't we go into the den? Kayla, you can go to your room and read a book while your father and I talk."

"This concerns me too." Kayla glanced up at Flex. "Don't I get a say in whether or not we'll be a family?"

Deidre looked at Kayla and counted to ten. The girl had just got off punishment for the stunt she pulled going to Body Bag. The situation with Deidre and Flex had Kayla being a little sassier than Deidre had the patience for. There was only so much more she could take.

Her eyes narrowed in on Kayla and she spoke between clenched teeth. "Kayla, I realize that this is a hard time for you. Trust me, that is the only reason you have been given this much slack." She paused to be sure that Kayla understood that was the only reason she hadn't given her a nice spanking to go along with the punishment. The young lady wasn't too old to be taught a lesson if she insisted on acting out.

"Flex and I need to talk about things that—while they will have an influence on you—are between the two of us. Once your father and I settle things between ourselves, we will include you in the conversation about how our decisions will impact your life. You need to go to your room now and read a book. Look at the wall. *I really don't care.* But you have less than a minute to get to it." The last words came out in a hiss.

Deidre took satisfaction in the fact that Kayla made haste running to her room. A few minutes ago the girl would have given a dramatic sigh first.

Turning to Flex, she let out a sigh of her own. "So let's chat, shall we?"

She had no idea what she was going to say to Flex. When she left his place a month ago and hightailed it back to her home in Minneapolis, she'd known exactly why she was running. "So, you're leaving the music business?" She sat down on the futon.

"Yes." Flex sat next to her.

"What are you going to do?"

He ran his hand across his head. "I thought I'd move out here and try to earn another chance with you and my daughter."

"You want to leave the Big Apple for the mini-apple?" Deidre asked incredulously. Somehow the thought of Flex living in Middle America did not compute. "Won't you miss all the excitement? Adoring fans? Being a superstar? Most important, won't you miss hip-hop?"

"I've been thinking a lot about what you said about how the music has changed. About how the culture can be found in more places than just music, and I have to agree. The truth is, I haven't enjoyed being a label owner for some time, if I ever did." He gazed at her, his eyes earnest.

"I loved being a deejay. I even loved being a producer. I loved making music. I don't have to own a label to do that. I can make beats and tracks from anywhere. If people take them, then that's cool; if not, that's cool, too."

"Oh yeah, like you're going to have trouble getting people to buy a Flex track." She made light of it, but the truth of what he was saying hit home. He really could leave it all behind and still do what he loved.

She shrugged. "There is still the fact that you lied to me, Flex. You had us followed. You tried to control my life like I was some kind of puppet, or worse, some brainless twit who couldn't know that she could possibly be in danger."

"I know. I should have told you. You were so dead set against moving back to the East Coast with me that I thought the less you knew, the better. Honestly, I had everything under control. Once I knew Stacks was getting out of jail, and that special came out that put you and Kayla out in the media connected to me, I made sure you were protected. That's why I wanted you close. I needed to know that you were safe."

While it warmed her heart that he'd felt the need to watch out for her and protect her, the way he'd gone about it was the issue. He had to understand that what he'd done was wrong, or they didn't stand a chance.

"That's just it, Flex. You can't just make decisions like that without discussing them with me. You knew I didn't want Kayla exposed to that. You knew that I no longer wanted to be around the danger." She felt her voice rise, and took a calming breath. "You wanted us there, so you lulled us into thinking we were safe and, all the while, Stacks was carrying this vendetta against you."

Flex closed his eyes and opened them again. "I had Stacks covered. It was only a matter of time before his label went under. His illegal dealings were being sabotaged from the inside."

"You courted danger, just like you did when you hung out with Stacks to set him up," she snapped.

"I was not courting danger. I was making things safe for the people I love."

"I know that. It was the way you went about it, Flex. You should have told me."

"Sweetness, just give me another chance. Let me prove to you that I've changed."

Shaking her head, Deidre said softly, "You almost killed him, Flex."

"He hurt you." Flex reached out and touched the side of her face that was once badly bruised and now held only a small, barely noticeable hint of the trauma that had been inflicted.

"You were out of control," she whispered to no one in particular.

Flex let his arm drop and sighed. It was time to lay it all on the line. If he couldn't make Deidre understand his thinking, no matter how twisted he now understood that it had been, then he would never have a chance to be the man she wanted him to be, *the man he wanted to be*.

"My mother met my father when she was a freshman in college and he was finishing law school. He says it was love at first sight. I don't know. All I really know is she got pregnant before she finished her sophomore year, and he did the right thing and married her. When she died during childbirth, he decided to raise me on his own.

"Sasha was my only cousin, my mother's only sister's only daughter. Even though I didn't spend nearly as much time with Sasha as I wanted to while we were growing up, we were close. In a way, until I met you, she was all I had." Flex paused, the ache in his chest almost halting his breathing.

He had never really properly grieved for his cousin, just thrown himself into avenging her. After her death, the sense of loss had become overwhelming at the very mention of her.

He looked up and saw tears trailing down Deidre's cheek. Although Deidre and Sasha hadn't become best friends, they'd shared a closeness that they had forged being the two women down with The Real Deal. When Sasha was killed, Deidre had had to grieve alone. When she'd reached out to him, he'd been unavailable. He saw the damage that had done for what it was now. He only hoped it wasn't too late to reconcile.

"When she died, I felt responsible. Something snapped in me, and all I wanted to do was make Stacks pay. I knew he had something to do with her being shot, but there was no way to prove it. I spent all that time hanging around him after it happened to try to get proof, hoping he'd slip." Flex took a shuddering breath to try to calm himself. He had to be strong. Too much was at stake.

"Why couldn't you have just told me that then, instead of coming in at all hours of the night and pushing me away?" Another tear rolled down her face, and he felt himself shiver.

He could handle anything but her tears. As tough as she was, he could count on one hand the number of times he had ever seen her cry. The fact that he was responsible for her tears pierced his heart.

"Because I was an idiot. I thought I could handle it and everything would be okay. That none of it would touch you. Even though you weren't signed to Body Bag records, thank God, I saw, with what happened to Sasha, how easy it was for Stacks to just wipe someone out. If anything had happened to you . . . it would have been one more person that I failed. Another woman dying because of me. I couldn't take it. First my mother, then Sasha, then . . . I just couldn't risk having anything happen to you."

"Your mother's death and Sasha's death had nothing to do with you. You weren't at fault." Deidre shook her head vehemently.

"Logically, I get that." He patted his chest in an attempt to soothe the ache that laying his soul bare to Deidre caused. "In my heart, in my gut, I feel that if I had never been born, my mother would still be living. I feel that if I had gotten my cousin away from that idiot Stacks instead of getting involved with him myself, she would still be alive. When I found out that she and Divine had hooked up with Stacks and they had a rap group that needed a deejay, I should have pulled her away instead of seeing it as my chance to be down with a crew and make music."

"As obsessed and twisted as Stacks was about Sasha, he would have ended up killing both of you back then if you had tried to get Sasha to stop seeing him." Deidre's voice of reason did nothing to halt the tremendous guilt he felt over what had happened to Sasha.

"Not only did I let my cousin hang around the fool, I also brought you around him and all that craziness. Sweetness, when I realized how out of control things were, I tried to clean things up and make it safe for you. I found enough evidence to get Stacks locked up for parole violation." He paused. Coming clean with everything was harder than he ever knew it would be, but he continued. "I got away from Body Bag and started Flex Time, hoping that you would eventually come back. When you never did, I was devastated."

Deidre rolled her eyes at that. "Couldn't tell based on all the beautiful women you dated over the years."

He couldn't blame her for being slightly annoyed. His injured pride and arrogance after she left him had made him do a lot of things he would have never thought of doing had they stayed together. He couldn't go back and change the past. He only hoped it wouldn't ruin his future with Deidre.

"None of them could ever measure up to you." He made sure to look her in the eyes so that he could be sure that she understood.

No woman would ever touch his soul the way his Sweetness had. She was the other half of him.

"Then I saw that special, and I saw my daughter for the first time. I wanted to be angry with you. Instead, I kept thinking how beautiful you were. I kept telling myself that I needed to marry you because it was the right thing to do, and Kayla deserved both parents. In actuality, I'd never stopped loving you, and wanted any chance I could get to tie you to me so that you could never run away again.

"I wanted you with me because I loved you. I knew that you didn't want anything to do with my lifestyle, and I kept my feeling about Stacks and my fears about him striking out at you or Kayla under wraps, because I thought you wouldn't come to live with me if you knew. I needed you with me. I told myself it was because I wanted to make sure you were protected, but the simple truth was I wanted you."

"I deserved to know. If Kayla had known the possible danger, she wouldn't have gone there." Visibly shaken by the thought, Deidre shuddered and wrapped her arms around herself.

"You knew that Stacks was dangerous, and you went there without coming to get me or telling me that you were going there." Flex tried to fight putting his hands on her and lost. He wrapped his arms around her and held her close. Even if she ended up throwing him out, at least he would have one more time holding her in his arms to add to his memories.

"Didn't you trust me to protect you and Kayla? Why didn't you come to me?" he asked.

She leaned into his embrace and he felt his heart stop and restart.

"He said come alone or the girls would be hurt. The crazy fool actually thought I was going to sign a recording contract for Kayla. He must have been out of his mind."

"Yeah, Teddy said he was losing it there toward the end. It was only a matter of time before he fully flipped. We have a pretty good idea that he was somehow involved with what happened to Louie. He got in touch with some people that Louie had wronged in the past and gave them some information that made them take Louie out. He wasn't about to come after us. He didn't have the ammo. It would have taken more than buzzing in a few ears. When Kayla fell into his hands, he snapped."

"Snapped is an understatement." Deidre shuddered again and he rubbed her arm as he held her. "So Teddy was still down with you guys after all?"

"Yeah, when he didn't come with us after I started Flex Time and he stayed on at Body Bag, even with Stacks in jail, I was through with him. I didn't speak to him for over a year. Divine slowly made me realize that I could trust Teddy. I had no idea about Teddy and Sasha. My cousin was full of surprises."

"So that wack album Teddy made . . ."

"Bogus. He was all about making sure Body Bag lost money and went into the ground. When Stacks got out of jail and decided to repay Teddy's loyalty by giving him a bigger role at Body Bag, we knew it was only a matter of time before we ruined him.

"I figured with Teddy on the inside, Stacks on his way out, and you and Kayla nicely protected, things would be fine. It never occurred to me that Kayla would turn up at some open audition for Body Bag." He knew, based on his daily talks with Kayla, that she had been punished, and he also knew that she was sorry for what she did. He didn't envy Deidre having to carry out the punishment on her own. If he had anything to do with it, he and Deidre would handle everything else when it came to Kayla as a couple.

"Knowing that the two of you were there and that anything could happen was the worst feeling I have ever experienced in my life. When I got there and I saw him hitting you, I experienced blind rage for the first time in my life. I know it scared you. Hell, it scared me. But you've got to know that I would never hurt you or Kayla."

"I know that."

Flex couldn't contain the sharp breaths that came with the hope that started to overflow in his heart.

"Then tell me you'll give me another chance. Tell me that it's not too late, that I didn't mess things up for good this time, that there's still a chance."

Deidre sat silently for a few minutes and then she gazed up at him. The expression in her golden brown eyes melted his heart because, looking in them, he knew that they had a chance.

"You have to promise me that you will be honest with me and not shut me out. When you shut me out and start acting like the puppet master, it takes me to places I don't want to go, especially not with the man I love."

His heart skipped and his eyes widened. "You love me?" He'd thought he was going to have to make her fall in love all over again, make her remember the magic they'd shared.

"I never stopped."

"So it's not too late?" He let out a shaky breath with no worry about appearances. Soul bare and heart on the line, he was done with the cool pose. The only thing he wanted was the love of the women sitting beside him. Hearing that he'd had it all along brought a tear to his eye.

She shook her head. "I really do believe that you did the things you did out of love. But I need you to see that in this loving relationship, we are upfront with one another."

"So that means no more running and leaving?" he teased.

She smiled. "No, no more running and leaving. Because if you pull some crap like this again, I'm going to get in your face so tough, you'll be the one on the run."

"Oh really?" He winked at her and pulled her close.

"Yes, really." She gazed up at him.

Then Flex really couldn't resist it. He had to kiss her.

CHAPTER 31

"Wifey"

Kayla couldn't believe it. Less than a year ago she didn't even know she had a father, and now her parents were tying the knot and she was standing up with them in front of the reverend.

Her entire family, including both of her grandfathers, was present for the wedding. Deidre even let Dr. James give her away. Flex and Judge Towns had smiled at each other and made jokes back and forth the entire weekend. Kayla felt like a part of a real family for the first time in her life.

"Deidre James, do you take Fredrick Towns III to be your lawfully wedded husband to love, honor, and cherish, forsaking all others until death do you part?" The reverend spoke the words as he looked at Deidre.

Kayla held her breath, crossed her fingers and her ankles, as she stood between Deidre and Flex. It had been a long haul getting to this point, and Kayla hoped that her mother wouldn't change her mind at the last minute.

"I do."

Whew! Kayla looked at her mother's face and had to admit that she had never seen her mom look happier. She had tears in her eyes, but they were happy tears, the kind she got whenever Kayla made her something in school and brought it home or gave her the perfect Mother's Day card.

"And do you, Fredrick Towns III, take Deidre James to be your lawfully wedded wife to love, honor, and cherish, forsaking all others until death do you part?" The reverend looked at Flex as he spoke.

"I do."

Kayla glanced at her dad. His wide smile went from ear to ear. He even had tears in his eyes and his voice had a gravely texture.

They were going to be a family. *Finally*! Kayla realized that, although she still had dreams of superstardom and being a famous rapper, being a family and having her mom and dad realize their love was a much better dream come true.

The honeymoon in Barbados couldn't have been better, even if Deidre had actually managed to see any of the beaches or the sea. They spent most of their time indoors, making up for lost time.

As she lay on the bed recovering from yet another wildly passionate encounter with the man she loved, she decided to turn on the television just to see if anything had been going on in the world during the week that she had been pretty much out of commission.

Flipping through the cable channels and finding nothing, she stopped on the Music Television channel when she saw the blonde black Barbie pseudo reporter/gossip monger at it again. The woman clearly hadn't had enough of talking about Flex and Sweet Dee.

"And last week super producer and former record label mogul, Flex Towns, married Deidre 'Sweet Dee' James in a small wedding ceremony in Minneapolis. Our sources say that the couple is honeymooning somewhere in the Caribbean. One would think that yours truly would have been first on the guest list since it was my stellar reporting that got Sweet Dee's skeleton out of the closet, thus bringing Flex back into her life. But alas, dear viewers, I was not invited to the small affair—"

Flex grabbed the remote and turned off the television.

Deidre laughed. "Hey, I was watching that. It seems I have been remiss. I should have invited her to our wedding."

Flex covered her mouth with his and kissed her senseless.

"I think I'll send her a thank you note anyway," she said breathlessly.

"What exactly will you be thanking her for?" Flex pulled her on top of him and she straddled him.

"For sending the love of my life back to me for one thing, and that kiss for another. If she hadn't blabbed her big gossiping mouth to the world, you might have never come back into my life, and I would never have had the pleasure of your kisses again." She leaned down to kiss his lips.

"Hmm. When you put it like that. I think I need to thank her too. I love you, Sweetness."

"I love you too, Flex."

He flipped her over on her back and gazed seductively in her eyes. "So, maybe I should make it good and give you a few other things to thank her for in this little thank you note of yours."

"You can do that. I'm all for starting a list. We have all night. I don't plan on starting the note until tomorrow morning."

He kissed her again.

"Or maybe tomorrow afternoon."

His lips connected yet again.

"Hell, she can wait until I get back from our honeymoon."

The next kiss lasted longer, and the only thing she could think about after he was done was that she was so glad to finally be where she'd always belonged.

Dear Reader,

I hope you enjoyed reading Flex and Deidre's story as much as I enjoyed writing it. I have been a fan of rap music and hip-hop culture ever since I was nine-years-old and the song "Rapper's Delight" was released. I even spent my teenage years wanting to be a rapper. In that regard, I have a lot in common with both Deidre and Kayla. This book was an exercise in trying to mesh my love of romance with my love of hip-hop. It was also an attempt at trying to tell a hip-hop love story. I'd love to hear from you to find out how you think I did. Many people would probably doubt the very possibility of love and romance having a place in hip-hop culture. I would have to disagree. The rap songs and hip-hop soul songs that serve as subtitles for the chapters of this novel all run the gamut from romantic love, love of family, love of hip-hop, and love of friends. The songs, from Tupac's "Dear Mama" to LL Cool J's "I Need Love," show that love and hip-hop can coexist. I hope Deidre and Flex's love story has added to those love songs and show-cased hip-hop love at its finest. Let me know what you think! Until next time, much love and peace!

Gwyneth Bolton

ABOUT THE AUTHOR

Gwyneth Bolton was born and raised in Paterson, New Jersey. She currently lives in Syracuse, New York with her husband, Cedric Bolton. When she was twelve-years-old, she became an avid reader of romance by sneaking her mother's stash of novels. In the 90s, she was introduced to African American and multicultural romance novels, and her life hasn't been the same since. While she had always been a reader of romance, she didn't feel inspired to write them until the genre opened up to include other voices. And even then, it took finishing graduate school, several non-fiction publications, and a six-week course at the Loft Literary Center titled "Writing the Romance Novel" before she gathered the courage to start writing her first romance novel. She has a BA and an MA in creative writing and a Ph.D. in English. She teaches classes in writing and women's studies at the college level. When she is not working on her own African-American romance novels, she is curled up with a cup of herbal tea, a warm quilt, and a good book. She welcomes response from readers. Please feel free to write her at P.O. Box 9388 Carousel CTR, Syracuse, New York 13290-9381. You can also e-mail her at *gwynethbolton@prodigy.net*. Or feel free to visit her website at *http://www.gwynethbolton.com*.

Sweet Sensation is the second novel in the Hip-Hop Debutantes trilogy. Alicia and Darren's story, *I'm Gonna Make You Love Me*, was the first and it is available now. She is currently working on the third, Troy and Jazz's story, which is tentatively titled *The Love You Save*.

SWEET SENSATION

2007 Publication Schedule

January

Corporate Seduction
A.C. Arthur
ISBN-13: 978-1-58571-238-0
ISBN-10: 1-58571-238-8
$9.95

A Taste of Temptation
Reneé Alexis
ISBN-13: 978-1-58571-207-6
ISBN-10: 1-58571-207-8
$9.95

February

The Perfect Frame
Beverly Clark
ISBN-13: 978-1-58571-240-3
ISBN-10: 1-58571-240-X
$9.95

Ebony Angel
Deatri King-Bey
ISBN-13: 978-1-58571-239-7
ISBN-10: 1-58571-239-6
$9.95

March

Sweet Sensation
Gwyneth Bolton
ISBN-13: 978-1-58571-206-9
ISBN-10: 1-58571-206-X
$9.95

Crush
Crystal Hubbard
ISBN-13: 978-1-58571-243-4
ISBN-10: 1-58571-243-4
$9.95

April

Secret Thunder
Annetta P. Lee
ISBN-13: 978-1-58571-204-5
ISBN-10: 1-58571-204-3
$9.95

Blood Seduction
J.M. Jeffries
ISBN-13: 978-1-58571-237-3
ISBN-10: 1-58571-237-X
$9.95

May

Lies Too Long
Pamela Ridley
ISBN-13: 978-1-58571-246-5
ISBN-10: 1-58571-246-9
$13.95

Two Sides to Every Story
Dyanne Davis
ISBN-13: 978-1-58571-248-9
ISBN-10: 1-58571-248-5
$9.95

June

One of These Days
Michele Sudler
ISBN-13: 978-1-58571-249-6
ISBN-10: 1-58571-249-3
$9.95

Who's That Lady
Andrea Jackson
ISBN-13: 978-1-58571-190-1
ISBN-10: 1-58571-190-X
$9.95

2007 Publication Schedule (continued)

July

Heart of the Phoenix
A.C. Arthur
ISBN-13: 978-1-58571-242-7
ISBN-10: 1-58571-242-6
$9.95

Do Over
Jaci Kenney
ISBN-13: 978-1-58571-241-0
ISBN-10: 1-58571-241-8
$9.95

It's Not Over Yet
J.J. Michael
ISBN-13: 978-1-58571-245-8
ISBN-10: 1-58571-245-0
$9.95

August

The Fires Within
Beverly Clark
ISBN-13: 978-1-58571-244-1
ISBN-10: 1-58571-244-2
$9.95

Stolen Kisses
Dominiqua Douglas
ISBN-13: 978-1-58571-247-2
ISBN-10: 1-58571-247-7
$9.95

September

Small Whispers
Annetta P. Lee
ISBN-13: 978-158571-251-9
ISBN-10: 1-58571-251-5
$6.99

Always You
Crystal Hubbard
ISBN-13: 978-158571-252-6
ISBN-10: 1-58571-252-3
$6.99

October

Not His Type
Chamein Canton
ISBN-13: 978-158571-253-3
ISBN-10: 1-58571-253-1
$6.99

Many Shades of Gray
Dyanne Davis
ISBN-13: 978-158571-254-0
ISBN-10: 1-58571-254-X
$6.99

November

When I'm With You
LaConnie Taylor-Jones
ISBN-13: 978-158571-250-2
ISBN-10: 1-58571-250-7
$6.99

The Mission
Pamela Leigh Starr
ISBN-13: 978-158571-255-7
ISBN-10: 1-58571-255-8
$6.99

December

One in A Million
Barbara Keaton
ISBN-13: 978-158571-257-1
ISBN-10: 1-58571-257-4
$6.99

The Foursome
Celya Bowers
ISBN-13: 978-158571-256-4
ISBN-10: 1-58571-256-6
$6.99

Other Genesis Press, Inc. Titles

A Dangerous Deception	J.M. Jeffries	$8.95
A Dangerous Love	J.M. Jeffries	$8.95
A Dangerous Obsession	J.M. Jeffries	$8.95
A Dangerous Woman	J.M. Jeffries	$9.95
A Dead Man Speaks	Lisa Jones Johnson	$12.95
A Drummer's Beat to Mend	Kei Swanson	$9.95
A Happy Life	Charlotte Harris	$9.95
A Heart's Awakening	Veronica Parker	$9.95
A Lark on the Wing	Phyliss Hamilton	$9.95
A Love of Her Own	Cheris F. Hodges	$9.95
A Love to Cherish	Beverly Clark	$8.95
A Lover's Legacy	Veronica Parker	$9.95
A Pefect Place to Pray	I.L. Goodwin	$12.95
A Risk of Rain	Dar Tomlinson	$8.95
A Twist of Fate	Beverly Clark	$8.95
A Will to Love	Angie Daniels	$9.95
Acquisitions	Kimberley White	$8.95
Across	Carol Payne	$12.95
After the Vows	Leslie Esdaile	$10.95
(Summer Anthology)	T.T. Henderson	
	Jacqueline Thomas	
Again My Love	Kayla Perrin	$10.95
Against the Wind	Gwynne Forster	$8.95
All I Ask	Barbara Keaton	$8.95
Ambrosia	T.T. Henderson	$8.95
An Unfinished Love Affair	Barbara Keaton	$8.95
And Then Came You	Dorothy Elizabeth Love	$8.95
Angel's Paradise	Janice Angelique	$9.95
At Last	Lisa G. Riley	$8.95
Best of Friends	Natalie Dunbar	$8.95
Between Tears	Pamela Ridley	$12.95
Beyond the Rapture	Beverly Clark	$9.95
Blaze	Barbara Keaton	$9.95

Other Genesis Press, Inc. Titles (continued)

Blood Lust	J. M. Jeffries	$9.95
Bodyguard	Andrea Jackson	$9.95
Boss of Me	Diana Nyad	$8.95
Bound by Love	Beverly Clark	$8.95
Breeze	Robin Hampton Allen	$10.95
Broken	Dar Tomlinson	$24.95
The Business of Love	Cheris Hodges	$9.95
By Design	Barbara Keaton	$8.95
Cajun Heat	Charlene Berry	$8.95
Careless Whispers	Rochelle Alers	$8.95
Cats & Other Tales	Marilyn Wagner	$8.95
Caught in a Trap	Andre Michelle	$8.95
Caught Up In the Rapture	Lisa G. Riley	$9.95
Cautious Heart	Cheris F Hodges	$8.95
Caught Up	Deatri King Bey	$12.95
Chances	Pamela Leigh Starr	$8.95
Cherish the Flame	Beverly Clark	$8.95
Class Reunion	Irma Jenkins/John Brown	$12.95
Code Name: Diva	J.M. Jeffries	$9.95
Conquering Dr. Wexler's Heart	Kimberley White	$9.95
Cricket's Serenade	Carolita Blythe	$12.95
Crossing Paths, Tempting Memories	Dorothy Elizabeth Love	$9.95
Cupid	Barbara Keaton	$9.95
Cypress Whisperings	Phyllis Hamilton	$8.95
Dark Embrace	Crystal Wilson Harris	$8.95
Dark Storm Rising	Chinelu Moore	$10.95
Daughter of the Wind	Joan Xian	$8.95
Deadly Sacrifice	Jack Kean	$22.95
Designer Passion	Dar Tomlinson	$8.95
Dreamtective	Liz Swados	$5.95
Ebony Butterfly II	Delilah Dawson	$14.95
Ebony Eyes	Kei Swanson	$9.95

Other Genesis Press, Inc. Titles (continued)

Echoes of Yesterday	Beverly Clark	$9.95
Eden's Garden	Elizabeth Rose	$8.95
Enchanted Desire	Wanda Y. Thomas	$9.95
Everlastin' Love	Gay G. Gunn	$8.95
Everlasting Moments	Dorothy Elizabeth Love	$8.95
Everything and More	Sinclair Lebeau	$8.95
Everything but Love	Natalie Dunbar	$8.95
Eve's Prescription	Edwina Martin Arnold	$8.95
Falling	Natalie Dunbar	$9.95
Fate	Pamela Leigh Starr	$8.95
Finding Isabella	A.J. Garrotto	$8.95
Forbidden Quest	Dar Tomlinson	$10.95
Forever Love	Wanda Thomas	$8.95
From the Ashes	Kathleen Suzanne	$8.95
	Jeanne Sumerix	
Gentle Yearning	Rochelle Alers	$10.95
Glory of Love	Sinclair LeBeau	$10.95
Go Gentle into that Good Night	Malcom Boyd	$12.95
Goldengroove	Mary Beth Craft	$16.95
Groove, Bang, and Jive	Steve Cannon	$8.99
Hand in Glove	Andrea Jackson	$9.95
Hard to Love	Kimberley White	$9.95
Hart & Soul	Angie Daniels	$8.95
Havana Sunrise	Kymberly Hunt	$9.95
Heartbeat	Stephanie Bedwell-Grime	$8.95
Hearts Remember	M. Loui Quezada	$8.95
Hidden Memories	Robin Allen	$10.95
Higher Ground	Leah Latimer	$19.95
Hitler, the War, and the Pope	Ronald Rychiak	$26.95
How to Write a Romance	Kathryn Falk	$18.95
I Married a Reclining Chair	Lisa M. Fuhs	$8.95
I'm Gonna Make You Love Me	Gwyneth Bolton	$9.95
Indigo After Dark Vol. I	Nia Dixon/Angelique	$10.95

Other Genesis Press, Inc. Titles (continued)

Indigo After Dark Vol. II	Dolores Bundy/Cole Riley	$10.95
Indigo After Dark Vol. III	Montana Blue/Coco Morena	$10.95
Indigo After Dark Vol. IV	Cassandra Colt/	$14.95
	Diana Richeaux	
Indigo After Dark Vol. V	Delilah Dawson	$14.95
Icie	Pamela Leigh Starr	$8.95
I'll Be Your Shelter	Giselle Carmichael	$8.95
I'll Paint a Sun	A.J. Garrotto	$9.95
Illusions	Pamela Leigh Starr	$8.95
Indiscretions	Donna Hill	$8.95
Intentional Mistakes	Michele Sudler	$9.95
Interlude	Donna Hill	$8.95
Intimate Intentions	Angie Daniels	$8.95
Ironic	Pamela Leigh Starr	$9.95
Jolie's Surrender	Edwina Martin-Arnold	$8.95
Kiss or Keep	Debra Phillips	$8.95
Lace	Giselle Carmichael	$9.95
Last Train to Memphis	Elsa Cook	$12.95
Lasting Valor	Ken Olsen	$24.95
Let's Get It On	Dyanne Davis	$9.95
Let Us Prey	Hunter Lundy	$25.95
Life Is Never As It Seems	J.J. Michael	$12.95
Lighter Shade of Brown	Vicki Andrews	$8.95
Love Always	Mildred E. Riley	$10.95
Love Doesn't Come Easy	Charlyne Dickerson	$8.95
Love in High Gear	Charlotte Roy	$9.95
Love Lasts Forever	Dominiqua Douglas	$9.95
Love Me Carefully	A.C. Arthur	$9.95
Love Unveiled	Gloria Greene	$10.95
Love's Deception	Charlene Berry	$10.95
Love's Destiny	M. Loui Quezada	$8.95
Mae's Promise	Melody Walcott	$8.95
Magnolia Sunset	Giselle Carmichael	$8.95

Other Genesis Press, Inc. Titles (continued)

Matters of Life and Death	Lesego Malepe, Ph.D.	$15.95
Meant to Be	Jeanne Sumerix	$8.95
Midnight Clear (Anthology)	Leslie Esdaile	$10.95
	Gwynne Forster	
	Carmen Green	
	Monica Jackson	
Midnight Magic	Gwynne Forster	$8.95
Midnight Peril	Vicki Andrews	$10.95
Misconceptions	Pamela Leigh Starr	$9.95
Misty Blue	Dyanne Davis	$9.95
Montgomery's Children	Richard Perry	$14.95
My Buffalo Soldier	Barbara B. K. Reeves	$8.95
Naked Soul	Gwynne Forster	$8.95
Next to Last Chance	Louisa Dixon	$24.95
Nights Over Egypt	Barbara Keaton	$9.95
No Apologies	Seressia Glass	$8.95
No Commitment Required	Seressia Glass	$8.95
No Ordinary Love	Angela Weaver	$9.95
No Regrets	Mildred E. Riley	$8.95
Notes When Summer Ends	Beverly Lauderdale	$12.95
Nowhere to Run	Gay G. Gunn	$10.95
O Bed! O Breakfast!	Rob Kuehnle	$14.95
Object of His Desire	A. C. Arthur	$8.95
Office Policy	A. C. Arthur	$9.95
Once in a Blue Moon	Dorianne Cole	$9.95
One Day at a Time	Bella McFarland	$8.95
Only You	Crystal Hubbard	$9.95
Outside Chance	Louisa Dixon	$24.95
Passion	T.T. Henderson	$10.95
Passion's Blood	Cherif Fortin	$22.95
Passion's Journey	Wanda Thomas	$8.95
Past Promises	Jahmel West	$8.95
Path of Fire	T.T. Henderson	$8.95

Other Genesis Press, Inc. Titles (continued)

Path of Thorns	Annetta P. Lee	$9.95
Peace Be Still	Colette Haywood	$12.95
Picture Perfect	Reon Carter	$8.95
Playing for Keeps	Stephanie Salinas	$8.95
Pride & Joi	Gay G. Gunn	$8.95
Promises to Keep	Alicia Wiggins	$8.95
Quiet Storm	Donna Hill	$10.95
Reckless Surrender	Rochelle Alers	$6.95
Red Polka Dot in a World of Plaid	Varian Johnson	$12.95
Rehoboth Road	Anita Ballard-Jones	$12.95
Reluctant Captive	Joyce Jackson	$8.95
Rendezvous with Fate	Jeanne Sumerix	$8.95
Revelations	Cheris F. Hodges	$8.95
Rise of the Phoenix	Kenneth Whetstone	$12.95
Rivers of the Soul	Leslie Esdaile	$8.95
Rock Star	Rosyln Hardy Holcomb	$9.95
Rocky Mountain Romance	Kathleen Suzanne	$8.95
Rooms of the Heart	Donna Hill	$8.95
Rough on Rats and Tough on Cats	Chris Parker	$12.95
Scent of Rain	Annetta P. Lee	$9.95
Second Chances at Love	Cheris Hodges	$9.95
Secret Library Vol. 1	Nina Sheridan	$18.95
Secret Library Vol. 2	Cassandra Colt	$8.95
Shades of Brown	Denise Becker	$8.95
Shades of Desire	Monica White	$8.95
Shadows in the Moonlight	Jeanne Sumerix	$8.95
Sin	Crystal Rhodes	$8.95
Sin and Surrender	J.M. Jeffries	$9.95
Sinful Intentions	Crystal Rhodes	$12.95
So Amazing	Sinclair LeBeau	$8.95
Somebody's Someone	Sinclair LeBeau	$8.95

SWEET SENSATION

Other Genesis Press, Inc. Titles (continued)

Someone to Love	Alicia Wiggins	$8.95
Song in the Park	Martin Brant	$15.95
Soul Eyes	Wayne L. Wilson	$12.95
Soul to Soul	Donna Hill	$8.95
Southern Comfort	J.M. Jeffries	$8.95
Still the Storm	Sharon Robinson	$8.95
Still Waters Run Deep	Leslie Esdaile	$8.95
Stories to Excite You	Anna Forrest/Divine	$14.95
Subtle Secrets	Wanda Y. Thomas	$8.95
Suddenly You	Crystal Hubbard	$9.95
Sweet Repercussions	Kimberley White	$9.95
Sweet Tomorrows	Kimberly White	$8.95
Taken by You	Dorothy Elizabeth Love	$9.95
Tattooed Tears	T. T. Henderson	$8.95
The Color Line	Lizzette Grayson Carter	$9.95
The Color of Trouble	Dyanne Davis	$8.95
The Disappearance of Allison Jones	Kayla Perrin	$5.95
The Honey Dipper's Legacy	Pannell-Allen	$14.95
The Joker's Love Tune	Sidney Rickman	$15.95
The Little Pretender	Barbara Cartland	$10.95
The Love We Had	Natalie Dunbar	$8.95
The Man Who Could Fly	Bob & Milana Beamon	$18.95
The Missing Link	Charlyne Dickerson	$8.95
The Price of Love	Sinclair LeBeau	$8.95
The Smoking Life	Ilene Barth	$29.95
The Words of the Pitcher	Kei Swanson	$8.95
Three Wishes	Seressia Glass	$8.95
Through the Fire	Seressia Glass	$9.95
Ties That Bind	Kathleen Suzanne	$8.95
Tiger Woods	Libby Hughes	$5.95
Time is of the Essence	Angie Daniels	$9.95
Timeless Devotion	Bella McFarland	$9.95
Tomorrow's Promise	Leslie Esdaile	$8.95

226

Other Genesis Press, Inc. Titles (continued)

Truly Inseparable	Wanda Y. Thomas	$8.95
Unbreak My Heart	Dar Tomlinson	$8.95
Uncommon Prayer	Kenneth Swanson	$9.95
Unconditional	A.C. Arthur	$9.95
Unconditional Love	Alicia Wiggins	$8.95
Under the Cherry Moon	Christal Jordan-Mims	$12.95
Unearthing Passions	Elaine Sims	$9.95
Until Death Do Us Part	Susan Paul	$8.95
Vows of Passion	Bella McFarland	$9.95
Wedding Gown	Dyanne Davis	$8.95
What's Under Benjamin's Bed	Sandra Schaffer	$8.95
When Dreams Float	Dorothy Elizabeth Love	$8.95
Whispers in the Night	Dorothy Elizabeth Love	$8.95
Whispers in the Sand	LaFlorya Gauthier	$10.95
Wild Ravens	Altonya Washington	$9.95
Yesterday Is Gone	Beverly Clark	$10.95
Yesterday's Dreams, Tomorrow's Promises	Reon Laudat	$8.95
Your Precious Love	Sinclair LeBeau	$8.95

Order Form

Mail to: Genesis Press, Inc.
P.O. Box 101
Columbus, MS 39703

Name _____

Address _____

City/State _____ Zip _____

Telephone _____

Ship to (if different from above)

Name _____

Address _____

City/State _____ Zip _____

Telephone _____

Credit Card Information

Credit Card # _____ ☐ Visa ☐ Mastercard

Expiration Date (mm/yy) _____ ☐ AmEx ☐ Discover

Qty.	Author	Title	Price	Total

Use this order form, or call 1-888-INDIGO-1	Total for books _____
	Shipping and handling: $5 first two books, $1 each additional book _____
	Total S & H _____
	Total amount enclosed _____
	Mississippi residents add 7% sales tax

Visit www.genesis-press.com for latest releases and excerpts.